COLTER'S
JOURNEY

LOOK FOR THESE EXCITING WESTERN SERIES FROM BESTSELLING AUTHORS WILLIAM W. JOHNSTONE AND J.A. JOHNSTONE

The Mountain Man

Luke Jensen: Bounty Hunter

Brannigan's Land

The Jensen Brand

Smoke Jensen: The Early Years

Preacher and MacCallister

Fort Misery

The Fighting O'Neils

Perley Gates

MacCoole and Boone

Guns of the Vigilantes

Shotgun Johnny

The Chuckwagon Trail

The Jackals

The Slash and Pecos Westerns

The Texas Moonshiners

Stoneface Finnegan Westerns

Ben Savage: Saloon Ranger

The Buck Trammel Westerns

The Death and Texas Westerns

The Hunter Buchanon Westerns

Will Tanner, Deputy US Marshal

Old Cowboys Never Die

Go West, Young Man

Published by Kensington Publishing Corp.

COLTER'S JOURNEY

WILLIAM W. JOHNSTONE
and J. A. Johnstone

PINNACLE BOOKS
Kensington Publishing Corp.
www.kensingtonbooks.com

PINNACLE BOOKS are published by

Kensington Publishing Corp.
900 Third Avenue
New York, NY 10022

All Kensington titles, imprints, and distributed lines are available at special quantity discounts for bulk purchases for sales promotion, premiums, fund-raising, and educational or institutional use.

Special book excerpts or customized printings can also be created to fit specific needs. For details, write or phone the office of the Kensington Sales Manager: Kensington Publishing Corp., 900 Third Avenue, New York, NY 10022. Attn. Sales Department. Phone: 1-800-221-2647.

PINNACLE BOOKS and the Pinnacle logo Reg. U.S. Pat. & TM Off.

First Kensington Books hardcover printing: June 2016
First Pinnacle Books paperback printing: July 2017

ISBN-13: 978-0-7860-5106-9
ISBN-13: 978-0-7860-3812-1 (eBook)

13 12 11 10 9 8 7 6 5 4

Printed in the United States of America

BOOK ONE
SOUTH PASS

CHAPTER 1

"**R**un, Tim! Run!"

R Tim Colter was buttoning his trousers after answering nature's call when he heard his mother's scream. He didn't even have time to slip the suspenders back over his shoulders. He peeked above the bush and felt all the color and all the blood drain from his face.

He had heard the stories. By Jacks, he had even imagined something like this happening, and had dreamed of being the hero. Saving the day. Having the newspapers back home in Danville write about him. Making Mr. Scott think a little bit more about him. Most important, feeling those ruby red lips of Patricia, Mr. Scott's daughter, kissing him after he had saved her life.

"Run!" his mother shouted again. "Ru—" The tomahawk slammed into her head, and she fell without a word onto the grass beside the Scott family dog, which looked like a porcupine or a pincushion from all the arrows sticking out of the poor mutt's body.

"Get that boy!"

Tim's eyes swung away from his mother. Another Indian was mounted on a big black horse with a perfect white star on its head. The man wore buckskins and long black hair that hung in braids. He pointed a smoking musket in Tim's direction.

Tim remembered hearing the gunshot a few moments ago and thinking how glorious it would have been if Indians had attacked the Scotts and Colters' camp, how he could run to the rescue and use his slingshot to drive off the Sioux or the Cheyenne or the Blackfeet or whatever they were.

Tim Colter they would say, and they'd compare him to David when he'd tackled Goliath.

He had sighed, figuring the shot had come from that Pennsylvania rifle of Mr. Scott's, who had been admiring a turkey he had seen off in the nearby woods.

From behind the bush, Tim saw Mr. Scott with his own rifle across his outstretched legs, leaning against the rear wheel of the Conestoga wagon . . . the one being repaired. Blood covered Mr. Scott's face, and his head tilted at an ugly, unnatural angle.

The Indian who had brained Tim's mother let out a curse, dropped the tomahawk, and pawed for a pistol stuck in a thick black belt.

Tim heard the screams of his sisters and Patricia Scott. He heard the shouts of men, Indians and probably his father. The grunts of the oxen and Papa's prized Percheron stallion, the one he had figured would be the envy of every settler in the Oregon Territory when they finally reached The Dalles and moved on to Oregon City.

He heard something else, too, and felt a bee buzz past his left ear.

The Indian had fired his pistol at him. Tim realized he had come just a few inches from death. Only then did he truly understand what was happening.

Only then did he turn and run.

The suspenders slapped against his woolen trousers as he scrambled down the hill. Behind him came *whoops* as the Indians chased him. He had a head start of maybe thirty yards on the savages, he figured, and he was going down a steep slope, picking up speed, feeling the wind in his face.

He felt terrified.

If he tripped, lost his balance, fell, he knew he was dead.

Another bullet sang over his head and exploded in the rotting trunk of a massive tree that had fallen over ages ago. Tim leaped over the log, and felt the brambles and saplings sting his arms, his face, and those cumbersome suspenders as he reached the patch of woods. Mr. Scott had said there might be a river or a stream beyond those woods. Certainly there had to be running water. Mr. Scott had said that he could hear it.

Running water? Tim had thought it must have been the wind rustling through the trees.

He ducked underneath the last branch, leaped over a boulder or something—he couldn't tell exactly what it was—and came out of the woods. Mr. Scott had been right. It was a river or creek.

Behind him came the curses of men, and he knew he had not much time to live. Unless he could find a hiding place.

Blinking, he spotted the mound of sticks in the middle of the running water, saw the pond that had pooled behind it, and then he remembered hearing all those stories about beavers and beaver dams. Quickly stepping into the water, he felt the iciness numb him, and suck breath out of his lungs. It was summer, late summer in fact, and he had never expected the water to be so cold. He moved quickly into deeper water, closer toward the beaver dam. Behind him, the noise of footsteps and curses came closer, and he drew in as much air as his lungs could hold, and disappeared underneath the water.

It won't work, he told himself. He was no swimmer. And surely the Indians would realize he was hiding in the dam . . . if he could even reach the dam. In the freezing water, he groped and found his way in the darkness. The beavers might even attack him with their sharp teeth. That would be his luck. Instead of being the hero who had saved his mother and his sisters and Patricia Scott from that dreadful fate worse than death, he would be killed by rabid animals.

In death, he would be the butt of jokes. He imagined someone saying, *"Did you hear the one about that boy from Pennsylvania who got killed by beavers?"* they would say at Fort Vancouver. *"Happened around South Pass in the summer of 'forty-five. Fool kid. They found his bones amongst the aspen and pines."*

He came up into the darkness, though he could see cracks of sunlight.

In the corner, a beaver glared at him. No, two beavers. But they kept their distance. They just stared. And stank.

The place had a musky odor that almost took Tim's breath away. Or maybe it was the cold.

Stop tapping those tails! Tim mouthed the words. He feared the Indians would hear the warning the beavers kept sounding. Then he realized that the sound did not come from the two animals. His teeth kept chattering.

Something splashed in the stream or the pond or the lake or the river. Tim ground his teeth so tight that his jaw ached, but he no longer heard that noisy clicking from his mouth. One of the Indians yelled something, and another answered. He could not understand the words. More Indians had joined the pursuers. A few ran down the creek. They shouted at one another in a mix of languages. He recognized a few curse words spoken in English.

"Mon Dieu!" one of the savages said in French.

Another answered.

"Forget him," said another, more of a grunt but spoken in English. "He's a kid. He'll be dead in two days out here."

An eternity later, Tim heard only the rippling of water. The Indians had left him. The beavers still stared.

He had dropped his slingshot. He unfastened the suspenders and brought them up to study them. *Can they be used as a weapon?* He shook his head and submerged them in the water, releasing his hold, hoping they might sink.

Worthless, these suspenders, he told himself. *Like me.*

His top teeth clattered against his bottom teeth, and he brought his arms out of the water and desperately tried to squeeze warmth into his body. He shook. He prayed. He thought he might cry, but no tears came.

What he wanted to do was to swim back out of the beaver dam, and reach the shore. Darkness would fall soon. The Indians were gone. He started to move, just to reach the shore, to feel the fading sun warm his body before nightfall came. A twig popped and he stopped. It could have come from a deer, or a moose, or maybe his own imagination, but he moved back toward the edge of the dam.

"Indians are stupid," Mr. Scott had said. "Some of them are probably smarter than Jenkins."

Jenkins had been the guide who had been hired back in Independence, Missouri, to lead the Scotts, the Colters, and other families to the Oregon Territory. Tim had liked the man he thought of as Just Jenkins.

"Ain't got no first name," the grizzled old man in buckskins had kept saying. "It's just Jenkins."

Tim wished Just Jenkins and the other twelve families were with him.

He listened. He heard nothing but the rippling of the water, and maybe the wind, and the two beavers moving around near him.

It would be so easy to slip out of the dam, wade

back to shore, and lie down. Wake up. Wake up from the awful nightmare.

Yet he did not move. He listened, and although he heard nothing, no Indian grunts, no flintlock being cocked, no curses, no horses, no shouts or screams, he decided he would have to spend the long, frigid night in the dam.

He wasn't sure he could do it. Wasn't sure the beavers would let him. He thought for certain that he had already lost all feeling in his legs. He could touch bottom, though, at least as long as he could remain standing. As long as the Indian that had remained behind. Tim was certain someone was out there, someone human. No. Not human. He remembered seeing his mother dropped by a tomahawk to her head. He remembered seeing poor Mr. Scott propped up against the Conestoga's wheel.

The screams of his sisters and beautiful Patricia Scott still rang in his ears.

Human beings did not do those kinds of things to other human beings.

Some animal was out there, probably at the edge of the woods, waiting for Tim to show himself. And be killed. Murdered.

Keep your head clear, he kept telling himself. *Don't fall asleep. Don't move around. You can do this. You can wait. You have to live.*

Sometimes, though, he wondered why he should live.

His mother's words echoed inside his head. *"Run, Tim! Run!"* He had obeyed his mother. That's what sons were supposed to do. He had run. He had hidden. So he was still alive.

He wanted to throw up, but, somehow, kept the bile down. He listened. He shivered. And silently he cried. The tears had finally broken free, and he could taste their saltiness as they ran over his lips.

Darkness came quickly, and the night would be lonely. He wanted to move around, just to make sure the blood still flowed and had not frozen in his legs and waist, but he knew better. Someone was out there, waiting. Waiting to kill him.

A man he had never met, never seen, never heard of. *Maybe,* he thought, *death would be welcome.* It had to be better than standing up in a smelly beaver dam in freezing water on a bitterly cold night. It certainly didn't feel like the summer nights he had enjoyed back in Danville, Pennsylvania.

Yet his mother had told him to run. She wanted him to live. He had to live. He would not be killed in some beaver dam and become a person men and women and kids all along the Oregon Trail laughed about.

He wanted to sing just to stay warm. He knew better, though. Knew that an Indian waited out in the woods with a weapon—pistol, spear, or bow and arrow.

He mouthed the words to "Home Sweet Home" and tried to remember how Patricia Scott had sounded when she had sung it time after time, night after night, all the way from Danville, Pennsylvania, to Independence, Missouri. To Fort Kearny to Chimney Rock to Scotts Bluff. To Fort Laramie and Independence Rock and all the way to South Pass. He tried to remember her voice, to recall the words to that sweet song that had often made him homesick for the iron works and the furnaces, and the forests and lush greenness of the summers in Pennsylvania.

All he could hear, though, were Patricia's screams.

He had run. He was no hero. Tim Colter was nothing but a miserable little coward.

CHAPTER 2

For nigh on two weeks, he had been drunk. But Jed Reno wasn't *that* drunk.

Lowering the brown jug and using his massive right hand to wipe off the whiskey—he was drunk enough to call that hooch *whiskey*—running into his beard, Reno stared hard at Malachi Murchison, who had only been drunk for a day or two. "What did you say?" Reno leaned forward.

"Start a war. That's what I say." Murchison stopped to burp. "Well, it's what he says."

He . . . Reno had to think. They had been talking about Louis Jackatars. Reno had never cared a fig for the man. Come to think on it, he never even liked Malachi Murchison, even after that old reprobate had bought the jug of rotgut they had practically finished.

"With the Blackfeet?" Reno snorted. "Ain't enough of 'em left to make much of a war."

Murchison leaned over to fetch the jug. He drank

a snootful and laughed. "Blackfeet. Sioux. Crow. Sho-shone. Jackatars don't rightly care one way or tuther. But it'd give us somethin' to do. Since nobody wants to buy no more beaver no more." He leaned forward and whispered into Reno's face. "Remember 'em times, Jed?"

His breath stank. Clapping his hands, Murchison leaned back, laughing, and rocking on his heels. "'Em was the glorious days of our youth, pard. When we'd trap those 'hairy bank notes' for all 'em dandies of the boulevard back east. Trap 'em, we would, all spring and fall, find some squaw to keep us warm in the winter and in the spring." Murchison lifted the jug, took another slug, and pitched the container back to Reno. "And in the summer, you remember, Jed? You recollect when the engages would show up on the Green. What a time we'd all have! Ain't that right, Jed? Surely, you ain't forgotten all 'em glorious days."

Reno managed to swallow some of the awful whiskey they served at Bridger's Trading Post to men like him and Malachi Murchison. The settlers who came flocking in on their way west, well, they'd get something more tolerable to drink.

"Remember?" Malachi Murchison reached for the jug, and Reno was happy to oblige the fellow.

"Hasn't been that long ago." Reno spoke the words softly. "I ain't getting so old I can't recollect four years back."

Four years. That had been the last time the cara-vans had come from the settlements, the last glorious

Rendezvous on the Siskeedee-Agie—the Green River, north along the Black's Fork of the Green.

Jed Reno had been at that last Rendezvous. Trappers—the free trappers and those working for the companies—got together, traded their beaver plews for whatever they would need for the coming year. Things like gunpowder and lead; coffee, kettles, and tobacco; flannels and awls and steel. Oh, the traders made off like bandits, but Jed Reno and the trappers he knew and respected—even those he didn't know or didn't respect—never minded one bit. The merchants had to return to civilization, while Reno and the trappers got to stay in the glorious Rocky Mountains, got to live the way they wanted to live.

Jed Reno had been at the first Rendezvous back in 1825 on Henry's Fork of the Green. He had hit every last one of them since, including the last, back when Bridger and Andrew Drips and Henry Fraeb had brought in the traders and even some missionaries. Father Pierre Jean DeSmet had performed a Catholic Mass.

Civilization had reached the wilds.

"Five years, Jed," Murchison said.

"Five years like he—" Reno stopped and shook his head in disgust. Malachi Murchison was right. It had been five years. Reno spit.

Back East, beaver hats had fallen out of fashion. Silk was what those dandies wanted atop their heads now, or something from South America called a Nutria, which was cheaper than beaver, or so folks said.

Whiskey kept befuddling him. Reno shook his head,

not liking that feeling. Time was when he could've been drunk for a month and not felt like he did.

"What do you say, Jed?" Malachi Murchison asked.

Reno blew his nose. "Jackatars tell you that?"

A shrug was how Murchison answered. "You know Louis. You know how that half-breed Métis is."

Sure, Jed Reno knew. He also knew how Malachi Murchison was, and would trust neither as far as he could throw them, which back in the day would have covered a considerable distance.

Reno was forty-nine years old, older than Jim Bridger. His beard, once black as coal, had streaks of silver in it, as did his hair. His face that wasn't covered with hair was clouded with scars, and one of his earlobes was missing, thanks to a Green River knife in the hands of a Snake Indian whom he had put under a few moments after getting his ear bloodied and mangled.

Like Bridger, Reno had joined General William Ashley back in '22 on that Upper Missouri Expedition, and he hadn't returned to home in Missouri or even closer than Fort Laramie in twenty years. More than twenty, he realized.

He had joined up with Bridger when they had bought out the General and founded the Rocky Mountain Fur Company, and then Jed Reno had decided that belonging to a company made him feel too civilized, so he had let Bridger buy out his interest, and he'd become a free trapper, that independent sort who came and went as he pleased, and sold and fought as he pleased.

His eye remained as blue as the mountain skies on a clear summer day. The one eye he had left, his right one. A black patch covered the hole in his head, a reminder of the eye he had lost early in his free-spirited days as a mountain man, when the Blackfeet Indians didn't cotton to being neighborly to anyone, especially a black-bearded young buck with blue eyes and the disposition of a Missouri mule.

He didn't feel old. Not in the summer, anyway. The winters were another matter. He stood six-foot-four inches tall, weighed right around two hundred and twenty pounds, and figured he could whip a silvertip grizzly bear if he felt like it.

"Jed," Malachi Murchison said as he corked the jug. "Louis wants an answer."

Reno turned his head and spit. "Wants an answer to what?"

"If you'll side him. Stir up that ruction with 'em heathens. Get us a war goin'."

Reno stared hard with his one eye. Murchison was a tiny man, no bigger than five-foot-two, with eyes like a rat and a nose like a hawk. His pockmarked face had a wicked gun powder burn across the left cheek, and his tiny hands sprouted only eight long, bony fingers if you counted the thumbs. He had lost both of his pinky fingers years back. Some say a beaver trap cut them off. Some said Louis Jackatars had removed them. Others argued that a Shoshone squaw had taken offense to Malachi Murchison's manners.

Jed Reno didn't care one way or the other. "No."

The black powder burn on Murchison's cheek

darkened. So did the rat's eyes, although he tried to smile with his busted and blackened and missing teeth. "Well"—he shrugged—"you know how that Métis can be."

Oh, Jed Reno knew that all too well. Reno had never liked Louis Jackatars and he had never cared for Malachi Murchison. For that matter, neither of those trappers had expressed or shown any affection or tolerance for Jed Reno, which was fine and dandy with him.

"Just as long as you don't go around spreadin' no wild rumors about Louis and his plans." Murchison tried that grin again. "You know. Don't need nobody tryin' to ruin our little plan, you see. That's all."

"I see."

Their eyes locked.

"I mind my own business, Murchison. You and that half-breed want to try to start an uprising, that's your doings, not mine. Way I figure things, you try to start a fight with the Shoshone or Crows or any tribe in these parts, and it'll be you and Jackatars who gets rubbed out. That'll set right well with me, too."

Malachi Murchison slapped his bony hands on his greasy buckskin trousers. "You make me laugh, Jed."

Reno rose. The whiskey didn't feel so warm in his belly anymore, or maybe drinking with a miserable cur dog like Malachi Murchison had soured his stomach. Besides, he had been at Bridger's Trading Post for two weeks, blowing whatever money he had brought in in skins. It was time to get out of civilization, if anyone ever considered that ramshackle affair civilized.

He left Malachi Murchison laughing and sipping the jug and wandered over from the corrals to the buildings.

Old Jim Bridger and his pard, Louis Vasquez, had established the trading post on the Oregon Trail maybe a year or so back. With the beaver trade dying out, Bridger had figured to make his mark in selling to those fool white emigrants and the Indians. Old Vaskiss, part French and part Spanish—or maybe just part Mexican—hailed from St. Louis, and had been trading with the Indians since he had first set up shop with the Pawnee. Neither he nor Bridger knew much about modern comforts.

The post had two double-log cabins about forty feet long, rough-hewn and papered with mud. The blacksmith shop was probably better built. No, the strongest structures had to be the pens that held the horses. Indians had set up teepees around the lodging, and wayfarers bound west kept stopping in.

A passel of prairie schooners had set up camp just in front of Bridger's post, and Jed Reno had to frown at the noise of the songs and the laughter of children from those camps. They still cooked with salt and pepper and allspice in their cook fires.

Bridger and Old Vaskiss had loaded up with flour and coffee and sugar to sell to those fools coming west to settle, but bringing in that big, black smithy might have been their biggest moneymaker because after all those miles from Independence, fixing wagons made a body lots of money. All that hammering the smithy done, though, bellowed and bounced about inside Jed Reno's head.

He reached the water trough, put his hands out on the rough wood, and buried his head in the cold water. There were times when water felt good on a body. Cleared the head some, washed out the hangover or the graybacks which might burrow into a man's beard and get to itching.

Reno pulled his head out, satisfied, feeling the water run off his hairy face. He blinked out the water and wiped his beard with his big hands. Those emigrants from back east likely were staring at him, stopping their bartering with Bridger to make some comment about what kind of white man would wash his face in a trough used to water horses.

Spitting out some of the water, he stared at the rippling water, waiting to see his face, to see just how old he looked. There had been a time when he could have stayed drunk for a month or six weeks, but that had been back in '35, when they had rendezvoused near Fort Bonneville, or '36, when they had met on Horse Creek near the Green.

He heard Bridger's voice from the front of the post, and Reno knew the lie the old mountain man was telling the greenhorns. By Jupiter, he had heard the story first in '32, after that set-to with the redskins at Pierre's Hole.

"Those red devils had me surrounded," Bridger was saying. "Me with nothin' but my hatchet and hair. They was forty of 'em, armed to the teeth. And all forty come at me of a sudden."

Reno waited for the question to come, and sure enough, one of the slickers from back East asked it.

"What happened, Mr. Bridger?"

Reno mouthed Bridger's answer as he said it. "Why, son, they kilt me, of course."

Everyone laughed.

Jed Reno would have laughed along with them, but the water had calmed and he saw a clear reflection. Malachi Murchison was right behind him, bringing the Green River knife in a lethal, slicing arc.

CHAPTER 3

Reno turned and spun away, but his age was show-ing. The knife's razor-sharp blade ripped through the buckskin and carved a ditch across his side. Al-most instantly, the curved blade of the knife came back. For a sneaky rat loaded up on rotgut whiskey, Malachi Murchison struck faster than a rattlesnake—and twice as deadly.

Reno lunged backward, catapulting himself over the watering trough and hearing the blade just miss as it sliced over the empty air where the mountain man had been standing a split second before. The momentum of the swinging arm spun Murchison around, like one of those toy tops from ages ago. The would-be assassin cursed as he fell.

Jed Reno did the same, landing on the hard-packed earth between the trough and the cabin's walls. He bounced up and reached for his pistol, only to catch himself. Like most trappers, he usually sported a belt pistol tucked in his sash. His was an old flintlock model, small enough to carry on one's person but powerful enough to stop a skunk like Malachi Murchison . . . if he had it.

That's one reason Reno had stopped at Bridger's Trading Post. The pistol had been misfiring, not even sparking, which could get a body killed in mountain country. So he had brought it to Bridger, who figured that the frizzen was worn through.

As he had said, "Jed, I've seen trees downed by beavers that wasn't as chewed up and gouged as bad as that frizzen of yourn." So the smithy was repairing Reno's pistol or maybe Bridger himself was hardening the frizzen.

Reno caught his breath.

Murchison had climbed back to his feet and moved around the trough, grinning his broken-teeth smile, moving the knife in his right hand. "Been meanin' to gut you for years, Reno." He hissed the words like a serpent.

"Have a try, old man." Reno backed up along the edge of the cabin.

"I don't try, boy. I get things done."

The clanging of metal from the smithy's shop had stopped. Reno kept backing up, out of the shade of the log cabin and into the sun. Behind him came the gasps of men and women—the settlers bound for the Oregon Territory—and a few grunts of approval from some of the Indians hanging out by the cracker barrel that had run out of crackers during the first month the post had been open.

"You need some hayseed farmer to help save your hide, Reno?"

Reno figured he had backed up far enough, so he stopped. Malachi Murchison did the same.

"They've been on the trail some months now," Reno said. "Figured they'd like to see the show."

"Pity you won't live to see the end."

The blade came quickly, but Reno moved faster. His right hand came up with the long knife he kept sheathed behind his back. Metal clanged, Murchison cursed, his face revealing the shock of Reno's defense. His eyes revealed fear. The rat had thought Jed Reno was unarmed. His pistol was being repaired and his Hawken rifle leaned against his traps, packs, and saddle by the corral.

Reno kept the charge. He moved forward, slicing one way, then the other, not saying a word, but controlling his breathing, working fast and keeping Murchison backing up.

"Stop it!" one of the wayfarers yelled.

"My goodness!" a woman in a blue bonnet gasped. "You men, stop this!"

Murchison grunted, kept moving back, away from the Conestogas and the oxen and the people. Reno never slowed his assault.

"Do something!" someone else yelled. "Before they kill each other."

Bridger's voice drawled out slowly. "Ain't stickin' my nose in somethin' that ain't my affair, ma'am."

"But what if they kill each other?"

"Then it'll be my affair, ma'am, and I'll bury the both of 'em."

"You mean you'll have one of your injuns bury 'em." That had to be Carroll Smith. Sounded like that trapper anyway.

"Buryin's work, Smith," Bridger said. "I'm a businessman these days."

"Ten buffalo robes says the weasel guts him," Carroll Smith bet.

Bridger laughed. "That's a bet, Smith, and I thank ye in advance."

The weasel, the rat, the conniving little cutthroat Malachi Murchison kept retreating, which gave Jed Reno pause. He had known the rat long enough and had seen Murchison bury more than his share of men, red, black, and white. Say what you would about Murchison, but he wasn't a fool, and he didn't run from a fight. Oh, he'd stab you in the back or cut your throat for the gold fillings in your teeth, but he was no fool, no idiot. He had to be backing up for some reason other than fear and survival.

Reno blinked away the sweat and stopped quickly. His side burned, and he felt the blood already staining his buckskin trousers. His lungs worked hard, and he wet his cracked lips with his whiskey-soaked tongue.

He grinned. Murchison did not.

Slow it down, Reno told himself. *You're bleeding like a stuck pig, and that's what the rat wants. So he can win Carroll Smith that bet.*

He saw Murchison's horse tethered by the corral and understood the weasel's plan. Two pistols would be handy in their pommels, along with Murchison's own long rifle. That's what the rat had wanted. Keep retreating back to his horse where he could fetch one of his weapons and send a heavy lead ball into Jed Reno's gut. Then slice his throat or gut him, as rats like Malachi Murchison were prone to do.

The eyes told Reno that the would-be killer understood what Jed Reno knew. After licking his lips, Malachi Murchison charged.

The blades glanced off one another. Reno backed up. Some emigrant yelled to get the children out of there.

Murchison shifted the grip on the elkhorn handle of his knife. He brought it up, swung it down. Reno's left hand shot up, and caught the rat's bony wrist in a vise. Simultaneously, Reno swung his own knife in his right hand, hoping to eviscerate the assassin's bowels.

But Malachi Murchison was no greenhorn when it came to knife fights.

He sucked in his gut, let the blade pass, and then his left hand locked on Reno's arm, just below the knife.

Both men squeezed as hard as they could. The strength in the weasel's hands surprised Reno. He had a savage, determined grip, and those bony fingers felt like hot iron.

Murchison's knee came up, trying for Reno's groin, but he deflected the blow with his thigh. They pulled each other closer, sweating, grunting. Reno felt his grip slipping, and he could smell the whiskey sweat on their bodies, smell the blood—his own— and the rancid breath of the rat.

Suddenly, Murchison went down. A purposeful move.

Reno felt himself sailing over. He landed on his left shoulder, came up quickly, pain burning in his side, and turned.

The rat grabbed a handful of sand, threw it into

Reno's eye, and backed away quickly, anticipating the knife blade that caught the knot on Reno's sash.

The sand blinded Reno, and he swore, spat, and swung blindly with the knife, which missed. Tears washed the sand from his vision, but it remained blurred as he kicked out with his moccasin, also missing. He coughed. Tried to catch his breath. He could see, slightly, but far from clearly, yet maybe just enough to stay alive.

Malachi Murchison's blade came up. Reno leaped back, feeling the steel just miss his stomach. He swung himself in a sweeping arc, hoping to luck out and maybe catch the rat's throat, but connected with nothing but air. Reno backed up again and slammed into something hard.

Some emigrant's prairie schooner. He could smell the wood, the canvas cover, and the dust that had been picked up from Missouri and across perhaps a thousand miles of the Unorganized Territory. Catching a glimpse of the knife in the rat's hand as it came down, he managed to move and felt the blade ram into the wooden frame of the heavy wagon.

Murchison swore, pulled, but his hand, slick with sweat, came away empty. The knife remained stuck in the wood. It was the break Reno wanted. He swung his own knife, but that weasel moved with luck and speed. The blade ripped the buckskin shirt, but caught no flesh. Reno had swung too hard and his momentum carried him spinning past the lucky rat.

The rat hit hard, catching Reno in the kidneys

and sending spasms of pain shooting from his bleeding side. A second blow followed the first, then another, and another, and another, driving him to his knees.

However, Reno still held his knife. With better than a foot and more than eighty pounds on the sorry cur, he turned on his knees and swung the blade, missing. Murchison danced back and kicked his moccasin up, slamming into Reno's aching, bleeding side.

"Arrghhhh!" Reno toppled over, but kept rolling. He felt Murchison's feet as the little runt tried to jump down and crush his head. He sprang up on his feet, backing away, trying to get some focus, find the assassin and plant him permanently.

"Stop them!" a woman screamed. "Stop them!"

"This is horrible," said another.

Reno heard the muttering of other voices, soft, quiet, reverent, and realized that some of the emigrants had gathered together to pray. Prayers. In that lawless trading post. How long had it been since he had heard a prayer? Back in '40 at the last Rendezvous when the padre had held that first Mass.

Reno feinted a charge, stopped, and swung back. He was learning. The handful of sand that Malachi Murchison threw was caught by the wind and sailed harmlessly to Reno's right.

"Iffen you boys have a mind, why don't we call this the first round. Get some water. Cool yourselves off a mite. Kill each other after me and these gents've concluded our business." Jim Bridger sat in his rocking chair next to the empty cracker barrel, the wide-brimmed, low-crowned black hat pushed back on his head, tapping the corncob pipe on his boot heel.

"I'll finish it right now, Jim." Murchison kicked out, trying to catch Reno's injured side again.

He missed, and Reno brought the knife down. He caught flesh and bone, and heard Murchison's high-pitched wail. The man fell back, spraying blood over the ground. He went down, came up, and took off, making a beeline for the horses.

Reno could never outrun a cat like Murchison. He started, thought better of it, and shifted the knife, then let it fly, arcing over and over, but missing when Murchison turned to his right. The knife landed on the ground, kicking up dust.

Reno swore. He was unarmed. Murchison would have those pommel pistols or his long rifle.

Reno looked around, trying to find something. He could run. That would be easy enough, dive into the trading post through the open door to Jim Bridger's right, but Jed Reno wasn't that type of man.

It would be a cold day on the Platte River in the middle of August when he would run from a snake like Malachi Murchison. He straightened, put his hands on his hips, careful to avoid the deep cut in his side, and watched Malachi Murchison leap into the saddle.

The rat's moccasins beat the horse's side, and he was galloping away. He did manage to fetch his rifle but never chanced a shot or a look in Reno's direction. Dust rose thickly as the horse thundered out of the yard, onto the trail, and the rat rode east.

Chest heaving, Jed Reno watched the coward flee.

He wet his lips and gently pressed his right hand against his aching, bleeding side.

"Nice fight, Jed," Bridger said. "But mind tellin' me what in blazes it were about?"

Jed Reno didn't answer. He dropped forward like a felled Ponderosa pine.

CHAPTER 4

For most of his life, Tim Colter had wanted to get away from Danville. Freezing in the water inside the beaver dam, he thought about the place. That was funny. Well, not funny. Nothing was funny anymore. It just seemed strange that he thought so longingly about Danville. His thoughts rambled as he grew colder and colder.

Some old man named Montgomery and his boy founded Danville back in the 1700s. The place seemed ancient, but, it wasn't that old a town. Pa always told me how William Montgomery had been thinking to the future. Why, Mr. Montgomery had the foresight to see how anthracite coal could be used to heat homes. He had used the coal to heat his own home, that old stone building on the corner of Mill Street and Bloom Road. Now, folks all around America and in the territories use anthracite coal during the winters.

Actually, Daniel Montgomery had staked out the town's

plot. That's why it's named after him and not his pa. All William did was buy some land about the time the American Revolution had started and opened a trading post called Montgomery's Landing. Before that, it was Iroquois land, but I never saw one Indian in Danville. Thanks to coal and canals the town grew. It's the seat of Columbia County, although grownups keep talking about how Bloomsburg is set on taking the county seat away from Danville.

I've never been to Bloomsburg. I never even set foot outside Danville . . . until we left it.

Tim shivered.

I never cared one whit about old man Montgomery or his boy Daniel. They're both long dead. I don't even care about coal. Or the Pennsylvania Canal System.

Danville is famous for that, too.

I think Daniel Montgomery was president of the Board of Canal Commissioners when he established the North Branch of the Pennsylvania Canal System. That was before I was born. Danville shipped a lot of wares down the canals, but what I remember most is the iron.

Iron furnaces. Oh man. I could use some of that heat. Black smoke. The stink of business. The noise and smell of the foundries—the one John C. Thiel established before I was born, and of course, the Columbia Furnace, which also uses anthracite coal. Pa worked for the Grove boys, Michael and John, at that furnace on the eastern end of East Mahoning Street. He always bragged that Mike and Johnny were the state's best furnacemen, maybe even the best furnace-men in America.

Well, that went without saying. The coal country of Pennsylvania is known for furnaces. Maybe the Groves are the best in the whole world.

Furnaces and mills and railroads and T-rails—what-ever those are—and canals. It wasn't much fun to be a kid in Danville. Oh, I thought it was pretty. Plenty of trees cover the ridges of the Appalachian Mountains, and the North Branch of the Susquehanna River flows on the south side of the city. Trees. That's what I remember most. Trees. Nothing but trees and hills, and that omnipresent smoke from the mills and foundries, train locomotives and riverboats.

I thought I'd be going to the Grove Furnace to work alongside Pa. That's what boys do in Danville. That's what everyone does in Danville.

Tim moved slightly in the cold water, trying to warm himself. His thoughts turned from Danville to the events that had started his future in a different place.

One evening about a year back, Pa burst into home, spun Ma around like a top, and announced that he had done it.

"Done what?" Ma asked him.

"We're going to Oregon," Pa said.

Ma sniffed Pa's breath, thinking that maybe he had decided it was still the Fourth of July and had found some Barbados rum or Appalachian corn liquor in one of the taverns.

"I'm sober, Ma. Sober and straight. I signed us up to go to Oregon."

"Where's Oregon?" my younger sister Margaret sang out.

Pa gestured toward the kitchen wall. "West. Yonder ways."

Ma rolled her eyes. She wasn't quite convinced that Pa wasn't in his cups.

"Why would we want to go to Oregon?" asked Nancy.

Only two years older, she thinks she knows everything.

"Because before long everybody's going to be bound for Oregon. It's the promised land."

"Don't be sacrilegious," Ma said.

Nancy didn't want to go to Oregon. I agreed.

"The Scotts are going," Pa said.

That silenced everyone, especially me. The Scotts' daughter Patricia has to be the prettiest girl not only in Danville, but in Columbia County, and maybe western Pennsylvania.

Tim closed his eyes. Thinking about Patricia, her blond hair and blue eyes, kept him from thinking about being in the cold water. Kept him thinking he needed to get warm, needed to find her. He let his mind drift back to that first conversation about leaving Danville.

"Doris going?" Ma asked.

"She's his wife, ain't she?" Pa said, shaking his head. "The boys, Will, Ben, and Richard'll likely be staying. They got jobs. Ben's married. Richard's engaged. Patricia will be going to Oregon. It's a better country, Matilda." Pa put a heavy arm over Ma's shoulders. "No furnaces. No sweat-

ing. We could have our own farm, Matilda. Not breathe black smoke eight days a week."

Pa had been listening to some old fur trappers and traders who'd returned east by way of the canal system and had lighted in Danville for the taverns and inns. He said most bragged about California, but some also told wonderful stories about the Oregon Country.

"You meet up in Sapling Grove. Then follow the trail to Fort Laramie. Then it's on to Independence Rock. They say we need to be there by July Fourth—that's how it got its name—to make sure we ain't stuck in the mountains when the snows come. On to Fort Hall. Then down to the Willamette Valley. It's a paradise. That's what they say. Horses and cattle. Sheep and hogs. Bushels of wheat. Orchards. Anything grows in that country. You just toss out a seed, and it's like Jack and the Beanstalk. Only no giants."

"But this is our home," Ma said.

"No, it ain't. We rent this from the Thiels. We should call 'em thieves. We can own our land in Oregon. Grow our own food. And it's our American duty."

"What do you mean by that, Pa?" Margaret asked.

"That's what Humpback Hallahan says."

"Who?"

"The trapper we've been conversing with. Me and Aaron. You should see him, Matilda. Dressed in buckskins so greasy he'd go up like pitch pine if he came close to a match. Hair down to here"—Pa touched about an inch below his shoulders—"and a beard like you ain't never seen."

"But why is it our American duty?" Ma asked.

"Because. We got to take Oregon for our own. If we don't, the British and the Canadians will outnumber us and then steal that veritable Garden of Eden for their own. It ain't right for country that great to belong to the English. Remem-

ber, my grandpa fought against them in the Revolution, and my pa battled them with Andy Jackson. We got to make Oregon a part of America—not England. Not Canada."

"Where's Sapling Grove?" Nancy asked.

In spite of the cold, Tim smiled. He had been more interested in those two forts—Hall and Laramie—or maybe even that Independence Rock. With nothing else to do, he resumed thinking about that first conversation.

"I'm not rightly sure," Pa admitted. "First, we got to get to Missouri."

"Where's that?" Margaret asked.

Once again, Pa made a gesture toward the kitchen wall. "West."

"Is it far?" Ma asked.

"Farther than Pittsburgh," Pa said with a chuckle. "But Aaron and I have it all figured out. We'll book passage on a steamboat down the Ohio River to the Mississippi. Then we'll sail up the Missouri to the City of Kansas. There's a settlement nearby they call Westport. Old Humpback Hallahan says he can meet us there and get us to Sapling Grove, but I doubt if he was that serious about hiring on with us. Guides are plentiful, though, he says.—Humpback I'm talking about—now that the beaver trade has gone bust. What do you think?"

Remembering his reaction, Tim smiled again. "When shall we leave?" he'd asked.

* * *

Pa took his arm off Ma's shoulder and slapped his thigh. "That's my boy. Always got the spirit of adventure, and Tim's not one to let Oregon fall into the hands of the British or the Canadians. Ain't that right, son?"

Tim nodded. He had already decided to go so he could be close to Patricia Scott.

"Claude," Ma said. "Steamboats cost money. Lots of money."

"That's a certain fact, Matilda. So do Conestoga wagons. We'll have need of one of those, too. One for us. One for Aaron, Doris, and Patricia."

The name *Conestoga* rang a bell in Tim's head, bringing his thoughts back to what had happened and why he was freezing in the water of a beaver dam. Not wanting to go in that direction, he remembered hearing of the Conestoga Turnpike. Said to be the shortest way from Philadelphia to Harrisburg, it was a windy, hilly road that connected the Lancaster Pike and the Ridge Road.

He'd traveled in the Conestoga that was a wagon—eighteen feet long from tongue to tail. Patricia had once paced off one that had been parked in front of Old Man Wessler's blacksmith shop on Bloom Road. The floor had been curved upward.

"Keeps the load from tipping or shifting," Old Man Wessler had told them.

The wagons, pulled by some of the biggest draft horses that Tim had ever seen, got their name from a river over in Lancaster County. Made mostly by Germans. Mennonites, Old Man Wessler had said, but he had not explained to Tim or Patricia exactly what a Mennonite was.

"Wagon like that," Old Man Wessler had marveled, "can haul twelve thousand pounds."

Tim shook his head. He remembered thinking that maybe a wheelbarrow would have held anything his Ma, Pa, and sisters owned. With nothing else to do, he let his thoughts drift some more.

"A wagon?" Ma asked.

"Yep," Pa said.

"Steamboats?" Nancy asked.

"Yep."

"That'll cost us a lot of money," Ma said.

Pa seemed to sober up. "I know. But it'll be worth it, once we have our own farm, our own cabin in the Willamette Valley in Oregon. I promise you."

"But . . ." Ma began, but her voice trailed off.

"We shall save. We shall skimp. We shall do what we must because what you and I both want is for our children, for Nancy and Tim and Margaret, to have better lives, to be able to breathe clean air, and to be free. Whatever it takes, Matilda. The way I figure things, in a year, we should have saved enough money to pay our way to Oregon."

Tim almost laughed out loud at that. Actually, it had taken them two years.

CHAPTER 5

"Thar ya go." Deftly, Jim Bridger pulled the stitch in a tight knot, and, holding the long bone needle in his fingers, clipped the thread with a pair of hand-forged scissors in his other hand.

Jed Reno studied the old mountain man. His fingers were long, calloused, filthy, and now stained with blood, Reno's blood.

Not sure he wanted to look at his side, Reno focused on the needle and thread. "Is that horsehair?"

Bridger dropped the suturing equipment into a wooden bowl and fetched a jug off the hard-packed earthen floor that served as a porch in front of the trading post. "Jed, a sorry cuss like you don't warrant no horsehair. But I plucked the finest hair I could find from a good mule I traded fer a couple weeks back."

Raising both arms, Jed Reno let one of the Indian squaws hanging around the post wrap the knife cut with a clean sheet. Clean? Well, in that country, cleanliness seemed a relative term. He grimaced when the short, squat, silver-haired woman tightened the make-shift bandage. She picked up the scissors, cut the left-over strip of calico, and walked away, dragging the cotton behind her without another word.

Bridger plucked the cork from the jug and took a heavy pull.

Reno looked at his side, surprised to see no blood already staining the bandage, and took the jug Bridger offered him.

"You do good doctoring, Jim."

Wiping his mouth, Bridger's wild eyes flashed. "Ol' Hoss, I've had me a passel of practicin'."

The liquor in the jug wasn't the Taos Lightning— red-eye rotgut of maybe two hundred proof seasoned with gunpowder, black pepper, tobacco juice, and a snakehead or two–Reno had expected. It went down smooth and sweet as bourbon.

"By Jupiter, that's pure Kentucky."

"Pennsylvania"—Bridger looked up from putting his own blend of kinnikinnick, more bark and leaves than tobacco into his pipe and pointed the stem of the pipe at the Conestoga wagons that were pulling away from the post—"or so some wayfarer told me. Won't blind you none, but I ain't used to such whiskey. Or such people." He found a match, stared at it dumbly, and then dropped it on the table, and fetched a branch from the fire at his side. He used that to light his pipe. After a puff or two, he again gestured toward the emigrants.

"Country's crowdin' up. In a year or two, this place won't be fit to live in."

Reno took another swallow of bourbon. It numbed the ache in his side. Since Malachi Murchison was long gone, he might as well rest his side, see if Bridger's doctoring and the mule-hair stitches would hold. Rest up. Not get too drunk. Then he would hit the trail, track down Murchison, and even the score.

He thought about what the rat had told him. "Jim, have you seen Louis Jackatars of late?"

The old trapper's eyes narrowed, and he slowly removed the blackened pipe stem from his mouth. "I patch you up, and you try to ruin my smoke?"

Reno grinned. Bridger didn't.

"Half-breed Métis rapscallion." Bridger spit into the fire. "Nah. Ain't laid eyes or fists on his sorry hide since . . ." His voice trailed off as he leaned back, staring at the roof over the porch, and seemed fascinated by the construction. "I recollect the times when I didn't remember what a roof was," he said wistfully.

Reno looked up too. "We'd build cabins." The roof did seem amazing, even if the lean-to over by the pens was probably better constructed.

"In the winter . . . unless we was winterin' with some red she-devil to keep us warm." Suddenly, Bridger leaned forward and slapped his knee. "You recollect that time ol' Broken Hand Fitzpatrick squared off ag'in' . . . who was it?"

Reno smiled at the memory. "It was Kit Carson."

"The hell you say." Again, Bridger's eyes flashed dangerously. "Carson wasn't no bully. He an' Broken Hand was good boys."

Reno slid the jug back toward Bridger, who lowered his pipe long enough to take a long pull. Pennsylvania bourbon could douse a fire before it got out of hand.

"No, Jim. I meant it was Carson who tangled with Chouinard." Reno thought back for the name. "Joseph. That's it. Joseph Chouinard."

With a grin and a nod, Bridger pushed the jug back to Reno.

"That's right. Chouinard. The Great Bully of the Mountains. When was that?"

Reno had to study on that. Years came and went, and Reno couldn't remember the last time he had seen a real calendar. Even the Indians would paint memories on a hide, something their grandchildren's grandchildren could use as a bit of history. Pictures like The Winter Three Foxes Killed The White Buffalo. The Year Of The Spotted Death. The Summer When The Fire Destroyed White Elk's Village And Killed Three Hundred Ponies. Things like that. But mountain men? They had nothing to fall back on. No written accounts, except if one counted maybe the ledger books of the purveyors who had come to the Rendezvouses to trade possibles for plews.

"It was after Pierre's Hole," Reno said at last, thinking *and before it all ended.*

"On the Green," Bridger said. "Or near it." A touch of melancholy could be heard in his ragged voice. Likely, he was thinking similar thoughts to those in Reno's memories.

"Most of 'em were," Reno said. "I'm thinking near Fort Bonneville."

Bridger shook off the doldrums and depression of years gone by, and grinned. "Where or when it was don't matter none. What matters, by grab, as that we remember it." He swallowed bourbon and passed the jug to Reno, who did the same.

He was right, Bridger was. And no one was likely to forget that time on or near the Green River, maybe back in '35.

That blowhard Joseph Chouinard, "The Great Bully of the Mountains," had been bragging and fighting, and whupping the tar and feathers out of most anyone who dared contradict him or argue with him. He had beaten up two of his own, or maybe three, leaving those French-Canadians bloodied and broken. And then, one afternoon, he decided to pick fights with any Americans, if they had the sand to stand up to a bear of a man like him.

"I shall take a switch," the Frenchie had bragged, "and switch them I shall, for Americans are nothing more than mewling school boys."

And who should come to the fire but a little rooster, a thin, wiry cuss who looked like a dwarf when he stood next to the big bully.

"Shut your trap," the rooster crowed, "or I will rip out your guts."

That was the challenge, and Joseph Chouinard accepted. Immediately, he rose and returned to his lodge. Kit Carson, that cocky little bantam, did the same.

It was on the Green River. Reno remembered. He knew the month—August—and the year—1835. He pictured everything perfectly, the open field enclosed by the lodges the traders and trappers and Indians had set up. Bets were being made as everyone gathered around to watch the fight.

Chouinard returned first, mounted on his big stallion, armed with his Hawken rifle. He studied the field, and laughed. "*Lâche.* The *Américain*, he has run back to find his *mère*, no? Ha! I would—" He swallowed his words, for there at the opposite end of the field rode the little bantam fighting cock, Kit Carson, on a wiry skewbald of an Indian pony.

Carson had been in such a hurry that he hadn't even bothered saddling his mount. He rode bareback and carried a big horse pistol in his right hand. His left held the hackamore.

The bully let loose with a curse and kicked his mount. Carson did the same. As they galloped toward each other, some Indian squaw began singing a death song. More bets were made, and then both riders pulled hard on their hackamores, and their horses slid to a stop. The mounts were so close, their heads actually touched.

Carson's voice carried across the open field. "Are you the French dog that aims to shoot me?"

"No!" Chouinard yelled, already lifting his rifle.

Carson brought his horse pistol up.

Two shots roared as one, and both riders disappeared in a cloud of white smoke. You could see the lower halves of the horses, feet dancing on the ground, and then a body slammed on one side. It was the body of the bully.

The smoke cleared.

Carson weaved in the saddle but did not fall, and slowly he tugged on the hackamore, neck-reining the pinto gelding into a turn. He trotted back toward his lodge, holding the smoking horse pistol in his right hand.

It had been a pretty good duel. Something to be talked about, to be embellished, over the coming years. Taos Lightning, other scraps, and other long drunks had fogged the memories of Jed Reno and Jim Bridger.

Both men agreed that Carson had fired first, which had saved the little trapper's life. His ball blasted through the bully's right hand. Bridger said it blew his whole hand off, but Reno thought it only took off a thumb, and maybe the top of the trigger finger.

"No," Bridger said. "The ball went straight through the arm and came out near the elbow."

The two did agree Chouinard had managed a shot, but since Carson's bullet struck first, it had spoiled the bully's aim. Otherwise, Kit Carson would have been dead and the bully would have won the duel. Instead of drilling the bantam cock straight in the heart, the French-Canadian's ball had carved out a good chunk of flesh along Carson's neck. And the powder burns had scorched Carson's eyes and singed his hair.

As Chouinard lay writhing on the ground, his horse wandering away, Carson dismounted, and still furious and full of fight, found another pistol. That's what Reno remembered.

Bridger disagreed. "Carson fetched his own rifle, a .50-caliber beauty."

Reno conceded that Bridger was probably right because not too many mountain men carried more than one horse pistol.

Either way, Carson returned to the field bound and determined to finish off the "Great Bully of the Mountains."

The two men on the trading post porch stared at one another, remembering. They drank more bourbon, and they smoked awhile for Jed Reno had put some tobacco in his own pipe, lighting it with the match Bridger had left on the table near the bowl that held the mule hair and the long bone needle.

"Did Carson kill the bully?" Bridger finally asked.

Reno blew a stream of blue smoke toward the beautiful roof over the porch of dirt. "That was a long time ago, Jim." *What has it been? Seven years? Eight?*

"He wanted to," Bridger said. "That much I recollects. Maybe that's when Broken Hand Fitzpatrick stopped him. Could be how come I got a mite confused over who was in the fight."

"Could be." Reno found the jug of bourbon and looked around. The last of the Conestogas was a quarter mile to the west. "Was Chouinard the one we had to chop his arm off when it took to festering?"

Bridger's head shook. "That was Thunder Bay Chadron. On the Pope Agie."

That was right, Reno remembered. "Thunder Bay. Another French-Canadian."

"Got his fingers took off in a trap. The gangrene set in. Jim Beckwourth cut off the arm with his hatchet." Bridger used the pipe stem to show where the blade had fallen.

"Jim Beckwourth," Reno said. Another name, another memory. "He still living with the Crows?"

"Was a chief or somethin'." Bridger sighed. "Nah. He taken off before '40, got civilized, took to tradin'. Last I heard tale, he'd set up shop at Fort Vasquez fer Bent and Saint Vrain and that lot of hoss thieves."

"Country ain't the same no more, Jim," Reno said. "People ain't the same."

"Peoples is stupid," Bridger lamented.

Reno figured they were both drunk enough, so he set his pipe on the table, belched, and asked, "So iffen a body had a mind to hunt down Louis Jackatars, gut him like a fish, and lift his topknot, where mighten he look first?"

CHAPTER 6

Tim Colter woke up with a start. He didn't remember falling asleep. In fact, standing in the freezing water, he didn't understand how he could have fallen asleep. His teeth chattered so relentlessly, he feared they might shatter. His waterlogged legs felt numb. He blinked and blinked, and heard the beavers snarling at him. He could see them glaring at him, telling him it was time to leave their home.

He sucked in a deep breath. It was morning. He could see the beavers and the few rays of sunlight that managed to sneak through the wooden dam the animals had constructed. He also smelled something besides the musky odor of the wild animals whose home he had invaded. His stomach began to growl and his mouth watered.

Someone had lit a fire and was cooking breakfast.

"Mama . . ." he whispered, and made his way out of the beaver dam.

Maybe it had been a dream. Yet he had spent the

night all alone standing inside a beaver dam, wet, cold, and crying. Sleepwalk? Had he? He wasn't sure. He did remember Old Man Peevy back in Danville. Everybody said the drunkard would roll out of his bed maybe once a month in the middle of the night, walk in his nightshirt all the way to the Grove Furnace. If you stopped him, he would talk to you as though he were wide awake and it was two in the afternoon, instead of three in the morning. Sometimes, he would even say that he was sleepwalking. Other times, maybe the night watchman at the furnace would tell him that it was a holiday, or that Mr. Peevy had the day off, or even that he was sleepwalking and needed to go to bed. Tim had always wanted to see Old Man Peevy sleepwalking . . . or anybody sleepwalking, for that matter. He thought it would be a funny thing to see.

Tim shook his head.

Sleepwalking. Yeah. That's what I must have done. Me and Old Man Peevy.

He heard the bubbling of the water as he sloshed through it, felt his shoes on the stones in the creek's bed as he came out of the water, breathing in fresh morning air that did not reek of animals, beaver scat, or wood felled by the sharp teeth of animals and stacked in a creek. The sun felt good, and his face warmed by the touch of daylight. Even though filtered by the trees, it also blinded him. He smelled the salt pork sizzling in a skillet.

"Ma!" he yelled. "Ma! It's me."

His eyes opened, shut tightly, opened again. He was surprised that he could still stand on his own feet. He blinked, and looked at his fingers, the skin shriveled up like an old prune he had been in that awful water so long.

"Pa!" he called out. He found the smoke, white and small and snaking its way through the trees. "Margaret! Nancy!" Another name came to him. He wet his lips with his tongue. "Patricia!"

Water pooled at his feet, and then he saw the shadow rise in front of the smoke. His heart pounded. He half expected to see his father striding toward him, scolding him for making his ma worry herself sick, that this territory was no place to play hide-and-seek.

The shadow moved toward him, slowly coming into focus. His heart stopped. His breath held. He shook with fright and the awful memories of what he had witnessed, what he had run from yesterday.

He was not sleepwalking. He had not dreamed anything.

The man in greasy buckskins standing before him was not his father.

That man sprayed tobacco juice on a sapling, wiped his mouth with the back of his left hand, and said with a wry chuckle, "I told the breed that ye was hidin' in that beaver dam."

Tim Colter heard himself say, "Huh?"

"The breed, he says, 'Nah. That squirt ain't Colter.' He says—"

"I am Colter."

Again, Tim heard his own voice.

The man's eyes narrowed. "What did ye say?"

Tim swallowed. He shivered. "Where's my ma?" he asked, trying to hide the fright in his voice. Trying, but knowing he had failed. "My pa?"

The bearded man grinned again. His teeth were blacker than his hair, which was braided, Indian fashion, and hung well past his shoulders. He wore buckskins and moccasins. A hatchet hung in the belt around his waist, along with a big flintlock pistol. Loop earrings of shiny brass and tarnished silver, hung in his left ear, and his hat was the head and tail of some wild animal Tim did not recognize. Red, yellow, and black markings were on his face not covered by the thick black beard. War paint of some kind. Vermillion. Whatever else Indians used.

Memories so horrible almost knocked Tim to his knees. He could hear his mother screaming again, and his sister, and those horrible yells of the Indians as they swarmed. His mother's shouts echoed. He put his pruny hands to his ears, hoping to block out her shouts. He didn't want to hear them, but they were in his head. Forever.

Run, Tim! Run!

Again, he saw the tomahawk slam into Ma's head.

The buckskin man with braids stepped closer, and Tim lowered his hands.

"Where's my pa?" he asked timidly.

The man grinned his black teeth. "Ye'll see 'im soon, boy. And yer ma, too." With that, he drew a knife that had been sheathed behind his back. "Real soon."

Tim blinked. He still wasn't sure it wasn't some horrible nightmare. Indians had attacked the wagons. Indians. But this man . . . he was dressed like an Indian with the war paint on his face and his hair hanging in greasy braids. Yet . . .

"You're white," Tim said.

"Aye. And yer dead."

With a scream, Tim turned and ran. Well, he tried to run, but the black-braided white man moved like a deer, and before Tim had covered five strides, he felt the breath leave his lungs, and he fell into the creek. He came out of the water, spitting and gasping for breath. Water cascaded off his face, and he saw the mountain man straddling him, laughing, while holding the knife in his left hand.

Tim tried to brace himself for the blade, wondering if the man would slice his throat or stab him in the heart. Maybe he would gut him like a fish. Whatever, Tim knew he was about to die. He wanted to pray. He wanted to close his eyes so he would not see the death coming. Yet his eyes felt frozen in fear. They would not even blink.

"Knife'd be too easy for a sister like ye, boy." The man tossed the knife to the bank. "Ye be as wet as a trout." He laughed. "Let's see if ye can swim."

The man leaned forward, planting both hands on Tim's shoulders, and shoved him into the water. Tim tried to suck in as much breath as he could. His head banged against the stones lining the bed. His lungs screamed for air. His eyes were closed.

The water muffled his hearing, but he could make out the man's laughter. Playing. Toying with Tim. Killing him slowly. Tim's fingers flexed in the water. He tried to bring himself up, but the man was too strong. He had maybe a good foot and more than a hundred pounds on Tim, and he was a man. Tim knew he was only a boy. In a moment, he would be a dead boy.

Just when Tim thought his lungs would explode,

that he would have to open his mouth and nose and drown, he felt himself jerked out of the water. His head hurt. His lungs burned as he sucked in fresh air while water poured off his face, his head, his shoulders, and his arms. He coughed and gagged.

The man laughed. "Not so fast. Not so fast. I had to spend all night out here, waitin' fer ye. I wants ye to die real slow. Then I'll cut off yer head and show it to the breed."

"But—"

Tim felt the wind rush, and felt himself being pushed back down toward the stream. Once again, he felt the cold water—though it did not feel quite as frigid—and his head hit the creek bed so hard he opened his mouth and swallowed a mouthful of the dirty water before his instincts took over, closing the airways and stopping himself from drowning. His hands groped. His brain worked. He heard the man's evil laughter, heard him say, "Die, boy, but die slow. Slowly. So ye shall remember me and yer death when yer dancin' in the fires below."

He almost opened his mouth and lungs, just to spoil his killer's fun. He could drown himself. End the misery. See his mother. His father. Maybe even Patricia Scott.

A second before he opened his mouth to end it all, something took hold of him. Something made him stop. A voice inside his head cried *No!*

It was the voice of Patricia Scott. Something told him that she wasn't dead, but she was in desperate trouble. She needed him. She needed him to save her from a fate ten thousand times worse than death. So did his two sisters.

His hands worked. So did his brain. He would not die. Not there. Not at the hands of the big piece of vermin.

Again, the mountain man jerked Tim out of the water, laughing.

"How's it feel, boy?" His breath reeked. "Ye ready now, kid? Ye ready to die?"

Tim's eyes opened. He saw the man's face. As he breathed in fresh air, Tim brought his right hand up as fast, as hard, as he could swing it.

From the corner of his eye, the man spotted the movement, and his expression changed. He turned and cursed.

Holding a stone, the largest one Tim could find, smoothed by the fast-flowing water in the creeks for who knew how many years, his right hand smashed the corner of the man's head.

Tim didn't realize he had that much strength in him. Maybe he didn't. Maybe the braided man with the black teeth just had not expected it, or maybe the stone was harder than even Tim had imagined. He heard the crunch, and the man's grunt, and felt himself falling back into the creek. But he was not being pushed. He was falling on his own, and the man with the beard and the Indian paint and the sinister laugh was falling to his side.

Tim splashed in the water and rolled over. He didn't figure he had hit the man hard enough to kill him, and hearing the man's roars of curses, he knew he hadn't even knocked out that murdering cur.

Coming up out of the water, Tim tried to stand, but his shoes slipped on the wet stones, and he went down again, stopping himself with his hands. He pushed himself up and glanced at the killer. Fear paralyzed him.

Blood gushing from a gaping slice in his forehead, the man pulled the big horse pistol and roared, "Die! Die, pig!"

Tim saw the hammer fall. He saw the flash in the pan, but it wasn't much of a flash. It fizzed, and that was all. Likely, water had fouled the powder. Again, the man cursed and threw away the useless weapon. He turned, searching for the knife he had tossed aside when he'd decided to drown Tim.

The killer found the knife and lunged, but Tim was no longer there. The man fell into the water, came up cursing again, slicing wildly with the lethal blade.

Tim was running. Running for his life.

He reached the woods. Briars and brambles slapped at his face, ripped his soaked sleeves. He ran. Ran to live. Ran to somehow find Patricia and his sisters and save them. Ran to save his own hide.

The man with the knife was right behind him.

CHAPTER 7

Something told Tim not to run into the clearing. Stick to the woods. In the open, the man would run him down and use that knife to send him to meet his Maker. Yet the man chasing him had lived his life in the woods, trapping, killing, hunting. Tim was a kid from Danville, Pennsylvania. In the open, rolling hills or in the little thicket, he had no chance.

Yet he had to try. He lowered his shoulder, leaned forward, and ran as hard and as fast as he could, using his arms to shield his face from the low branches and brambles.

Tim's mind worked. Worked better than it had at the subscription school in Danville, or when his mother had taught him ciphering and helped him with his reading and writing on the long journey from Pennsylvania to the Oregon Country. Even as he ran to stay alive, his brain worked.

For the moment, he was outrunning the killer but he knew he couldn't outrun a grown man, an experienced woodsman. Not for the long haul. Sooner or later, the mountain man would be on top of him, and then Tim would die. He understood something else. He had gotten out of the stream, gotten past the man with the black teeth and braids, for one simple reason. He had surprised the murdering dog.

He needed to surprise him again.

He slid down a little knoll of straw and rocks, and picked up a piece of old wood from a tree branch. Wielding the stick, maybe four inches in diameter and three feet long, he turned on his knees and looked up the incline.

The man with buckskins and braids exploded from the woods and slid down the knoll, his eyes widening when he saw Tim. The surprise had worked.

Tim swung the limb and smelled the tar of the pine. The wood splintered as he slammed it into the mountain man's face. Blood spurted as the nose broke. The limb flew apart, but the mountain man fell, sliding past Tim.

As Tim leaped over him, he saw the knife, and desperately wanted to pick it up. The knife would give him a chance. But again, his brain worked, telling him not to stop. Not to attempt making a play for the knife. The man with the braids was experienced. He could grab Tim's legs, jerk him to the ground, and finish what he had started.

Run.

That's what Tim's brain told him to do.

That's what Tim Colter did.

He leaped over the man still on his knees groping and spitting and cussing, and sprinted back up the trail—if you could call it a trail—hoping and praying that he wouldn't slip and slide back down into the mountain man's arms. At the crest of the incline, he reached up and grabbed a little sapling. It held, did not come up by its roots, and Tim pulled, lifting himself to the top.

Something whistled over his head and smashed into a tree. The man had thrown a piece of rotting wood at him, but he had missed. Tim lunged forward, his feet digging as hard as they could as he carried himself back through the woods.

To his left stood the clearing, the prairie, the hills and the camp. He knew better. With no place to hide, something even worse would meet him there. He would see his mother and his father—maybe even his sisters if he was mistaken in believing that they might still be alive—and that would stop him. He would freeze, and the man would be atop him, and Tim would indeed join his parents in death.

To his right flowed the creek. The woods did not go on forever. Stones. Stones had stopped the burly man with the knife. Stones were in the creek bed. He remembered the story he had read and heard so many times during his life. *David and Goliath. David has slain the giant with a slingshot.* Tim had no slingshot, no weapon at all, but he could use those stones in the creek. He had already used one, and that was why he still breathed and his heart still beat.

He turned that way, bursting from the woods, looking at the sun reflecting off the river. He didn't see the dam the beavers had made, at least, not at first. Because he had come out well before it. He had run a lot farther through the timbers than he had believed. The dam, and something else, was down the stream. Tim saw it, blinked, and ran.

Behind him, the big man with the knife burst out of the forest.

No longer did Tim feel cold. His clothes remained wet—he didn't know if he would ever feel completely dry after spending all night inside that beaver dam—but at least he was warm, even sweating as he ran. His muscles burned and his breath came harder. He knew he was slowing down and the mountain man was closing in on him.

Tim's side screamed in agony. He was leaning to one side as he ran. Behind him, the man felt too close to snatch a stone from the bed of the stream. Tim saw what he thought might help and lowered his arm as he ran.

It might have been a mistake. The action slowed him, and he needed all the speed he could summon. His hand gripped the walnut stock of the pistol the man had dropped, and he brought it up as the man dived behind him, reaching out with his hand that did not grip the knife. His fingers caught just enough of Tim's left leg to send him tumbling to the ground.

He rolled, grunted, tumbled, and his head boomed with pain—he had hit something, but didn't know exactly what. He came up and saw the man coming at him on his knees. His face was bloody and scratched and flushed from heat and exhaustion. Yet Tim could see murder in the man's eyes.

He could also see the knife in the man's right hand.

He waited, trying to find pride and strength within his heart. When the man, still walking on his knees, raised the knife, Tim swung.

The iron barrel of the fouled horse pistol smashed into the man's jaw, splitting his lip and knocking out a few teeth. Again, the man dropped like a felled tree and the momentum carried Tim to the ground.

He wanted to lie there to catch his breath, to rest until he could move again. But to do so meant death, and Tim was not going to die. He rolled just in time. The blade came down with a *whump*, and the mountain man cursed and screamed. The blade was buried to the hilt in the damp earth. Tim came to his knees, his lungs heaving, working and trying to grasp what little oxygen the air held. He fell backwards onto his buttocks and saw the man, his face bloodier than before, jerk the knife free from the dirt.

The man was exhausted. He had to be. The knife left his grip and flew a few yards away. That was enough time—or all the time Tim had—to make himself stand, turn, and run.

Three times he had surprised the mountain man. The killer would be even more wary and would have enough hatred to not make any more mistakes.

Tim forgot about the stones and ran back toward he woods. The man swore, said something that Tim could not understand, and went after him.

Luck. That's what Tim needed. Luck or someone to come to his rescue. Maybe his father was still alive. Maybe Mr. Scott had loaded his Pennsylvania rifle and was waiting for the man with the buckskins and braids to show himself. Tim ran, but his brain had stopped working. He ran into the woods and made a straight path along the animal trail into the clearing. He ran to the campsite where his mother had yelled as the Indians—*no, not Indians. Is the man with the knife a renegade white man, running with the red savages?* He tried not to think.

He saw the two wagons, the one belonging to his family and the one that the Scotts had purchased. He saw his mother's dress. Again, he tried not to think. He tried not to run toward the camp, the last camp his family had ever made. Yet he could not help himself.

His mother was lying there and she might need him. She might still be alive. He ran toward her, and saw her eyes staring at him. He saw the blood that had poured out of her mouth. He saw the blood on her chest, and the arrows pinning her into the earth. She looked like a pincushion. Her head had been split open, too, and her scalp had been removed.

She was dead.

Dead.

He knew that. He did not stop, but leaped over her body. His feet and legs gave out, and he dropped, rolling, spinning, heading toward the left rear wheel of the big Conestoga. He saw his father when he stopped rolling.

They had slit his throat. They had taken his scalp.

Tim had never seen anyone so butchered. Oh, he remembered the stories. Western Pennsylvania had not always been so civilized. White settlers had tangled with Iroquois and other Indians over the years. Even some men in Danville had fought them in past years. He had heard and read about scalpings. About death.

These were the first scalped bodies he had ever seen, though, and to see his own parents so small, so tiny, so dead.

He was played out. He pulled himself up by gripping the spokes of the wheel, and leaned against the big wheel. Grinning, the man with the buckskins and braids was coming at him, his face still red with hatred. The big man leaped over the dead body of Matilda Colter, and it seemed as if even in death, Tim's mother had tripped the man with her outstretched hand.

It didn't happen that way, of course. His mother did not move. She could not move. She was dead. But the man had tripped over her hand, and down he went, screaming and cursing and landing on his stomach.

Tim felt his heart banging against his ribs. He was still breathing, but he could not move.

He watched the man with the black teeth and black braids push himself up with his right hand. He came to his knees. His left hand held the bone-handled grip of the knife and pulled, but the sweaty hand could not pull the knife out of the man's own chest.

Tim blinked. He felt confused.

The man with the black hair and buckskins looked just as confused, and his face no longer burned red, but was pale as the ash from a fire that had burned all night.

The man looked at the knife sticking out of his chest. He stared back at Tim.

Blood stained the man's buckskin shirt and dribbled from a corner of his mouth into his beard.

"Ye . . ." The man coughed. "A kid . . . Ye . . . It can't . . . It . . ."

He fell to his side. His eyes never closed. And his heart never beat again.

CHAPTER 8

West of the Continental Divide, the Big Sandy flowed south and southwest—when it had water. So late in the year, it was a mere trickle. Although the land was gently rolling and the white-capped mountains of the Wind Range to the north and Essex Mountain to the east could be seen, mostly all a body ever saw were antelope, Indians, and sagebrush—which is why Louis Jackatars had set up camp there. Nobody could sneak up on him. He could see forever.

It was a land of contrasts. Nearby Boar Tusk served as a landmark for travelers across the Red Desert; the rugged high country to the north and the verdant valleys of the Green River, which the Big Sandy fed into; the wondrous Flaming Gorge carved by the Green River to the south; Sinks Canyon in the Popo Agie at the southeastern edge of the Winds; the valleys that surprised a person traveling across what seemed like a vast, flat wasteland—Alkali Wash, South Packsaddle Canyon, Blind Canyon, Split Rock Canyon, and Box Canyon. The sand dunes, the creeks, and the springs—Indian Spring, Ox Yoke Springs, Deer Springs, Hillside Springs, and Rock Springs down to the south—where a man could find water when the creeks ran dry.

Louis Jackatars had always loved that country, especially the Red Desert. The high-elevation badlands were spectacular with sandstone buttes, deep canyons—even the sand dunes that rain (but mostly wind) kept shifting.

It was where the Continental Divide split, then rejoined. You could see a herd of desert elk, not the mountain variety, but a herd that lived and survived in the windswept, harsh country.

He loved the sage grouse. They weren't too plentiful around that time of year, but come fall, a person could hunt them forever amid the open plains, grass pastures, and all the sage that grew.

Antelope and deer—both white-tailed and muleys—called that area home. Great eating. Great country. Too bad people had to ruin it.

All of the country in the unorganized territory could be spectacular. The towering Rocky Mountains, the Tetons, and the Absaroka Range off to the northwest and those hot springs and geysers. That magnificent gorge cut by the Green River down south. The Big Horn mountains off to the northeast, and the wild Yellowstone River.

Jackatars had seen most of it. Indeed, he had seen places no eyes had beheld before his. He remembered seeing the Owl Creek Mountains for the first time, and how intimidating the canyon cut by the Shoshone River had made him feel. How the country changed far off to the east where the hills still rolled and the wind always blew. He remembered the grass that fed the buffalo and those Black Hills to the northeast.

Yes, it was a country of contrasts . . . and a place that Louis Jackatars, mad as he knew he was, wanted all for himself. If he could not have it, then no one else could.

He considered the contrasts in the men who lived there, too. There were plenty of good men. And there was Louis Jackatars. And the vermin who rode with him.

Jackatars said that he came from a long line of *coureurs des bois*, those fabled "runners of the woods" who left the civilization of Montreal to explore the land to the west and south, to trade with the Indians, and learn the ways of the natives. They were *voyageurs* who traveled by canoe who didn't believe in acquiring a trading license from the government but, when it came to Indian maidens, did believe in *marriage à la façon du pays*.

In reality, Louis Jackatars knew nothing about his heritage beyond the fact that his mother was a Red River Métis Indian from Canada and his father was a fur-trading vagabond who had been killed by Blackfeet when Jackatars was ten years old. He did not remember much about his father, who was around only every two or three winters, but he had followed in his father's footsteps.

He lived among Indians and white men. He trapped, traded, robbed, raped, and killed.

Standing in the wet sand along the creek bed, he watched the dust rising from the south. One horse, still coming at a hard trot. He figured it to be Malachi Murchison, and the dumb sot had better be bringing good news, along with the head of Jed Reno. Turning, he looked off toward South Pass, but saw nothing.

That troubled him. Baillarger should be back by now, bringing good news, and the scalp of that boy who had escaped their well-planned massacre. Jackatars could send another man to see what was keeping Baillarger, but that could prove risky. Another train of emigrants could already have discovered the two Conestogas and the remains of the butchered travelers. That much Jackatars knew would happen, and wanted to happen, but he didn't want one of his men to be found, alive or dead, near the site.

Again, he looked back at the dust. Footsteps sounded behind him, but the half-breed Métis did not turn around.

"Dust," said Dog Ear Rounsavall. The Frenchman spit. "Murchison."

Jackatars nodded.

"What if it is Reno?" Rounsavall asked.

That caused Jackatars to laugh. "Jed Reno would not make so much dust. He is no fool."

Jackatars was a slim, lithe man. Folks said that the buckskins he wore, heavily beaded blue, red, and white, weighed more than he did, especially when soaking wet after fording a river. Fringe hung in foot-long strips around his shoulders, sleeves, and the sides of his *mitasses,* as his people called the leather leggings. His moccasins were well worn and on their third set of soles. The bright red sash, sporting the pattern known as a *ceinture fléchée,* carried a small bone-handled weapon more dagger than knife, a large-caliber horse pistol, and a longer, curved knife. A wide-brimmed, low-crowned tan hat with three eagle feathers sticking out from the left side, topped his head. Jackatars's black hair, always cut evenly, hung to just above his shoulders, unlike most fur trappers of the region. Likewise, instead of sporting a full beard, he kept his dark face clean-shaven except for the small, thin mustache.

In his buckskins and fur hat, Dog Ear Rounsavall towered over Louis Jackatars, but no one in the camp would have bet against the half-breed Métis in a fight.

A woman screamed from the center of the camp, and, with a vile curse in the Métis language, Jackatars moved away from the Big Sandy.

He saw the circle of men—if even a rogue like Louis Jackatars would call these animals *men*—and drew the little dagger from its sheath in his left hand and the flintlock pistol in his right. He knew what the men were up to, and blood rushed to his face. "Imbeciles!" he yelled.

Two rough-looking white men turned and quickly parted, allowing Jackatars to move into the circle.

Three girls still in their teens cowered on a saddle. Their hair resembled the nests of rats, and their pale faces and arms had been burned by the sun after a hard day and night of traveling. They wore only chemises for tops, and their skirts had been ripped between their legs so they could ride. Their feet were covered with stockings, but Jackatars had pulled off their shoes and pitched them miles back.

If they tried to escape, they would not get far without shoes, and not without hats or bonnets to protect them from the sun. The oldest girl, the one called Patricia, had an arm around the other girls, two sisters. All three were quite pretty for white girls, despite the dirt and grime and blood that covered their bodies. Jackatars had told them that they could bathe in the Big Sandy. It had been a pretty good joke, he had thought, knowing that the creek would not have enough water to wash one's hands in so late in the summer. The snowmelt from the mountains was practically in the Pacific Ocean.

The petrified girls were looking at the two men whose backs were all that Louis Jackatars saw. Beneath one of the men's legs, a slender, bare leg dug ditches in the sand. The men laughed.

Jackatars strode toward them, furious. "Smith!" he called out, his voice savage.

The big red-bearded man with the pockmarked face—the one hovering over the woman's leg—turned his face, his grin fading. He started to stand, but Jackatars never gave him the chance. The pistol boomed in the half-breed's hand, and the man's beard erupted in a blaze that quickly died. Smith also died quickly.

The shot replaced the mountain man's nose with a bloody hole, and Jackatars had fired the pistol at such close range, powder blackened what was left of the dead man's face. His body flew backwards and landed on the woman.

The other idiot, a renegade Crow with only one ear, came up quickly, clawing for his big stag-horn knife, but Jackatars moved in quickly. He punched the man with the dagger just above his navel, and the

Crow Indian's knife slipped from his grip, landing in the sagebrush.

"I told you," Jackatars said with a whisper, "that we keep our hands off the ladies."

He never told anyone anything twice. He brought the blade up to the rib cage, and then used the smoking pistol still in his right hand to push the Crow away. The Indian fell to his knees, trying to hold his belly together while attempting to sing his death song. The words were choked with the blood pouring from his mouth, and he fell to the ground, pushed himself up once, only to collapse in the sage, staining the green shrubs and brown sand with his blood.

The woman, with her blond hair wet with sweat, crawled from underneath the dead man.

Jackatars turned toward the men who had gathered to watch and cheer and laugh. He dropped his empty pistol in the sage and pulled the curved knife with his right hand. He had killed more men with knives than with pistols, anyway. One look at his gang and he knew he had nothing more to fear.

He repeated in English, French, Métis, and Crow, what he had told the dead Indian and gestured at the corpses behind him. Using the small knife as a pointer, he picked four men and ordered them to bury the dead men deep, so no wolves and no white men would ever find their bodies.

Finally, sheathing both blades, he walked to the woman. She was good-looking, even with her busted lip and a face paled with fear. Trembling fingers held her chemise together, keeping her breasts from spilling out where the fiends had ripped the undergarment, but the two men had not done anything else—thanks to Louis Jackatars. He shook his head.

Idiots. Did they think they could have gotten away with it? Were they that drunk or that lustful?

Kneeling beside the woman, he held out his hands. "You are safe now."

Color returned to her face and life suddenly filled her eyes. She spit between his moccasins.

Jackatars laughed. "You have spirit. That I like in a woman."

She came up to her knees quick as a rattlesnake and struck out with her right hand. He caught her wrist with his left and jerked her forward, close to him, then took her left hand and squeezed like a vise until she cried out and tears ran down her cheeks.

"Spirit I like, but only so much. Too much salt spoils the food."

He shoved her to the ground, admiring her breasts for a moment, before rising. "Go to your child and her friends, wench. Fix your chemise so no one else gets any fool notions. Remember that I saved your life and the lives of your daughter and those other two girls. Remember that I, and only I, Louis Jackatars, can keep you alive."

He tried to remember the woman's name and the names of the three teenage captives. *Lois. No, Doris.* She was the mother of the girl named Patricia. The other two girls, the sisters of the brother who had fled into the woods when they had attacked, he could not remember. There had been another woman, the mother of the two other girls and the boy who had escaped death—unless Baillarger had found him and killed him and was on his way to join Jackatars and his renegades. But she had fought against Dog Ear Rounsavall too hard to live. He regretted having to kill the woman. None of the men had any regrets about killing the two men.

They had been fools, as most of the emigrants were, and had died easily. After filling the men's bodies with arrows, the renegades had taken their scalps—and even the scalp of the dead woman—and ransacked the trunks they had found in the wagon. They'd considered burning the wagons, too, but decided against it, in case a hunting party was in the area and came too quickly to discover that white men and renegades had been responsible, and not the relatively peaceful Indians to the north.

By the time the mother was being comforted by the teenage girls and four of his men were carrying the dead men away, Jackatars saw the horseman riding in from the south.

It was Malachi Murchison, and from the looks of the trapper and his horse, he had ridden hard—too hard—from Bridger's Trading Post on the Green.

CHAPTER 9

Jed Reno rode along Bitter Creek on the rim of the Red Desert, heading east. Eventually, he would turn north and ride toward the Popo Agie country, probably cutting through along the divide between Essex and Steamboat Mountains. His mule was fully packed and restocked after his visit with Jim Bridger and run-in with Malachi Murchison. If Louis Jackatars was around, Bridger had told him, he'd likely be around Sinks Canyon or heading north into the Tetons and Colter's Hell.

Murchison's trail had made a beeline northwest from Bridger's place, turning north after swimming the Green, toward the Big Sandy, Father DeSmet's mission, and those old Rendezvous sites that held so many memories for men like Jed Reno and Jim Bridger.

Reno didn't follow Murchison's trail, however. They would be expecting him, he figured, and Jackatars could lay an ambush with the best of men. Instead, Reno would try to sneak up on the evil Métis and knife-slashing Murchison by making a roundabout trip in country scarce of people, pick his way to South Pass, and then into the Rocky Mountains.

Jed Reno was no fool.

His bones creaked and his muscles ached as he shifted his weight in the saddle. *Old bones,* he figured, and not so much from the fight with Murchison. He tested his side, but those stitches of mule hair still held. No blood had leaked from the knife slash, though Malachi Murchison would give Reno another scar. Still, he was alive. He would make Murchison pay, partly thanks to old Bridger. Yep, Jim was mighty handy when it came to patching up his old pards.

If Murchison wasn't lying, Louis Jackatars was set to start an Indian uprising. But how? Most tribes had been feeling relatively peaceable of late, and even those long lines of prairie schooners trodding across the Great Plains and greater mountains did not trouble the Indians too much. The white men and women kept moving across the country of the Pawnees and Arapahos and Shoshones and Cheyennes and Paiutes and Utes . . . or whomever claimed it at the moment. The emigrants didn't scare off that much game, or take too much meat from Indian bellies, and they left behind a lot of interesting trinkets—blankets and mirrors and boxes and books, even furniture, when the fools traveling west realized that they had packed too much in their wagons for such an arduous journey.

The whites did not stop, so the Indians usually let them go.

The whites did not stop . . . yet. Jed Reno was a white man—at least, he had been once—and he understood that before long, the whites *would* stop. Oregon could not hold them all. Even fool emigrants would soon learn the land they were crossing was mighty good. When they started settling there, and when the Army sent its Dragoons and cannons and idiot soldier-boys to protect the new white settlers, war would come. It would be bloody, ugly, and last a long, long time.

Oh, the Indians would eventually lose. Whites would try to grow crops, or raise pigs, or something. The elk and the buffalo would disappear like the beaver. The country would not be fit for a man like Jed Reno. And Jed Reno did not see himself minding a store and swapping stories like Jim Bridger was doing down by the Green.

Of course, Jed Reno had once been like many of those starry-eyed white men, taking his family across the Great Plains and through the Rockies. Back when he had two eyes, wore duds made of muslin and wool, and learned his letters and to do his ciphering thanks to his mother. As he rode along, he gave in to long ago memories.

Bowling Green, Kentucky, had not been much of a place compared to Independence or St. Louis or Cincinnati, but it was home. It hadn't been called Bowling Green back when his ma and pa had settled on the north bank of the Barren River back in 1783. Back then, folks called the settlement McFadden's Station.

Jed came along in April of '96, four years after Kentucky had become the first state west of the Appalachians. He was the fifth child and fourth son to live. Two more girls followed.

Jed was not quite two years old when Warren County had been carved out of the wilderness, and Robert Moore, one of the first homesteaders, donated a couple acres for county trustees to put up some public buildings, and then some thirty or forty acres to plot out a new town. Bowling Green was incorporated in 1798. Of course, by the time Jed could count and even knew his ABCs, nobody could quite remember exactly how that name had been chosen.

He remembered turnips and beets the most about his hometown. Oh, there were plenty of people—maybe a hundred and fifty back when he was fourteen—not to mention riverboats. Folks had already been talking about erecting canal locks and building dams to make the Barren River easier to navigate and thereby making Bowling Green more important.

He dug up turnips that had a circumference of better than thirty inches, and beets weighing upward of fifteen pounds. Corn sprouted up like weeds. Sweet corn, too, some of the best a man would ever eat. He chopped down hickory. He hunted in the woods. To a teenage boy, Kentucky was paradise.

Yeah, I'd probably still be in Bowling Green, with a fat wife, a farm of his own, a couple coon dogs, and a brood of young'uns, attending camp meetings regular and frequenting the tavern only twice a week . . . if Pa hadn't been such a miser and a fool.

His pa decided to apprentice Jed to a wheelwright in Louisville. After all, even fifteen-pound beets and giant turnips couldn't feed seven kids. One less mouth to feed seemed a good financial incentive, and, well, Jed Reno always was on the wild side. He got the most whuppings and was prone to talk back to his elders, even the circuit-riding preacher.

Louisville was huge and right on the Ohio River. The wheelwright wasn't a bad fellow. In fact, Jed probably liked Mr. Sneed better than he liked his own pa. The food wasn't bad, either. Even if Mrs. Sneed made Jed wash on Saturdays and took him to church on Sundays and wouldn't let a body do a thing on the Sabbath except listen to the boring sermon and then read the Bible and pray and eat and sleep, they did let him go exploring for a few hours on Saturday afternoons.

It was on one such Saturday afternoon that he sneaked aboard a steamboat and went down the Ohio.

The crew quickly found him, but just worked him like a dog until they reached New Madrid on the north side of the Mississippi River's Kentucky Bend. That's about the time they got sick from bad pork and blamed Jed as a jinx. He hadn't been taken with vomiting and the runs, but only because the crew hadn't let him eat supper that night. But you couldn't tell a bunch of ruffians that, and Jed was sick of living on a keelboat, anyhow. They might have flogged him or just left him at the landing, but they kept him until the keelboat had pulled out and turned south toward New Orleans. After that, three men tossed him overboard about a mile downstream.

They figured he wouldn't know how to swim, but he had three older brothers who loved tossing him into the Barren back in Kentucky. Of course, the Mississippi was a whole lot wider, with a stronger current, but Jed made it to the Missouri side and walked back to the settlement.

He stole at first, but quickly got caught doing that, and the store owner put him to work, though he did let him sleep on a blanket in the storeroom and took to feeding him like a stray puppy dog after a couple days. About a week later, the

*owner, a man called Chester, started paying Jed five cents a
week.*

*Jed might have worked his way up to becoming a re-
spectable citizen in Missouri. New Madrid was small, and
the forests and river kept a boy active when he wasn't clerk-
ing, but something wild happened on December 16, 1811.*

Jed shook his head, surprised he remembered the
exact date. He'd been looking at the calendar on the
wall, making an *X* over the date, and suddenly he realized that his *X* was straying out of the sixteenth box
and the jar of sugar beside him was crashing to the
floor. The whole store kept shaking, spilling ax han-
dles he had carved, and Mrs. Chester was clutching
her throat and screaming that the world was coming
to an end.

He fell back into the memory of that day.

*Earlier, while sleeping on the floor, the floor seemed to
shake. He thought he was dreaming. That morning, the
ground began rumbling and the building kept rattling a
whole lot worse.*

*It didn't last long. When it was over, and Mrs. Chester
stopped screaming, and Mr. Chester brought out the broom
to sweep up the spilled sugar, everyone settled down. New
Madrid went back to business.*

*About a month later, the world shook again. Things were
a bit different. Jed was in the street, leading a mule to the
stable across from the store, when the mule stopped dead in
its tracks about a half-minute before the ground shook. Jed*

saw the ground, well, it seemed to be warping. He dropped the hackamore, dropped to the ground, and the mule bolted toward the river. What he saw almost caused him to soil his britches. A ditch was carving straight down the road toward him, but nobody was digging the ditch. Mrs. Chester said it was God's work. Mr. Chester blamed the devil.

When the world stopped shaking, Jed had gone hunting the mule. He didn't find the mule, but he did see uprooted trees, caved in banks of streams, and a few more ditches, either dug by God or Lucifer.

Well, that got folks talking about earthquakes and what might happen next. He hoped that the Chesters would decide to light out for somewhere the ground did not shake so hard and so often.

They decided, though, that they would keep right on running their store. Most of the handful of people who lived in New Madrid felt the same.

Till two weeks or so later.

Late that night or early in the morning, well before dawn, anyhow, when most folks were asleep, the ground started shaking and didn't stop so soon. Jed made it out of the store just before the chimney collapsed. Being February, cold as a coonhound's nose, the store went up in flames. The Mississippi flowed backwards. Waterfalls sprang out in the middle of the river, and water moved inland. A keelboat moored at the landing swayed up and down and sideways. Trees crashed in the forests surrounding the town. Birds screamed as they flew away. Dogs howled. Horses whinnied. People screamed and prayed. The air smelled of sulfur. Someone shouted that the gates of hell had opened. Above the roar and panic, Jed thought he could make out the church bell in Cahokia pealing.

"It's Judgment Day!" someone shrieked.

More chimneys toppled. The ground stopped its roaring, and settled down, while the river kept roaring.

After dawn, another quake shook the earth, but by then, there wasn't much left of New Madrid.

Jed and the Chesters and several more lighted out for St. Louis, wading through knee-high water, saying at least they didn't have to worry about snakes. They did find a few dead bodies and buried them in shallow graves, but by the time they reached Cape Girardeau, things seemed to be a little more normal and a whole lot safer. The Chesters decided to stay there, but Jed kept on with others to St. Louis. Any place where the ground shook so violently that the river ran backwards and formed new lakes, well, that wasn't where he wanted to live.

For the next eleven years, he worked odd jobs in St. Louis. He worked on the waterfront, and saw the first steamboat arrive back in 1818. He even served as a mate for about six months, but didn't take to riverboat life. He found his calling when a restaurant hired him to bring in game. That Jed could do. In fact, he was soon hauling in so much fresh meat, the restaurant owner couldn't handle it all, so he sent him to three other cafés, and Jed finally had enough money to do as he pleased.

He was in a tavern on the waterfront one evening when he picked up a copy of the Missouri Republican. *He couldn't recall reading any articles, but he did remember the advertisement. A hundred "enterprising young men" were sought to "ascend the river Missouri to its source, there to be employed for one, two, or three years." Applicants needed to be well-armed, tough, and good shots.*

The next morning, he sought out William Henry Ashley. Jed wasn't the first to sign up, but he did become one of Ashley's Hundred. Ashley and his partner, a bullet maker named Andrew Henry, were looking for furs. They provided everything a trapper needed. For that, they split the profits fifty-fifty with the men they hired.

Reno managed to keep his eyes moving, clearly watching and looking for anything that might cause him difficulty. Not seeing anything, he smiled, thinking of the men—the hundred and fifty whose blood ran just like his own.

Jim Beckwourth and Hugh Glass. Thomas Fitzpatrick and Jim Bridger. Jedediah Smith and the Sublette boys, William and Milton. Kit Carson and Joseph Meek. And men he would never call friends—Malachi Murchison and Louis Jackatars.

Reno set out with Henry, some twenty-odd men, sixty horses, and a keelboat. The next boat, captained by Daniel Moore, sank. Ashley took the third keelboat. Once they reached the mouth of the Yellowstone River that autumn, they put up a post they decided to call Fort Henry.

Jed Reno found his true calling. He became a trapper. He became a mountain man.

Nothing lasts forever. That was a saying he heard enough. Well, he knew that for a fact. Fort Henry was around maybe a year. Andrew Henry quit the company after a couple years, went back to mining lead and making bullets. He died sometime back in '32 or '33, maybe '34.

Ashley sold his share of what had become the Rocky Mountain Fur Company to David Edward Jackson back in '26. Ashley had, of course, not retired back to St. Louis just to dabble in politics. A former lieutenant governor, he did run for the big office in Missouri but didn't win. But he had helped set up the Rendezvous system. He had set up a few other trading posts, too, and done his fair share of exploring, to the Great Salt Lake and down south in the Colorado country.

Reno sighed. Ashley and Jackson, those two old rich Virginians, were also dead. He decided he better stop reminiscing and think about living.

Six Indians were loping toward him.

CHAPTER 10

Tim Colter slept next to his mother, hoping that when he woke she would be alive.

Of course, she wasn't.

He had looked all around for his sisters and Patricia Scott, but they were gone. What looked like horse tracks—except the horses wore no iron shoes—led off to the northwest. The Indians must have taken the girls away. Remembering what all the white men he had met had said what a red-skinned savage would do to a white girl made Tim sick to his stomach.

The Indians had also taken Pa's prized Percheron stallion and all of the oxen that had been pulling the wagons since Independence.

He found the bodies of his father and Mr. Scott, but couldn't figure out why he did not find Mrs. Scott. *Maybe she got away.* He shook his head no and felt sick again. More than likely, the Indians had taken her with the girls.

Indians? Tim stopped and leaned against the Scotts' prairie schooner. *No. Not Indians.* He looked back toward the creek, where he had dragged the man with the black braids and black teeth, and the knife in his gut—the place where that piece of filth lay dead. A white man. A white man who had been dressed like an Indian.

Tim walked away from the wagon.

White men had killed his parents. White men had taken his sisters, Mrs. Scott, and sweet Patricia. But those white men looked like Indians. They had scalped his mother and father and Mr. Scott. They had filled their bodies with arrows, and left the long shafts with the bird feathers affixed to the ends in their bodies. Did they want to be Indians? Why would anyone want to be an Indian?

Well, Tim remembered when he was much, much younger.

The boys from Danville, and sometimes a few girls, would play. We would be Continental Army soldiers fighting Indians, and, of course, some of the boys always wanted to be Indians.

Those were kids games, though.

This is real.

He looked at one of the arrows sticking in his mother's back. He bit his lip, and gripped the arrow with his left hand. Then . . . he jerked.

The arrow came out with an ugly sucking sound, and he saw the shaft all covered with his mother's congealed blood. There was no arrowhead. It remained inside her.

The bile rose again, and he hurried away. He threw up, heaving until nothing remained in his stomach—not much remained anyway—yet still he retched. He gagged and threw up until he thought his ribs would break.

Finally, he made himself stand, and, tears flowing down his face, he returned to his mother and pulled out another arrow. It still had the arrowhead, a black stone stained with blood. He tossed it aside, wiped his mouth, and went back to work, until all the arrows were out of his mother's body.

Next, he went to his father's body. The white renegades had chopped off his father's arms, carved gashes in his thigh, and slit his throat. Tim tried not to look at the corpse, tried to tell himself that what he saw on the blood-soaked ground was not his father.

"Pa is in a better place, walking the Streets of Gold, hand-in-hand with Ma," he said aloud.

He knew what he had to do, so he pulled the arrows out of the mutilated thing that had once been his father, and dragged the bloated thing around the wagon until it lay next to his ma. He had to go back.

Somehow, he did not gag as he picked up the severed arms and brought them back to his pa, and tried his best to make the arms look natural—an impossibility.

The raiders had ransacked the two wagons, stealing what they thought they could sell or use, letting the wind carry off most of the clothes. Mirrors had been broken, and his mother's favorite rocking chair smashed. Tattered ruins, now unrecognizable, littered the campground, and the tops of trunks had been ripped off their hinges. His father's Lancaster rifle was gone, naturally, as were Mr. Scott's fowling piece and long rifle. The raiders had even made off with Tim's hatchet, which his father had bought for him before they had left Pennsylvania. The slingshot he had dropped? It was gone, as well.

Still, he found a spade, though the handle had been snapped off till it stretched less than two feet long, but that would do. It would have to do.

Near his parents, Tim began scraping away earth. The rough ash handle soon blistered his palms, but he worked through the pain until he could dig no deeper. It wasn't deep at all, certainly not.

What did Pa always say about the dead? Six feet. Six feet under. So no. Not deep.

Maybe a foot and a half, but Tim made it wide enough. So gently, he moved his pa and his arms into the right edge of the shallow grave. Reverently, Tim placed his ma beside his father.

Back home in Danville, folks got separate graves, but Tim knew he didn't have the strength for that. He couldn't even give his parents a fitting grave. But at least they would be together. He put the dirt back around them, and then walked through the woods to the creek. He knew about wolves, and other animals—even Indians, some of the men had said—and how they would dig up bodies. That chilled him. Careful not to look at the body of the dead man, he found the heaviest stones he could lift and brought them back to the grave, laying them on the mounds of dirt he had piled up beside his parents. And back to the creek he walked.

Over and over he walked, back and forth, like a machine. Not thinking. Just doing. Scrapes covered his knuckles, and blisters formed on his fingertips, but still Tim worked. His muscles soon screamed in agony, for he was a city boy, not used to that kind of labor. Maybe he should have worked in the mills or headed up to the mines. That would have toughened him up.

It took him all day and into the night, but he kept on walking, finding stones, gently making a grave over the bodies of his parents. When the moon rose, he was still at it, though he had started to find the stones in the creek itself, and not just on the bank. The water soothed him, cleansed the cuts, popped blisters, and slaked his parched tongue, mouth, and throat. He worked until he could no longer walk.

Then he lay beside the unfinished grave, and cried himself to sleep.

Sometime in the night, he woke up with his muscles burning, and cried out for his mother, then he remembered everything. The pain in his arms did not lessen, but at some point, tired as he was, he fell back into a deep sleep.

* * *

When morning came, he went to the river, drank, and thought about trying to catch a fish. But he had no bait, and no clue how one fished out in the overpowering West. He stared at his hands.

Sighing, he picked up a smooth stone from the creek and carried it back to his parents' grave.

At some point, he realized wolves and coyotes and bears, and, yes, even Indians, would have a hard time digging their way to the bodies. The grave, he determined, was finished.

He bowed his head, trying to recall the words he had heard preachers read at the funerals of the friends of his parents, or the siblings of his own friends who had been taken to heaven by disease or fever. He remembered Cindy Leonard, who had drowned in the river when she was twelve and he was seven. No words came. He couldn't think anymore.

"Amen," he said.

He picked up the spade and walked to the body of Mr. Scott. He had been a good friend of Tim's father, and he had brought up a beautiful daughter. Tim could not, would not, leave him for wolves and ravens. Once again, he dug.

Probably not as deep as the shallow grave he had managed for his parents, and certainly not as many stones from the creek, but it would suffice. He had picked up the arrow-riddled body of the Scott's old dog, too, bloating and heavy already, and starting to stink. The dog he had laid beside Mr. Scott, because Patricia's father had sure loved that old dog. It had been a miracle the dog, lazy, old and feeble as it was, had even lived as long as it had on the Oregon Trail. Tim figured that Mr. Scott would enjoy spending eternity with his old friend.

Tim, on the other hand, had never cared much for that dog, especially now. The cur had not even managed to bark out a warning when those raiders had struck. Mr. Scott and the dog were together, buried.

He looked at Mr. Scott's grave, then at his parents', and realized something was missing.

A tombstone.

He had seen death on the trail before. The wagon train had buried five people since Independence. That's how he knew about wolves and Indians. He entered the woods and found some fallen branches.

Using the broken branches and strips from clothing the killers had left littering the camp, he fashioned three crosses, and shoved the long ends in front of the graves, one for Mr. Scott, and two for his parents.

He wet his lips, his bones and muscles aching, and his stomach growled. When was the last time he had eaten? At some point, he remembered the smoke he had smelled back in the beaver dam. The man with the black braids had been fixing breakfast or something. He backed away from his parents' grave and looked at the woods, trying to remember where he had seen the smoke wafting above the trees.

He moved through the forest, his hunger intensifying, turned when he knew he must have gone too far, and walked back. Twenty minutes later, he almost walked right past the small circle of cold ashes. He stopped, dropping to his knees and picking up a stick with some sort of meat on it. *Rabbit?* He jerked it up, and quickly brushed off the ants that had covered the meat. His first instinct was to take it to the river, wash it off. His second quick thought was to throw it away, fearing it had spoiled after a day or two, but his hunger won out. He tore through the meat, and finished sucking the bones.

Chapter 11

Once Tim had pitched the last bone into the ash, he saw the gear at the base of a tree. On his knees, he moved to the tree and picked up the small sack, which he held up with his left hand and dumped into his right. Tobacco. And a pipe. *Worthless.*

He tossed the pipe away and wiped the flakes of tobacco off his hands. In the bigger pouch, he found an awl, a bullet mold, a smaller pouch that held musket balls, and a ring upon which he found a small brush, a black pick, and a hard rod. Tiny. He didn't know what they were for, but he dropped them back inside the pouch. He also discovered a handmade screwdriver and another smaller pouch, inside of which he found flint and even some tinder. This he knew he would need, and dropped it back inside the larger leather bag with the rest of the stuff, pulling on the drawstring to close it.

Throwing the leather sack over his shoulder, he spotted the powder horn on the other side of the fire pit. This he grabbed and tossed it over his other shoulder before turning back to the tree and seeing another sack. It held salt, flour, dried meat, stale biscuits and another pouch, which held some kind of greasy substance. Pinching a little bit, he brought it out. He saw the bits of berries in some disgusting thing that smelled vaguely of meat. He didn't like that smell or the grease, and dropped the leather pouch on the ground.

After wiping his fingers on his trousers, Tim ate a handful of salt, washing it down with water from the canteen. He wanted to devour the dried meat and biscuits, but figured that he had just eaten and that he had better save the rest of the food. He rose with his plunder, looked around for anything else, but found only a long bow and a quiver of arrows.

He could not keep his eyes on the quiver, remembering how his ma and pa had looked and how Mr. Scott had been. The meat he had just eaten began roiling in his belly. Swallowing, he kicked the quiver to the ground, and found an arrow. He wanted to throw it away, too, to block out those nightmares, but he needed a weapon for hunting.

Most men in this country, he had been told, carried long rifles. The man with the black braids had carried only pistols and knives, but possibly he had left a rifle in his camp. That would serve Tim better, perhaps, than a bow and arrow. Scanning each tree, he saw no Hawken, no Lancaster, no shotgun, nothing but bark and leaves.

The bow came to his shoulders. Well, a rifle would likely be that tall or even longer.

He picked up the bow and found the spot wrapped in leather where he figured he was supposed to grip it. He tried to pull back the string. Tried again. Pulled harder, but he could not get the string to hardly budge.

"I ain't no Indian," he said, and tossed the bow to the ground.

He started back toward the wagons and grave, then stopped as another thought occurred to him.

The killers and kidnappers were riding horses. He turned, looking through the forests, wondering if his foes had been left behind. Maybe he was a runner. Maybe the horse had run off. He saw no trace of animal—no saddle, no bridle, nothing.

All right, he said to himself silently. *The man is a runner. Or those evil men left him here to die. No horse.*

After traveling about twenty yards through the forest, he stopped again.

His stomach and bowels rebelled, but he made himself look back toward the river. He turned quickly away, and stared up the embankment toward the Conestogas, wondering if what waited for him there was any better than what lay by the creek.

With a heavy sigh, he moved through the woods.

The man still lay where he had fallen, but he had company.

Tim's mouth moved, but emitted no sound. He swallowed, thought about running away, but knew what he had to do if he wanted to live. After clearing his throat, he yelled, "Hey!"

The big black birds ignored him. He dropped the sack containing the food and grabbed a branch. This he flung at the black birds, and then he ran toward them, waving his arms, and yelling at the top of his lungs.

His ma would have made him wash his mouth out with soap for using the words he shouted, but the birds took flight, squawking their hideous cries. They did not go far. A few lighted in trees, and some landed on the ground across the creek. Most stayed maybe thirty yards away, staring at him with their hideous eyes.

Trying to avoid looking at the dead man's body, Tim grabbed the bone handle of the knife that had been buried in the man's chest. He gagged, and pulled, and got the blade out, then wiped the blood on the man's greasy leggings. Climbing over the dead body, he found the sheath that had held the knife stuck inside the sash. He pulled it free and slid the blade inside the leather sheath that was fringed and heavily beaded. He pulled the hatchet from the sash around the dead man's waist. Without looking at the man's face, he looked about the body for anything else he might need before deciding that the only thing he wanted from this man he already had. With knife and hatchet, he walked away, stopping to pick up the big pistol the man had carried. He stuck it in his waistband, and gathering again the knife and hatchet, Tim stumbled back to the abandoned wagons and the graves he had dug by himself.

Before reaching camp, he fell to his knees and vomited. Maybe it was the rabbit, or whatever the man with the black braids had cooked. Perhaps it was the dead man by the creek. There was more. Hurriedly he pulled down his trousers and underwear, and squatted, purging the sickness that ran through his body.

When that had passed, he fell onto his side and wished he were dead.

Tim made it back to the camp. Sick as he felt—the vomiting and diarrhea would continue well into the night—he made himself work. He found a blanket, which would serve him well during the cold, and fashioned a sash out of one of Mrs. Scott's scarves. He slipped the knife's sheath through it, and tied it around his waist, making sure it was tight.

Then he worked on the pistol.

He had never fired a weapon before, but he had seen many men in Danville and especially on the trail from Independence shoot and load.

Once he figured out how to get powder from the horn, he held the pistol up and poured down the barrel what he figured would do the job. Pulling the rod from beneath the barrel was easier, and he tamped down the powder. He fingered a round lead ball out of the dead man's pouch and seated it atop the barrel. Once again, he used the ramrod to seat the ball.

He studied the flash pan. It had to be primed. He remembered that much, but decided to wait. Be safe. He didn't want the gun to discharge accidentally and send the ball into his leg, groin, or gut. He shoved the pistol inside his waistband.

His hat was missing, but in a bush, he discovered the wide-brimmed, dirty, once-white hat that had been Mr. Scott's. It was too big, but he used another scarf to tie on the hat. It pulled the brim down to his ears, and he expected that he resembled some sort of clown, but it would keep his ears from burning in the sun.

He laughed.

And got sick again.

The next morning, Tim tested his stomach by eating more salt and a biscuit. He thought about the dried meat, but decided against it.

Again, he looked about the wagons, found a gourd, which could be used for water. He did not have to go back to the river and risk seeing the black birds and the man with the black braids. He dipped the gourd inside the water barrel on the side of his parents' prairie schooner and watched the bubbles until they stopped. Corking the barrel, he used strips of Mr. Scott's blue calico shirt that a spoke of his wagon's wheel had caught. He made a sling and wondered if he could carry all of it.

"I have to," he said.

He wet his lips.

Stay. That was one thought. *Stay. Another wagon train will be making its way here. Maybe even our party will come back wondering what kept us.* He tried to remember what the plan had been. *The train's captain said they would wait for us at Bridger's Trading Post.* Tim could not remember how far away the post was.

Typically, the wagon train had made eight to ten miles a day, sometimes a little less, rarely any more. *How long have I been here? Two days? Three? Four? Longer?*

Three. He decided it had been three days. Three

days since his ma and pa and Mr. Scott had been killed. That would put the train thirty miles down the trail. The ruts in the trail would be easy enough to follow. He had food, even weapons.

Carrying all his plunder, he walked back to Mr. Scott's grave, took off his hat, which he had not yet secured with the scarf, and bowed his head. He could remember a little more than *Amen.*

"Ashes to ashes and dirt to dirt," he said, which was all he could recall anyone ever saying at a burial. He knew his Bible. His ma had used it often enough to teach him how to read, but his mind remained fogged from the past few days. "You were a good man." He looked at the cross. "You raised a good—" He couldn't finish. He choked on the words and felt tears well in his eyes. Hat in hand, and carrying everything else, he went to the other grave.

"Ma," he said, sniffing. "Pa. I love you. Know you loved me."

He remembered hearing something else when the father of a friend in Danville had been killed when his horse threw him and broke his neck. *You're the man of the house.*

"You were good parents. Both of you. And I reckon you'll always be with me. I'll try to make you proud. Rest in peace."

Quickly he turned away and felt the wind drying the tears on his cheeks. He moved down from the camp, the graves, the horrible memories, and straddled the first rut. He faced west and stared at the trail so many wagons had left. *How many have come this way?* he wondered. *How many men, women, and children have died?*

It was, he knew, an easy trail to follow. He might live. Maybe he could even make it to that trading post the train's captain had mentioned. Bridger's. Many a night some man around the campfire had told a story about Jim Bridger. Tim had been excited about the chance to meet the famous mountain man.

That's the way he should go. *That's the way Ma and Pa would have told me to go.*

Tim tightened the scarf over his hat and tied the knot under his chin. The morning sun felt warm, and the breeze wasn't kicking up much dust. He stepped to the center of the trail and crossed the next rut.

A few yards off the road, he found the tracks left by the raiders' horses, and that's the trail he followed.

Ma and Pa might be frowning on my decision. I might regret it shortly. But I have to try. Nancy, Margaret, and Mrs. Scott are out there. So is Patricia.

Tim Colter wasn't going to leave them in the hands of those butchers. He would find them.

Or die trying.

CHAPTER 12

Reining up, Jed Reno held up his right hand in a peaceful greeting and let the Indians come. Most were shirtless, and wearing only breechclouts. Some wore eagle feathers in their hair, and their braids were long and black, glistening in the sun.

They rode good ponies, which they stopped a few yards in front of him.

"Pave-vooná-o," the oldest one said. *"Ne-pevo-mohta-he?"*

Reno knew the first part, but the second sentence he couldn't fathom. They were Cheyenne. That much he could tell, not just from the guttural language, but from their clothes and features and the horses they rode.

"English?" he asked. "Speak white-man language?" He remembered one of the few words he knew in the tongue of the Cheyenne. *"Vé-ho-é-nestsestotse?"*

The one who had first spoken shook his head. So did the five others. The leader moved his hands. He had much practice at communication, and, after spending more than twenty years in that country, so did Jed Reno.

Nodding, he swung out of the saddle. After ground-reining his horse and hobbling the pack mule, he took his Hawken rifle and sat cross-legged in front of the Indians, who sat in a semicircle around him. Reno kept his rifle across his lap, but did not think he would need it. Still, to stay alive in a country as wild as that, a man wanted his long gun handy, just in case.

The oldest Cheyenne, who probably had yet to see twenty-five winters, spoke in his native language as he talked with his hands. Reno did not understand a single word, but the hands he could read.

Rubbing his right cheek in a counterclockwise circle with his four fingers meant red. Holding his hands together in front of him, palms up, then spreading the hands apart was prairie. The brave's name was Red Prairie.

Reno signed that he was glad to meet him and the others. His name, he signed, was Plenty Medicine. It was the name the Utes had given him back in '28 on his way to the Rendezvous in Bear Lake. He had needed plenty of medicine to survive that little set-to, and when he finally reached the agreed-upon site, glad to have his hair, the supply trains had not arrived. The trappers and Indians grew annoyed, and Reno had wound up in another fight with two Frenchies who worked for Pratte, Chouteau, and Company. After that, even some of the white men took to calling him "Plenty Medicine."

All that, and the trains did not arrive till late fall, meaning men like Jed Reno and other trappers wouldn't get their supplies until the next spring.

Reno read the Cheyenne's hands. They had been hunting.

Probably ponies and scalps, he figured, as more Crows and Shoshones could be found in that part of the country. Red Prairie did not say, and Reno did not push. He let the Indian keep on.

"North"—the Indian pointed, and Reno guessed he meant the South Pass or maybe the Popo Agie—"the hunting party had found bad medicine. Two wagons that lumber across the country had been attacked."

Reno leaned forward.

"Just two wagons?" he signed.

Red Prairie's head nodded in affirmation.

Only fools would cross this country with only two wagons.

Likely one of the wagons had broken down, and the men in the other had stayed behind to help make repairs. That, in itself, was dangerous. The whole train should have stayed behind, but maybe the captain thought they needed to make good time. Greenhorns were scared of getting caught in the winter. Not that Reno could blame anyone for that.

"Did your party do this bad thing?" Reno asked with his hands. Using the word "bad" might have been risky, but he felt these Cheyenne warriors weren't a bad lot. After all, they had approached him, and had ridden up to him showing the signs of peace.

All of the braves shook their heads adamantly.

Reno believed them, having learned a few things about Indians. Not all of them, but most of them, had a thing about telling the truth. "Who did it?" he signed.

"Indians," Red Prairie signed. "But not Indians."

Leaning back, Reno tried to comprehend exactly what the Cheyenne brave meant. He watched closely, focusing on the hands and fingers, their movements, and not the Cheyenne words Red Prairie and others spoke.

He learned that Red Prairie and his friends rode down a hill and saw off the train two wagons the white men used to cross this country. No oxen were with the wagons anymore, but Red Prairie saw smoke in the woods. The Indians dismounted, and Red Prairie and another fine Cheyenne named Big Beaver—Big Beaver grinned and puffed out his chest—sneaked their way to the wagons.

Big Beaver found a white man wearing his hair in braids in the fashion of the Cheyennes and other Indian tribes, and with his face painted for war. Red Prairie carefully, silently, walked around the wagons. He looked at, but did not touch, the bodies of two white men and a white woman. All had been scalped. All had been filled with many, many arrows.

"Whose arrows?" Reno signed.

"Arapahos," Red Prairie signed.

Reno frowned, then sucked in a deep breath when

Red Prairie's hands kept moving. After making the sign for Indian, he put his hand, palm down, under his chin, and then pulled it away. That was the sign for the Sioux.

Red Prairie was not done. Again, he signed "Indian," and then held up his right hand, the pointer and middle fingers pointing up, close to his shoulder, and lifted his hand a few inches up and forward. The sign for a wolf. Pawnee Indians.

Still, Red Prairie's hands moved. He made signs for the Utes, and the Crows, and the Blackfeet, and the Paiutes.

Lastly, Red Prairie did the sign for "Indian," the left hand flat and up, palm down, in front of his body, then using his right fingers to rub the hand from the wrist to his knuckles, up and down, but only twice. After that, he made the sign of the finger choppers.

"*Tse-tsethése-staestse,*" Red Prairie said. The Cheyennes, too.

"A confederacy of Indians," Reno said. His stomach felt sour.

"This bad thing," Red Prairie said with his hands and fingers, "we did not do."

"I know you didn't," Jed Reno said, and began to make the signs that he knew Red Prairie spoke the truth.

Malachi Murchison had said that Louis Jackatars wanted to start a war with the Indians, and he did not care which tribe. The rat had been lying. Jackatars wanted to start a war with every Indian tribe in the West, it seemed.

"We must go," Red Prairie signed, and he and the other braves rose.

Reno had to use the butt of the rifle to push himself to his feet. His joints popped as he rose, holding out his right hand to shake with the Cheyenne warriors.

"We wanted to find a white man we could trust, and one who would trust our words," Red Prairie signed and spoke. "We are glad that we found you, Plenty Medicine. Now we must go."

"Tell your chief," Reno signed. "But stay in your camp. Stay away from white men."

Red Prairie stiffened. "We are men," he reminded Reno.

Reno nodded. "I will do what I can." He watched the Cheyennes mount their ponies and gallop off toward the north. "What I can," he whispered, "which ain't much."

He flipped up the patch covering the hole where his eye should have been, and rubbed the eyebrow. After putting the patch back in its proper place, he went to work, removing the hobbles from the pack mule, sticking them in the leather sack, and gathering the hackamore to his horse. Once he had climbed into the saddle, he started to sort through his options.

He could ride back to Bridger's Trading Post. Ol' Jim knew the Indians, liked them probably more than he cared for his own kind of people. He was a man Reno trusted and might need. Bridger could also help calm down those feelings for revenge that the emigrants would likely have once they found the remains of those three dead white people, and all the arrows sticking out of their bodies.

He could forget about the Cheyennes and the emigrants. Just keep right on after Malachi Murchison and Louis Jackatars. What Jackatars was doing, trying to start up a war—it would be one unholy war—was one thing, and not really any of Reno's business. But Murchison had tried to kill him, and Jackatars had sent him to do it.

Or he could read what would be happening to this land if Jackatars got that war going. Whites against Indians . . . in the country Reno had called home since 1822. The whites would win. The Indians would be wiped out. That country could be ruined.

He looked south.

Old Bill Williams had raved high and low about the country down that way, south and west of Taos, in that Spanish country of giant gorges and mountains and desert landscapes that were something to behold. It would be new. It would be different. That appealed to him, especially since the beaver were pretty much played out and that country was filling up with people, although, granted, most of them were just passing through.

Unless a war started. Then the Army would come with cannon and Dragoons. And the British up north would get scared. And before long, the United States would not be at war with just every Indian tribe out here. They would be fighting the British and the Canadians, too.

"C'mon." Jed Reno kicked his horse into a walk and tugged on the lead rope that pulled the mule behind him. *Find Jackatars. Kill him.*

That would satisfy his revenge and stop the war the half-breed Métis was bound and determined to start.

CHAPTER 13

"Reno?" Malachi Murchison leaned back his head and laughed as hard as he could. When that was done, he shook his head and looked at Louis Jackatars. "His guts was hangin' out of his belly when I was finished with him." He drew his knife and showed off the blade to Jackatars and the other men gathering around him.

Then he saw the women—three children and one grown woman, it appeared—all of them something to look at.

"Aha! I see you were successful. You sell them to the Blackfeet, no?"

Jackatars frowned. "Do you want to see the graves of the two fools who wanted the women for themselves?"

The smile vanished from Murchison's face. He sheathed the knife.

"I asked for you to bring me the head of Jed Reno."

"That I could not do, Louis," the leathery man said. "Jim Bridger is an old man, but he remains quick. I did not have time to even lift Jed Reno's scalp."

Murchison was lying. Jackatars knew that. Not about Bridger—even Jackatars would not care for a tangle with that old mountain lion—but about Jed Reno.

"Your face betrays your words," the part-Métis said.

The scarred hands of Malachi Murchison reached up, and he flinched when he touched the bruises and cuts. "What?" he said, forcing himself to sound jovial. "These." He stepped forward, laughing, but even that seemed to pain the man. He realized it and turned. "I promise you, Louis. I cut Jed Reno across his side. He fell, bleedin' like a pig before slaughter. If not dead when I rode out of Bridger's Trading Post, he was dyin'. This I swear on the grave of my sainted mother."

"You don't even know who your mother was." Jackatars turned.

Malachi Murchison called out his name, but Jackatars waved a hand and moved toward his prisoners. "There is nothing to fear today, you lying dog. I have killed two men this day, and I should not kill any more. To start my plan, to get my war bloody and furious, I need every man I have. Even a scoundrel such as yourself."

Suddenly, he stopped and turned back. He raised his arm and pointed a long finger at Murchison. "But come near these women, touch one of them, and this to you I swear. Your guts will be spilling out of your belly when I leave you for the wolves and the ants."

He went to the women and motioned away the two Spaniards who had been guarding them.

The woman the two fools had attacked was sitting up. She had pulled another shirt over her torn undergarments and brought two of the girls under her arms. The girls she protected did not look anything like her. It was the other girl, the one standing, who resembled her.

"What do you want?"

The mother did not speak. Her daughter did. She stood off to the side, holding a wet cloth that she had used to wash the scratches on her mother's face and arms left by the dogs who had tried to rape her.

"What is your name?" Jackatars asked.

The girl flattened her lips.

Spirit. A lot of spirit. She was strong. She would be the one to watch, not the mother or the two frightened girls of the woman they had been forced to kill back near the South Pass.

Jackatars smiled. "Obey me. Answer me. Three women are all I need to give to the Blackfeet. You, I can leave behind. Or let my men have you."

He spoke as if he were teaching a toddler how to behave in public. Slowly. Pleasantly. But with a voice to let the kid know how serious things would be.

The girl understood.

"Patricia. My name is Patricia Scott."

She was tall, slim, with blond hair that would have been quite beautiful if she had had a chance to wash it. Her eyes shone as blue as the cloudless sky, and as big and bright as this wild country. Her face and arms had been burned by the sun, her neck even more so.

The underclothes she wore had been dirtied by the rough camps and rougher long rides across the country. Yet she remained pretty.

Since attacking the camp and killing the fools, Jackatars had not spoken to the captives. They had simply made hard rides for days, covering the country they needed, before stopping at the Big Sandy.

"You are her daughter?" He pointed a knife's sharp point at the woman.

"Yes."

He thought of something else. "Do you speak French?"

"No."

"A pity. It is a much more pleasant sounding language."

"Spoken by the likes of you, it would still sound ugly—even if I understood it."

When Jackatars stopped laughing, he showed the blade of his knife to Patricia Scott, and narrowed his eyes.

"Careful, little lady. It is a long way to the land of the Blackfeet. And I might tire of your sass."

The girl sat down, crossing her legs like an Indian squaw.

Maybe, Jackatars thought, *this one I can keep. Too young, yes. Too skinny. But what a beauty with some practice and seasoning.*

"Your mother's name? Doris is it not?" He remembered the wench's husband calling out that name before he had killed the fool.

"Yes."

He turned toward the woman. "Doris. You are the

woman. These others are children. I hold you responsible. You are a mother, so you know children. You know how to discipline them. If one of them runs away, if they do not obey what I tell them to do, or what my men tell them to do, there must be punishment. It is how boys learn to be men and girls learn to be women. Is that not so?"

"They will not run away," Doris Scott said flatly.

"That is good. That is the way it should be. If one of them disobeys me or my men, or if one of them runs away, it is you, Doris Scott, who will be punished. You got a taste of that earlier, but I do not think you enjoyed it. Am I right?"

He was testing her, but Mrs. Scott had a brain in that head of hers. She knew to answer. "I did not enjoy it."

"Did you hear what I said would happen to that piece of filth who just joined our group of merry men?"

"I heard."

"What did I tell him?"

"You said"—she swallowed—"that his guts would be pouring out of his stomach when you left him alive for the wolves and ants."

Jackatars enjoyed watching the two other girls grow suddenly pale.

"You listen well, Doris. Remember to do so."

His eyes found the youngest girl, for his words, though directed at Mrs. Scott, had been meant for the children. Children were the ones apt to run away. Children would cry. Children would scream.

"What is your name?"

The girl's face, filled with fright, looked at Mrs.

Scott, and Jackatars considered letting her know then that when he asked a question she must not look at Doris Scott but must face him. But he merely tossed the knife from one hand to the other. *In time,* he told himself. *Girls must learn the ways, but they are slow. It will take a few days before they know what is really expected of them.*

"Tell him," Doris Scott whispered.

"Mar"—the girl swallowed—"Mar-ga-ret."

"And your age?"

"Thirteen."

"Thirteen." Jackatars stopped playing with his knife. "Girl, when I was twelve, I had killed five men. Would you like to see the scalps?" He grinned evilly and waited for Mrs. Scott to tell the child to answer.

"Answer him, Margaret."

Margaret was a cute kid, even with freckles. The sun might burn off those freckles before long. She wasn't very old or tough, and the long ride ahead might be hard on a kid like that. She would be the one likely to die, long before they reached the Black-feet country.

Then, Louis Jackatars thought, *she would be the lucky one.*

The girl had to wet her lips. "No." Tears fell down her cheeks, and Doris Scott pulled her closer.

"Some other time, then." Jackatars turned to the older sister, a pretty girl, and said carefully so that everyone would hear, "And let us hope that your scalp is not one I am forced to add to my coup stick. Or even worse, that I give you to Dog Ear Rounsavall and you feel the blade of his knife. Or hatchet."

The third girl had brown hair and green eyes. Not quite as tall as Patricia Scott, not quite as pretty, but a good-looking girl. Had her fool parents not taken her away from whatever Eastern state they had called home, she would have grown up to be a pretty woman till she married and had a dozen kids and grew fat and lazy and old and ugly.

The Blackfeet would love her, though.

She probably wouldn't care much for them.

"And your name?"

"Nancy," she said just loud enough for Jackatars to hear.

He didn't care much for that name. Too plain. He sheathed his knife and clapped his hands. "Very well. I am Louis Jackatars. I bid you welcome to my camp. We have a hard way ahead of us, so sleep when you can, eat when we feed you, do your business before we put you on the horses and before you go to bed. Do as I say, and when I say it. Do this, and you live. Disobey, and you die. Do you understand?"

They were well-trained.

"Yes," all of them—even stubborn Patricia Scott—answered in unison.

"We ride in an hour," he said, and moved back toward the main camp, motioning for the Spaniards to return.

"Mr. Jackatars?"

He turned on his heel and smiled at the girl named Patricia Scott.

"Yes?"

"What about the boy? The one that ran from the camp when you . . . you . . . attacked?"

"The coward?"

He liked the anger that flashed in the girl's eyes.

She knew better, however, than to contradict him. Swallowing down anger and pride, she ignored his insult and asked, "What happened to him?"

Jackatars shrugged. "As they say to the south, '¿Quién sabe?' Who knows? The coward is dead, of course. Baillarger . . . the man I left behind . . . he kills everyone and everything. He has killed more men than I have." Laughing, he walked away, barking out his orders to get ready to ride.

He ordered Dog Ear Rounsavall to ride out ahead, on a scout, make sure no Indians or no trappers were to be seen. The gravediggers, he yelled, would have to catch up with them, and they had better make sure no one could ever find the two bodies of the men Jackatars had killed.

He beckoned one of the Spaniards, the Basque called Abaroa. In a mix of Spanish, English, and sign language, Jackatars told him to wait until they had gone, mount his horse, and ride back to South Pass. Find out what had happened to Baillarger. "But be careful. Don't be caught by white men. If they find you, tell them that you saw a raiding party of Indians, and that they were headed northwest."

As Abaroa walked to find his horse, Rounsavall approached Jackatars and whispered in French, "Any man who is not blind can follow our trail from South Pass." He pointed at the camp they had made. "You seem careless, my friend. Once you would make a camp where no one would ever be able to see that you had camped here."

Jackatars clapped the French trapper hard on the back.

"This time, my friend, I wish to be followed." From his possibles sack, he removed a Ute headband and feather, which he slipped into a sagebrush, making sure the wind would not carry it away.

Let the white men find that, he thought, moving quickly to his horse.

CHAPTER 14

Climbing up the hills was tiring. Tim found himself stopping for breath a lot more often than he thought he would. The captain of the wagon train had said South Pass was something like seventy-five hundred feet in elevation. His pa had joked to the family that that was only seven thousand feet higher than Danville.

Tim drank some water, but it didn't help his headache. It would be easy to stop, to rest, but he didn't want those raiders to get farther away from him.

His chest heaved, his legs ached, and the country seemed to get higher and rougher, but he made himself keep walking. It was slow-going, but at least he moved in the right direction. Following the horse prints seemed easy enough, and when the ground got too hard for any tracks, he found horse dung, broken twigs, and overturned stones. He couldn't be certain, but he seemed to think he was moving in the right direction.

As he walked, he remembered.

* * *

"Horses and mules aren't what people are using any-more," Mr. Scott told Pa. "Oxen. That's what you'll need to reach Oregon. Not that Percheron."

"Oxen." Pa shook his head. "They move so slow, we'll never get there."

Mr. Scott laughed. "Slow, but sure. They are not prone to being stopped by mud and snow. They don't get as sick as horses and mules."

"You have to shod them."

"Yes. And that's no easy chore, but few people moving to Oregon use horses or mules anymore. Most of the leaders of the wagon trains won't allow the Conestogas to be pulled by anything but oxen."

Pa glanced at the Percheron. "I'm taking that stallion."

"Of course. He'll make you rich in Oregon. But he won't be pulling your wagon."

Tim continued walking . . . walking and remembering.

The Colters and the Scotts said their farewells, loaded their wagons with furniture and supplies, and left Danville, traveling in their mule-pulled wagons—Tim's pa bought the oxen later in Kansas—to Pittsburgh, the biggest, wildest, roughest city Tim had ever seen. One of the largest cities west of the Alleghenies, it was filled with wooden homes and factories belching smoke. It was as though storm clouds always blocked out the sun, but coal dust and fibers of cotton rained instead of moisture . . . and the air smelled of soot and ash.

* * *

Tim shuddered, glad he did not live there. Too many people—maybe 20,000, his pa had said—and lots of them foreigners. He'd heard Scottish brogues and what he took as German. Most of the people worked on the Pennsylvania Canal or in the iron- or glassworks. "Traveling down the Ohio River all the way to the Mississippi was a lot more fun than Pittsburgh, even if it was named after William Pitt, whoever he was. I liked the river. It was amazing."

Tim leaned against the railing and watched the river and the ever-changing land sweep past.

"Nine hundred and eighty-one miles," a burly deckhand with a face and beard blackened by soot and tattoos covering his forearm, told him and Patricia. "All the way to Cairo, Illinois."

"La Salle called it La Belle Rivière,*" the ship's captain told them on another afternoon. "But it ain't always so beautiful, children, especially when heading downstream back when we had to deal with the Falls of the Ohio. But the Louisville and Portland Canal has eliminated that hazard. Still, I like the name* Ohio *better than the name La Salle give her. That's what the Iroquois called it.* Ohio *means 'The Great River.' And she is that."*

It seemed like an adventure. Tim had seen hardly anything other than Danville, but on the river, he saw more— amazing towns, landings, and cities. Parkersburg . . . Wheeling . . . Huntington . . . Steubenville . . . Marietta . . . Gallipolis . . . Portsmouth . . . Cincinnati . . . Madison . . . New Albany . . . Evansville . . . Mount Vernon . . . Ashland . . . Covington . . . Owensboro . . . Paducah. It was the most amazing piece of water Tim had ever seen . . . until they reached Cairo, Illinois and he gawked at the Mississippi.

Cairo was not much—nothing like Pittsburgh, although you could breathe the air without coughing too much, even if you might suck in a pound or two of gnats and mosquitoes. The banks were flat and low—like the houses. Even the trees did not appear tall. The land was swampy, and the air was hot.

But the river?

Strong and wide, a mile from bank to bank in places, and even wider elsewhere, muddy, the current slow—six miles an hour, on average, said the second mate of the second ship Tim found himself on—with logs shooting down the river like battering rams.

"Aye," the mate said, "'tis the snags ye have te watch. The snags and the sawyers . . . they can send a boat and all hands aboard to watery graves."

On one dark night, when Tim had ventured out, another mate had let him stand by him, and they stared at the dark water in front of them, his hand near a bell.

"You look for the ripple," the mate said. "That tells you when—" Immediately, he rang the bell, and a moment later, the ship seemed to slam to a stop so suddenly, so unexpectedly, that if the mate had not grabbed the waistband of Tim's britches, he would have fallen overboard.

The bell rang seven more times that night before Tim went to bed to hear his father cursing that it was impossible to sleep when he kept being pitched off his cot.

Tim smiled. He remembered most the times he'd spent with Patricia Scott. They'd strolled the decks, watched men fishing from the banks and the islands, looked at the land, the river, and the men working the boats. Sometimes, when they were certain no one had been looking, they'd held hands, fingers together, and now and again he had squeezed her hand and smiled when she'd squeezed back. Twice, when the moon shone down upon them and the Mississippi River, they'd even kissed.

Thinking of those moments made him more determined than ever. He kept walking . . . and remembering.

They left the ship in St. Louis, a raw, ugly town full of rough-looking men, mosquitoes, and a city that reeked of dead fish, smoke from the steamboats, mud, smoke, urine, and dung. Pa exclaimed that since this would be their last touch of civilization, they should eat at the finest hotel the city offered. So they spent a small fortune at The Planter's House.

Granted, they saw most of the towns only from the river, but St. Louis seemed different from any other they passed. It wasn't strictly frontier, since Main Street and the sidewalks were paved, although part of both desperately needed repairs. Tens of thousands of people lived there—men in buckskins, homespun, or the finest clothes Tim had seen since Danville. Soldiers, on leave from Jefferson Barracks south of the city, sang out drunkenly from cafés and dram shops; pack mules carried furs and hides.

"Used to be practically all beaver plews," one man in a silk hat and spectacles told Tim and Patricia, "but 'tis now mostly buffalo."

They saw more Irish and Germans, and for the first time in their lives, they stared at slaves.

St. Louis, their mothers decided, was too raw a place for anyone to travel alone, so after breakfasting at the Planter's Hotel the Sunday before they boarded their last steamboat and headed across the state along the Missouri River, traded their mules for oxen, and began the long, arduous journey to Oregon, the two families walked the streets of the foul-smelling city together.

A tall man of color, dressed resplendently in a garnet waistcoat, stood at one corner, reading from a newspaper to a crowd of black men and women. Some were dressed in ragged muslin and had no shoes; others would have fit into white society if not for the color of their skin.

"I was told that the coloreds have their own church," Mrs. Scott said, *"and that it is attended by slaves and freemen and freewomen."*

"Their masters allow the slaves to attend church?" Patricia asked.

"This is a day of rest," Pa said. *"For slaves and regular folks."*

"I have never seen our domestic institution," Ma said.

"I have seen enough of it," Patricia said under her breath, and walked away from the wretched slaves in their worn clothes and bare feet.

Barber emporiums and shops of all kinds lined the streets. A fight broke out between a man in patched woolen britches with a hook for his left hand and a bearded man in buckskins. Tim felt disappointed that he did not get to see the fight, as Pa and Mr. Scott hurried their wives and children across the street and then back down toward the Planter's House.

They ate supper at their camp that night and slept un-

*derneath their wagons. The next morning, after a breakfast
of hotcakes and coffee, they watched the Conestogas loaded
onto the last steamboat, the* Chautauqua, *then the men
paid for their passage and freight up the Missouri River.*

*Tim had thought if a person had seen one river, he had
seen them all, but he realized how different rivers were. Of
course, until he had started out for Oregon with his family
and the Scotts, he had known only the North Branch of the
Susquehanna. Traveling cross-country, he had seen the
Ohio, Mississippi, and Missouri.*

*They disembarked at the Town of Kansas where they
heard rumors that Pittsburgh had been destroyed by a great
fire just a few weeks after they left it. Pa and Mr. Scott
agreed that God must have been watching after them. If they
had started out later, they might not have gotten out of Pittsburgh in time.*

"It's a blessing," Mr. Scott said.

Tim frowned. As he followed the trail of the
raiders, he wasn't so sure about that.

*They went on to Westport where they sold their mules,
bought oxen, and met Henry W. McConnell, who had been
voted captain of the train of wagons due to leave in the next
week.*

*That first night in camp, he introduced the families to
their guide, Just Jenkins.*

"We must leave by the fifteenth," Jenkins told them.

*He wore his thick red hair to his shoulders, with streaks
of blond in the long beard. His clothes were buckskins from
foot to shoulders, and a wide-brimmed hat the color of the*

earth topped his head. One eye never moved, and Tim discovered it was made of glass. The other eye missed nothing.

A brace of pistols Just Jenkins wore in a yellow sash—the one piece of his wardrobe not made from a wild animal. He spoke forcefully, as if he had been guiding wagon trains all his life. "Fort Kearny in a month, Fort Laramie by June, Independence Rock by July, South Pass a short while later. That will get you to Oregon in early September. Leave later, you might not get there at all."

Pa said that Jenkins was a man who knew what he was doing, though Mr. McConnell kept saying—when Jenkins could not hear—that the uncouth scout was a simpleton and that he, as train captain, would question the idiot's every decision.

Tim settled in for the night, alone in a wilderness, sick from the altitude, and missing his dead parents.

They had done everything Captain McConnell and Just Jenkins had told them to do, but his parents and Mr. Scott would never see Oregon. They were buried some miles back to the south. Patricia, Mrs. Scott, and Tim's sisters might never see that promised land, either.

The way Tim felt, by morning, he might also be dead.

CHAPTER 15

Most folks gave Robert Stuart and his Astorians credit for finding South Pass. After all, the Astorians, trappers with the Pacific Fur Company under Stuart's guidance, had crossed there back in 1812—when Jed Reno was just a boy in Bowling Green, Kentucky—delivering dispatches to John Jacob Astor back in St. Louis from Oregon. The men Jed Reno called friends, however, said credit should be given to ol' Broken Hand Tom Fitzpatrick and Jedediah Smith, because they had found it again back in '24 when they and Reno had been part of General William Henry Ashley's One Hundred.

Reno, of course, always believed that long before Ashley's One Hundred or a bunch of Astorians were in those parts, Indians had to have known about the pass. Sioux, Cheyenne, Shoshone. Maybe the Crow. Or some ancient tribe the Sioux or Cheyenne had long ago sent retreating to some other safer clime. It didn't rightly matter, Reno figured, who discovered it. South Pass had been discovered likely by accident, considering how hard it was to see. It was deceptive. A wayfarer could see the Wind River Mountains, just north of the pass, for days before ever getting here, but when they went through the pass—actually, two passes, cutting through the Wind River range and, to the south, the Oregon Buttes—they would be sorely disappointed. The pass didn't feel like a pass, and once they had pretty much entered the Oregon Territory, that land of promise, what stretched out before them for an endless amount of miles wasn't much more than sand and sagebrush.

Still, no matter who discovered it and no matter what people thought, once they had reached South Pass, the point was that it had been discovered. Even worse for men like Jed Reno, ever since Captain Benjamin Bonneville had shown that wagons could reach the summit back in '32, the pass was being used regularly.

Reno reined in his horse, and the mule stopped behind him.

"Hell." Sighing heavily, he rode up the trail toward the train of prairie schooners that stretched for about a mile. Any game he might have found had long been frightened off by the bellicose shouts of the men—those fool emigrants—pointing and cursing until one of them happened to notice Jed Reno, riding easily in their direction.

One of the men lifted his fowling piece, but a man in buckskins stepped forward, putting a massive hand on the barrel and forcing it down. As Reno drew nearer, he recognized the old trapper.

"Terrance," he said with a nod as he reined in.

"Well, ol' Plenty Medicine is still kickin'," Terrance Jenkins said warmly. Reno was the only man who knew his given name. "But it won't be if you keep callin' me by that handle."

"You guiding emigrants these days?" Reno asked, and added with a smile, "Just?"

"Man's gotta eat, Jed." Just Jenkins looked ashamed.

"Reckon so." Reno tried to remember when he had first met Terrance "Just" Jenkins, a latecomer to the beaver business, but not a bad sort. Must have been in '38, when they had rendezvoused up on the Popo Agie, not too far from hereabouts. The prices of beaver plews were already dropping by then, and Jenkins had been one of the men who had guided some missionaries bound for Oregon. The Hudson's Bay Company had hired him, but he quit them at the Rendezvous, called to this wild, glorious land like so many others. Problem was, Terrance Jenkins got the calling a bit too late. Beaver were playing out, and so was the demand for beaver hats. The last rendezvous was held only two years later.

"This your rabble?" Reno asked.

Jenkins grinned, and looked at the wayfarers, a bunch of hayseeds from Ohio, he told Reno. "Nah. My party should be listenin' to Bridger's lies by now. This here party is being capt'ned and guided by Mr. Zacharias Hetzel yonder."

Hetzel, a tall, gangly man in spectacles and a big black hat and coat, stepped forward.

"He's got hisself a book."

Yep, Hetzel held some book in his hand, and it wasn't a Bible. Reno had heard of such trail guides. There weren't that many, yet, but he figured they would be selling faster and faster as more and more people left the East for that Garden of Eden called Oregon. Books like that told the fools back east what they needed to carry along the trail, how much food, what kind of clothes, what kind of weapons. He studied the weapons most of the men had. The fowling piece held by the old farmer was flintlock, but Reno spotted at least one Mississippi Rifle held by a man in a plaid shirt and britches patched at the knees.

He had seen only one Mississippi Rifle before, carried by some Dragoon, and he had to admit that it was a fine piece, with a thirty-three-inch barrel of .54 caliber. He looked around and spotted some others, shouldered by the Ohioans or butted on the ground. Problem was, a rifle like that used those new-fangled percussion caps.

Mighty fine invention, percussion caps. Not as prone to misfire as a flintlock like Reno and Jenkins and others carried. Meant you could reload a damn sight quicker, and wouldn't have as many parts you might have to replace.

But at South Pass, and even in the Willamette Valley, just where did these wayfarers think they could find percussion caps for sale?

Reno also figured that the guide book Mr. Hetzel held would also showcase the sites where emigrants should camp, where they could find wood, grass, water, the best places to ford a river, probably described the route, and provided an educated guess as to how far it was from one place to the other. Some of the guides had been taken from diaries or newspaper accounts published from diaries or letters by folks who had traveled to Oregon. But a lot of them, probably the bulk of them, were fiction. If Reno had one, about the only use he would find would be to help get a fire going.

He saw the two Conestoga wagons off the trail, how the wagons had been ransacked, clothes littering the sage, and noticed the big cairn and the cross some deer or elk had likely knocked over.

As he dismounted, Jenkins introduced him to the men. The women, and most of the children, kept a safe distance from a wild creature from the mountains like Jed Reno.

"It's Indians!" Mr. Hetzel exclaimed. "They massacred those poor men and women who were traveling with Mr. Jenkins's party."

Reno reached the cairn and knelt beside it. He felt Jenkins's shadow fall over him. "That true?"

"They was with us, sure enough. Couple families from Pennsylvania. Some town I ain't never heard of. Man named Scott had a wife and daughter and 'nother family called Colter."

"Colter." Reno smiled at the name, and he looked up at Jenkins. "You remember John Colter?"

The trapper's head shook. "Just stories is all. Way before my time."

"Mine, too. But I saw him once when I was a kid. In St. Louis. Had a farm or something at Miller's Landing. Fine life he lived. Seen this country when it was really wild."

Reno looked back at the grave.

Jenkins kept talking. "Colter family was bigger. Man, wife, three kids. Two boys and a girl. No. That ain't right. Two girls and a boy."

"And the Indians killed them all!" That wasn't shouted by Jenkins or Hetzel, but one of the other emigrants.

Reno looked up again at Jenkins. "You bury them?"

Jenkins's head shook. "And they didn't, neither. 'Nother grave by the other wagon, and more arrows plucked out of the body, I reckon. Smaller grave, though. Likely only one body buried in it. Me? I figure there be two in this one."

"We found the site of this tragic affair this morning when we arrived," Mr. Hetzel said. "Mr. Jenkins arrived shortly after. He is the one who found the arrows, and told us about them."

"I done tol' you, Hetzel, there ain't no *Mister* to my name. It's Just Jenkins."

Reno had seen the shafts of several arrows in the wagons, but Jenkins gestured to a mound of arrows, shafts, and obsidian heads darkened by dried blood near the grave.

Reno's stomach gurgled at the sight, not because of the blood or any imagination he might have had about what had happened, but because he began to understand more of Louis Jackatars's nefarious plan.

"Ain't just one band, Jed."

"I see that," Reno told Jenkins.

Shoshone. Arapaho. Cheyenne. Sioux. And others. Just like Red Prairie had told him earlier.

"We're going to find the butchers," the loudmouth said, "and make them pay."

"Somethin' else you oughta see," Jenkins whispered.

Reno let Jenkins lead the way through the woods, and the hayseeds from Ohio began gathering in a circle, talking in angry voices that carried. Reno couldn't understand most of the words, but he did not need to.

"You left those folks"—Reno tried to remember the names—"the Scotts and Colters, behind?"

"Wasn't my idea, Plenty Medicine." Jenkins pushed a low branch ahead, and held it until Reno had passed. "They voted this gent named McDonnell as captain, and he give the orders. Me? I only given advice. Told 'em we should stick together. But you know those folks. In an almighty big hurry to get through this country. He told Scott that they would wait a few days at Bridger's Trading Post. About a day's ride from Bridger's, I talked the capt'n into lettin' me ride back and see what might be keepin' 'em folks. This be what I found. And this."

He stopped, pointing toward the creek.

The body—or what once had been a body—lay strewn about the creek, among piles of buckskin remnants and bones.

Reno studied the carnage before walking toward it, looking for sign before giving up.

"The hayseeds found it, too," Jenkins said. "Fools don't know nothin' about tryin' to find no sign."

"No chance of reading much now," Reno conceded.

The wolves and other carrion had done their work quickly and neatly. He looked at the ripped garments but could not tell if they had belonged to a white man—which he guessed—or an Indian. Mountain men often let Indian squaws make their duds.

"Folks with that train," Jenkins said, "they think he was injun."

"That's what they want to think." Reno thought

about telling Jenkins about Louis Jackatars but decided against it. Just Jenkins would want to tag along, and Reno did not want anyone to get hurt or killed on his account. Besides, Jenkins needed to get that fool McConnell and whoever was left in his wagon train to the Willamette Valley.

"Found a horse," Jenkins said. "And ashes from a fire."

"And?"

"Horse was a pinto. Indian saddle. But that don't mean nothin'. Hawken rifle. Which an Indian could have owned."

Reno pointed at the bones. "But Indians don't leave their dead behind."

"Aye. Horse was well from that little camp. Upstream, staked where he could get water."

"With the Hawken?"

"Yep."

"That ain't like an Indian or a woodsman."

"Confident," Jenkins said. "He had a bow and quiver of arrows at that camp."

"Wanted to be quiet," Reno said.

"Yep. And 'em Ohioans didn't get to ruin all that sign. They don't even knows 'bout that horse." He pointed in the general direction.

Reno nodded. He would find the horse after the wayfarers were gone.

"The bow? The arrows?"

"Shoshone."

Left behind, he thought. *Maybe. As a sign. And this man?* He looked at the remains.

"He chased some kid," Jenkins said.

Reno straightened. "Kid?" He was thinking that

the man, likely one of Louis Jackatars's fiends, had found a woman, maybe one of the daughters, and— He shuddered. Maybe another piece of vermin had then killed this man in a jealous rage.

"Boy," Jenkins said. "The Colter kid. Good boy, though greener than a tree frog. From the looks of the sign, be my guess. But then 'em wayfarers come along and wiped out most of the other sign."

"Colter, you say?"

"Be my guess," Jenkins replied.

Reno let out a mirthless chuckle. "You mean to tell me that that square-head, snot-nosed kid from Ohio—"

"Pennsylvania," Jenkins corrected. "'Em square-heads up yonder hail from the Ohio country. Train I was leadin' come from Pennsylvania mostly."

"Pennsylvania, then. You're telling me that a kid— how old?"

Jenkins shrugged. "Twelve to sixteen, I reckon. We wasn't all that sociable, and I ain't got much of a head when it comes to judgin' no age of no white kids. Indian kids, now that be different."

"A kid, though. A boy. You think he killed that man?"

Jenkins shrugged. "Well, you always tell that story about Kit Carson and that Frenchy fella at that Rendezvous way back when. How Kit was thinner than an aspen sapling, yet he out that big cuss under."

"All right." Reno wasn't going to debate. He would find the trail and figure out what had happened. He headed back toward the shouting white men.

"You think Indians done this, Jed?" Jenkins asked.

"No. But I think someone wants us to think it was Indians."

"Makes no sense."

"Hatred usually don't make any sense whatsoever."

"What you talkin' 'bout?"

"Just a hunch, Jenkins. But I want you to get them square-heads to Bridger's. And when you do, you tell Jim that I'm gonna find out what happened, but don't let no war start before I get back. Tell him to give me two weeks. If he ain't heard from me by then, he can do as he sees fit."

"Two weeks ain't much time, even for you, Plenty Medicine."

"Might be long enough for me to stop a war. Or get killed."

CHAPTER 16

"I'm figuring," said the loudmouth Ohioan when Reno and Jenkins reached the campsite, "that we send the women and children on to Bridger's. The rest of us go after those red devils that killed the entire families. By thunder, this could be you and your family, Wilson. Or yours, Leonard. Or even you, Hetzel. We'll wipe the dirty heathens off the face of this earth."

Reno spit and shook his head.

"You're probably no better than the savages who did this dastardly act," the loudmouth said. "You likely lived with the Indians."

"I have," Reno said, and that caught the white men from back East off guard. "But you'd do best to just go on to Oregon." *And get the hell out of this country that I so admire.*

The loudmouth recovered. "Two families—white families—murdered by savages. All of them!"

"All of them?" Reno asked pleasantly.

"Look around you, you damn fool!" the loud-mouth cried.

That caused Jenkins to take a few steps back. He knew the code of men out there, which the Ohioan surely did not. Men who had been called far less insulting than *damn fools* had found themselves in a fight to the death. But Reno decided to let the loud-mouth live.

"I see two graves," Reno said, nodding at the big one and the smaller one off to his left.

"That's right."

"Who you reckon buried these folks?" Reno asked.

That shut everyone up.

He could have gone on, let the Ohioans know that, most likely, the raiders—be they white or red—had killed the two men, maybe the two mothers, and made off with three girl captives, but Reno knew better. That would fire up these fools who belonged back East even more. That would start a war, and after the Indians had killed these fool white folks, the Army would come in. The country would be scorched with cannon and musketry. The people would be dead, and the land would be ruined.

Nah, Reno wanted to stop that from happening. He had to.

"You boys get your families out of here. Jenkins here will get you to Bridger's place, then Mr. Hetzel and his fine book will get you to the Willamette Valley. Maybe." He whispered the last word. "I'll go after the vermin that did this. No matter what color they are, they'll pay for this. That I can promise you."

The loudmouth stepped forward. "Maybe you

were one of those butchers. Man who lives with injuns, he ain't a man I'd trust. Maybe—"

Reno belted the man with his left hand and heard the teeth smash. The loudmouth went down, dropping his fowling piece, rolling onto his hands and knees, spitting out blood, a piece of tongue he had bitten clean off, and teeth that Reno's solid fist had busted.

When the man turned around and clawed for the long gun, Reno stepped forward, sighing, and slammed the stock of his Hawken across the man's skull.

"Goodness gracious!" Mr. Hetzel shouted. "You've killed him."

"Nah." Reno tucked the big rifle back underneath his arm. "But if you folks don't get moving right quick, I'm likely to start killing. And Jenkins here knows. When I get the bloodlust, it ain't likely slaked."

Somehow, Jenkins managed to keep his face straight. He clapped his hands, gathered the hackamore to his own horse—a fine, high-stepping blood bay mare—and swung into the saddle. "Let's ride, folks. Ride and walk. We're burnin' daylight, and it's a fer piece to Bridger's." He looked at the unconscious Ohioan on the ground. "Best cart him to his wagon, fellers. Don't look like he'll be walkin' none this fine day." He looked back at Reno. "*Slaked*. You sometimes use big words, Plenty Medicine. Musta read a lot of books before you come out here to God's country."

When the square-heads and Just Jenkins were maybe a quarter mile down the pass—which sure took that long train of prairie schooners long enough—Jed Reno unsaddled his horse, grained it and the pack mule, hobbling both. Grabbing his Hawken, he cut through the woods to the creek and followed the water upstream, as Jenkins had indicated. Soon, he found the horse that had been picketed by the river.

Jenkins was right. Indian horse. He found the Hawken rifle leaning against the saddle. Some Indians had found long arms—most of them spoils from a battle they had won with a white man—but Reno shook his head at the dead man's audacity. Leave a fine weapon like that. Leave a good horse without food. Must have been quite confident that he would finish his job in a hurry.

Well, he was dead. Fools often paid a price in that country.

Reno saddled the horse, fetched the rifle, and led the horse back to the camp where it could eat. The saddle he shoved in with his packs and then went to find the camp the man had made.

Just Jenkins had been right. Back in Kentucky, when he wasn't traipsing through the woods, Jed Reno had done his share of reading. His ma had often made him read. And he still read, only not books, but the land itself.

If the train of emigrants from Ohio had not shown up, he figured Jenkins would have read the sign. But he had guessed correctly. The boy had survived the massacre, probably hidden somewhere in the woods. Jackatars had left one man behind to kill the kid, and that man had been killed instead, and been food for wolves, ravens, and whatnot. Reno could not guess how a kid from Pennsylvania—who lacked enough

sense to find the horse the man had left behind—
had come out ahead in that scrape, but the evidence
was there. The boy had won, through pluck or luck
or a mixture of both, and had buried the dead.
Three, Reno guessed, two men and a woman.

And he had found this camp. Reno could tell
where the kid had sorted through the dead man's
traps, carrying off what he needed, leaving behind
what he didn't need—at least, what he thought he
would need.

Reno returned to the camp and examined the two
graves. He wondered how long it would have taken
the kid to haul all those stones from the creek to
cover the bodies. Keep the wolves off.

Boy had grit. Plenty of it.

'Course, Reno figured he would have done the
same for his mother. But his pa? Maybe not. At least,
not after his father had apprenticed him to that
wheelwright in Louisville—although that had led to
Reno's discovery of himself and the Rocky Mountains.

If what he could read after the Ohioans had
traipsed all over the campsite was right, the boy had
lighted out from camp after burying the dead, and
that in itself took a lot of effort. Jackatars's bandits
had ransacked the wagons, taking anything of value—
spades, weapons, even the oxen and a trailing large
horse—which meant the boy had dug those two graves
by hand, even made a cross for each burial site, before setting off afoot. Only instead of following the
ruts all the way to Bridger's Trading Post, he had
walked among the tracks of unshod ponies.

The kid's tracks sure weren't steady, at least as far

as Reno got—no more than a hundred yards. *Was he delirious? Did he think that would take him to civilization, or what passed as such in this rugged patch of earth?*

Reno laughed as he walked back to the campsite. *No, the boy knew what he was doing. At least, he thought he did.* Reno shook his head as he realized, the boy wasn't trying to find Bridger or some other white men. The fool kid was going after his sisters, and the other women—likely two, if Jenkins was right. A mother and her daughter, and the boy's two sisters. Or the kid's own mother.

"Guts," Reno told the horses and mule. "Boy's got a ton of guts. I'll give him that."

Back among the abandoned prairie schooners, Reno led the mule and two horses to the creek—away from the scattered bones of the dead idiot—and let them drink. He also refilled his canteens and drank himself—upstream from the animals—and splashed the cool water over his face and neck.

He stood, led the mule and horses back to the camp, then looked around some more. From the look of the tracks, Jackatars had better than a dozen men riding with him. Leaving a trail anyone could follow. Reno knew that had been purposeful. The half-breed wanted white men to follow them. Probably to some Indian camp, so he could start his war. The tracks led northwest. Toward the Popo Agie.

Off down the pass, Reno could still see the wagons as they lumbered over the dusty country. At least, at that rate, it would take them a while to get to Jim Bridger's post—perhaps buy Reno some extra time to find, stop, and kill Jackatars. Maybe even get those women and girls back before it was too late.

He saddled his horse, fashioned another lead rope, and secured the dead man's pinto behind the pack mule. He could rest there, but time might mean life. A wolf wailed in the distance, reminding him of the dead man's bones along the creek. Jackatars would likely send someone to see what had happened to his killer. And whoever that man was would likely find the boy, who would walk straight into another killer's gunsights. Pluck and luck would get a man just so far in the Rockies.

Reno swung into the saddle, keeping his Hawken in his right hand. "C'mon!" he barked, kicking the horse's side, and loping away from the abandoned Conestogas, following the trails left by Louis Jackatars, and a fool boy named Colter from Pennsylvania.

CHAPTER 17

What was it her mother had said?

Patricia Scott tried to remember. It had been back in the desert country, after the leader of the gang that had kidnapped them had spoken so harshly— and had brutally killed the two men who had attacked Patricia's mother.

"Find a pleasant spot. A happy memory. Lock onto that, children," her mother had told her, Margaret and Nancy. "That will keep you alive. That will keep you sane. We will get out of here, girls. I promise you that. We will survive this. We must survive this. To survive, find that happy place. Go to it. Go to it . . . and keep it"—she tapped her heart—"here."

How long had they been traveling with this pack of dogs who maybe once, eons ago, had been human? Patricia wasn't sure.

Happy. She thought. *Danville? No. Not home.* After crossing so much of the country by riverboats and then Conestoga wagons, she could barely even remember what she had done, what had pleased her, why anyone would even think about living in Danville, Pennsylvania.

Happy. She tried again and almost smiled. But Patricia Scott figured she would never smile again.

Independence. Yes, Independence, Missouri.

She tuned in to memories. They had traveled five days on steamboats—maybe it had been six, she wasn't sure, and it didn't really matter.

They stepped off the boat and onto the banks of the wide Missouri River. They could see the boats, the trees and thick brush that grew along the banks, and they could see the town—a beehive of activity.

It was small, maybe smaller than Danville, certainly much, much smaller than Pittsburgh or St. Louis or several of those river towns. Yet the town's square brought in scores and scores of people. She had listened to merchants hawking everything anyone would need on the way to the Oregon Territory. She had even seen a couple Indians.

"Tame as candy, li'l lady," a man in buckskins told her.

Those Indians sure were tall, though. Osage, someone called them. Even Patricia's father looked small standing next to those Indians.

Independence maybe had two hundred residents—and many, many more emigrants just passing through. The town wasn't old. In fact, Patricia's mom and dad were older than Independence. It had been founded in 1827, only to become that "jumpin'-off dot on the map," as somebody had called it, to send folks to Santa Fe or Oregon. It came about, Patricia heard, because the riverboats couldn't get much far-

*ther west. It had something to do with the Kansas River,
which flowed into the Missouri a little west of town.*

The town had been named after the Declaration of Independence. Patricia liked that. It made her feel good.

*There was a spring, where anyone could draw water, and
even a gristmill so the merchants could make a fortune selling flour to those emigrants.*

Her father bought a blue-tinted book titled The National Wagon Road Guide, *with a sketch of a buffalo, a
covered wagon, and an Indian—certainly not friendly—on
its cover. He said the book would come in handy.*

*Mr. Colter bought some grain for his prized Percheron
stallion. One of the merchants had asked if he wanted to sell
the big animal, but Mr. Colter had said no.*

*"You should leave early," the man told Mr. Colter. "Horses
and mules can feed on the short grass. It'll take you four or
five months to reach Oregon. If I were you, I'd sell that big
stud horse of yours."*

*"No, thanks," Mr. Colter said. "And don't worry. We
have oxen to pull our prairie schooners. The stallion is to
make me richer than a king when we get to our new home."*

"If you get there," someone loitering in front of a sod saloon said.

*Tim Colter grabbed Patricia by the arm and raced her to
look at the wagons. It seemed like thousands of them along
the banks of the Missouri, parked in various sections like little cities.*

*"Think about it, Patricia," Tim said excitedly. "All these
people. All of them. Traveling west. For a new life. Think
about it."*

"I'm trying," Patricia said.

Tim shook his head and let his fingers interlock with Pa-

tricia's. "*We're making history. Did you ever figure we'd make history?*"

History. *Patricia had not considered that. History was something she learned at school.* People didn't live history. Did they? *History was George Washington and King David. It was the* Mayflower *and King Arthur. Yet as she looked at all those wagons, and so many people, she began to think that maybe Tim had a point.*

Each family. One Conestoga wagon. Four or six oxen. Well, some of the emigrants insisted on using horses or mules. Each person had two sets of clothes, and that was all. Already people were leaving boxes and crates and bundles of clothes on the ground. Patricia and Tim could see other people—those not going to Oregon and even a few Indians—sorting through the abandoned merchandise.

Maybe a milch cow. A few had chickens. Of course, the Scotts had old Wilbur. That dog that might have been older than Patricia herself. Shotguns. Rifles. Lanterns. Bonnets. Coal oil. Fatwood to help get the fires started, although a lot of people kept saying that was a waste, that these wayfarers would find plenty of buffalo chips for fuel. A few, but not many, had pistols. A bucket or two of axle grease. Candles. Bonnets and straw hats with very wide brims. A churn for butter. And sacks of food stores: flour, bacon, vinegar, beans, coffee, yeast powder, hardtack, potatoes, carrots.

Patricia and her parents and Tim and his folks and siblings were bound west for riches, but to her, it seemed as if the merchants in Independence were making all the wealth.

"*You need mules,*" *a burly man in suspenders called out.* "*Mules is tough. Oxen is too slow.*"

"*Tougher than mules, though,*" *another man yelled back.* "*Oxen eat lousy grass. Mules won't. Oxen can get you out of a mud hole. Mules can be stubborn.*"

"Only if you don't know how to work them!"

Oxen were costing emigrants forty-five to sixty dollars on that day. Patricia didn't know how much a span of mules would run because the man selling the mules got into a fight with the man selling the oxen.

She also understood why they would be traveling in those giant covered Conestogas.

Flour? Six hundred pounds. Bacon? Four hundred pounds, and packed in barrels of bran so it would not melt. Melt?

"Whoever heard of bacon melting?" Tim said with a laugh.

Coffee? Sixty pounds. Tea? Four pounds. Sugar? One hundred pounds.

Then came sacks of beans and sacks of rice. Dried peaches. Dried apples. Someone, Patricia heard, was even loading saplings of fruit trees in his wagon . . . to start an orchard when they reached the promised land.

Knives were being sold. Axes. Seeds for corn or wheat or whatever. Tools migrating farmers would need when they finally arrived in Oregon Territory—plows, rakes, hoes, scythes—and tools they would need on the long journey across this country called America—shovels, hammers, mallets, planes, saws. A spare axel. A spare wheel.

If you could afford those.

Most in the train the Colters and Smiths joined could not afford that. They had spent practically their last penny just to make it to Independence.

But they had made it.

Patricia and Tim returned to the wagon train. Its newly elected leader was busy announcing his plans.

"First," Captain McDonnell was saying, "I have drawn up an obligation that all members will sign. It binds every-

*one to the rule that all will abide by my orders and decisions,
and that each and every one of you will aid me by every
means, so be it. We will also form a company that will guard
our herd and other animals, and protect us, God willing
from red heathens. And . . ."*

The kids stopped listening. Indians? Those would never
attack a wagon train of their size.

Tim led Patricia away, toward the spring. He carried a
bucket, said he had told his mother that he'd go and fetch
some good water—not that muddy slop from the river—and
Patricia walked with him.

A man in a wide-brimmed black hat stopped them as they
made their way along the trail that led to the spring. He had
two pistols stuck in his waistband and no right ear. "You
two ain't Mormons, are ye?"

Tim blinked.

Patricia asked, "What's a Mormon?"

The man laughed. "Well, that's the question, ain't it? I
reckon y'all can have some of our water. Don't like givin' it
to no Mormons, though. You see, little lady, we had us a
scare a few years back. Mormons . . . crazy cusses . . . figured they could take all of our good decent white women for
their own brides. Preaching this and that. Saying it's their
right to have as many wives as they want."

"Goodness," Patricia said.

"No, ma'am. There ain't nothing good about them folks.
So they come here, decide they's gonna build up this temple.
Right here. In our good, decent, God-fearin' town. Well, by
thunder, we're Christians in this town. So we run them folks
out. Killed as many as we could." He pointed. "Just follow
that trail, younguns. You'll find the water, and help yourself to it."

When they passed the man, he called out.

"Kid."

Both Tim and Patricia turned.

"You best watch out for any Mormons, kid. They'll take that gal of yours for their own. That's why we Christians just figure we have to kill them all."

When they reached the spring, Tim said, "That man's crazy."

"You think he was joshing us, Tim?"

"I don't know." He filled the bucket. *"Mormons. Maybe I did hear tell of something about them. Or read something in a newspaper."*

Patricia smiled. "Maybe you'd like to become a Mormon. Have a bunch of wives."

Tim grinned. "You think so?"

She batted her eyes. "I don't know."

"Get me a haram?"

"A what?"

"A lot of wives."

She shrugged.

Tim lowered the bucket, glanced down the trail to make sure no one was coming to the spring, and walked up to her. She looked down.

He put his hand under her chin and lifted her head so that she looked up at him. "No haram for me, Patricia Scott. When I get to Oregon—even if the whole territory is filled with Mormons and harams and the like—I only want one woman. One wife. For all of my life."

Tears welled in her eyes. "Oh," she said, her voice weak, body trembling. "Oh, Tim."

She felt him lean over, and his lips met hers. Tim Colter didn't taste like her grandfather had, back when he had kissed her on her birthday. Grandfather Scott had tasted

*like snuff. Tim's lips were gentle, sweet, and tasted like . . .
well . . . maybe honey.*

Yes. That was the place Patricia Scott wanted to return to. That was her private place. It was the happy
place she chose to keep in her heart. The public
spring in Independence . . . where Tim had kissed
her and practically proposed to her.

She needed to remember that. More than Father
and poor old Wilbur. More than the riverboats across
Pennsylvania and the West. More than anything.

That could keep her alive.

She wanted to stay alive . . . because Tim Colter
was still alive, no mater what everybody else said. And
she knew Tim. He would be coming for her, his sisters, and her mother.

He had to be coming. He had to be.

Just remember, Patricia kept telling herself.

So she tried. As hard as she could.

Within a few days, she could remember nothing.
Nothing except the daily hell the captives had to en-
dure. It felt like they had been living through it for
an eternity.

CHAPTER 18

"**M**a, I don't want to be sick!" he cried.

His mother removed the damp rag over his forehead, helping him up, leaning him over as he vomited into the chamber pot.

Tim wailed. He despised being sick. It seemed so weak, and he didn't like how he felt—hot and clammy, his stomach roiling—yet his mother pulled him close, using a handkerchief to wipe his mouth.

"Ma—" Tim sniffed.

"It's all right, Tim. Everybody gets sick."

"But—" He said no more, letting his mother pull him closer and run her fingers through his sweaty hair.

Tim woke up, staring at the morning sky, praying that everything that came flooding through his memories had been a dream. He wet his lips, chapped and crusted with the vomit from last night. That much had not been a dream. After sucking in a deep breath, holding it for a moment, and then exhaling, he slumped.

He knew what he would find when he sat up. He would find himself alone on a hilltop, a long way from Danville, Pennsylvania, where his mother would always comfort him when he was sick with fever or a cold, and a far distance from the two Conestoga wagons he had walked away from yesterday afternoon. *Had it been longer? How long have Ma and Pa been dead?*

Making himself sit up, Tim used the cloth that served to protect him from the sun to wipe his mouth. He found the canteen and drank some water then looked at his options for breakfast. *Dried beef? One final biscuit? The bad-smelling greasy mix in the leather pouch? Or do without?*

He ate the biscuit, figuring that if he waited much longer, the stale, tasteless stone might break his teeth. Another sip of water, and he stood, stretching, looking down the trail, and wondering how many miles he had traveled. It didn't matter.

Late in the afternoon before, he had thrown up, although he had little in his stomach to force out. At first, he thought he might have found bad water—the mountain man of a guide on the trail, Just Jenkins, always worried about bad water, said it could kill a man, even wipe out an entire train. Tim soon decided that he wasn't dying of cholera or poison water and remembered something else Jenkins had said.

"Air's thin. Gets thinner the higher you go. Make a body sick, it will, iffen he ain't careful."

He had not been careful. So determined to put some miles on him, to catch up with Patricia and his sisters and Mrs. Scott, he had walked and hurried, climbed and slipped, driving himself to keep moving and rarely stopping to slake his thirst.

Just Jenkins always advised to drink water. "Don't get too thirsty," he'd warned, adding, "but don't waste water. It can be hard to come by."

Tim did not know that country or when he might happen upon another creek or water hole. What he had, he could carry. So he'd felt conserving water would be the wisest option.

And it had made him sick.

After throwing up, however, and drinking a few swallows, he felt better. Eventually, his pounding head had stopped aching, he'd eaten a bit of dried beef, and had fallen asleep. To dream of his mother and how she had always been there for him when he was sick.

But . . . he was alone.

He looked at the trail of horses. He gathered his belongings, securing the makeshift bonnet over his head. He walked. *Today, though,* he told himself, *when I need to drink, I will drink.*

About two miles later, he stopped.

He had dreamed of his mother. He had remembered her. But he had not cried. He frowned.

Healing? Disrespectful?

Tim didn't know. He just kept walking, trying to remember her voice, how she sounded, picturing that smile of hers until he had it chiseled into his brain. He thought of his father, tried to recall his face— the face before the bandits had butchered him—and how he had laughed.

He thought of the journey.

* * *

They left Independence early in the morning, twenty-four Conestogas carrying families west. Mr. McConnell was the captain of the train, and Mr. Jenkins was the scout.

He always told Tim, "Mr. Jenkins was my pap, boy. You call me Just. That's me name, Just Jenkins."

"He'll do no such thing, Mr. Jenkins," Ma said. "You hear me, Tim?"

"Yes, ma'am."

Yet when they were alone—which did not happen often— the man in buckskins would whisper, "Yer Ma cain't hear us now, boy. Call me Just."

"Just." Tim grinned.

"Beats bein' called a son-of-a-Pawnee, and that's fer sure."

It caused Tim to laugh.

The first night, they camped at a place called Lone Elm. It had been aptly named, for on this small rise, he found only one elm tree, but the grass reached his shoulders, and the water from a nearby spring tasted sweet. One night out, and he felt awestruck. It was actually happening. They were going to Oregon, starting a new life, a good life, and Patricia Scott would be there with him.

A mile or two out of camp, Mr. Scott pointed out the junction of two trails. The Santa Fe went to Mexican country, off to the west, but he pointed at the ruts that led northwest, and he whipped off his hat, bellowing, "I'm a-goin' to Oregon, folks. If you want to eat hot chile peppers, go yonder way. Iffen you want to see paradise, foller me!"

So they went, keeping the wagons on the high ground. The trees slowly faded into a memory, and all Tim could see were rolling hills, tall grasses, but mostly an endless sky. He marveled at the country, but soon found it dull and dusty.

Maybe he grew homesick. In Pennsylvania, he had always taken trees for granted. He never thought he would actually miss them, their leaves, their smell.

Before long, he was given a sack and sent out of camp to find dried buffalo dung to use as fuel for their fires. He began to wonder if the beans Ma cooked up tasted like—He grinned at the word he did not say, but one Just Jenkins would use quite frequently when the women could not hear.

At Blue Mound—a hill that shot from nothing but flat grasslands—Tim and Patricia had walked up to see what lay ahead.

"What did you see?" Mr. Scott asked when they returned.

"More of the same," Patricia answered.

Tim added, "A whole lot of nothing."

Later, they crossed the Kaw River, which some folks had started calling the Kansas, using the ferry Joseph and Louis Papin had build at the Topeka crossing. Lucky, Mr. Jenkins had said, that the Papins had settled there.

"The river is raging from snowmelt," Jenkins said. "You do not want to ford this stream when she's mad."

Rivers, and even small creeks that did not look so dangerous, soon brought fear to the settlers, because there were no more ferries to be found.

By the time they crossed the Red Vermillion, their grand adventure had turned into nothing short of drudgery. Up before dawn, a quick breakfast, oxen hitched, and by the time the sun was rising, they were rolling westward. Walking. Walking. Those prairie schooners had no room for passengers, just furniture, supplies, and water barrels. The sun baked. The wind blew. They ate sand.

At one place along the Little Blue, Just Jenkins called out, "Last chance to turn back, folks! This here be the junc-

tion of the road back to Independence, or you can take that one to St. Joe."

To Tim's surprise, and to the annoyance of Captain Mc-Connell, two families had had enough. They went the way of St. Joseph, saying to hell with Oregon, they were going back to Scranton.

By the time the train reached The Narrows of the Little Blue River, Tim sometimes wished they had joined those two deserters.

Then, he saw the Platte River. It looked wider and certainly bluer than the Mississippi.

"Mile wide," Jenkins said, "and 'bout an inch deep."

"It's big." That's about all Tim could find in his vocabulary.

"We won't cross her for a spell," the guide said. "Just foller alongside the south bank."

That led Captain McConnell to his first disagreement with Mr. Jenkins at a place called Plum Creek, even if Tim and his sisters found nothing even resembling a plum.

"We have to cross this river at some point," Captain Mc-Connell said. "Here is a likely place."

"Not here, Capt'n," Jenkins said. "She'll split a ways up the trail, and we'll cross the South at the Upper Crossin', then ford the North near Ash Hollow."

"That means we have to cross the river twice. I say we do it here."

Jenkins shook his head.

"By thunder, sir, this is only an inch deep, as you say."

"And full of quicksand. The channels move like the dust that eternal wind's always ablowin'. It'll be dangersome even at the Upper Crossin'."

It was. The Fuller family broke a kingbolt, and the Scotts,

the Colters, and even the Fullers watched as the Conestoga, stuck in the middle of the river, settled deeper and deeper into the sandy bottom. The water reached the axle, then the sides, and Tim could hardly breathe as he watched the water soon cover most of the canvas tarp.

The Colters had crossed second, after the McConnell family, followed by a family from Buffalo, New York, and another from Lancaster. The Fullers tried next and failed.

They had no wagon left, no supplies.

"They'll have to ride with one of you good folks," Just Jenkins said. "Till we can leave them at Fort Laramie."

"We have not enough food," Captain McConnell said, "to spare."

Tim's pa stepped forward. "Are you saying we must leave these good folks behind?"

"They knew the risks."

"It's a long walk back to Independence," the guide said.

Captain McDonnell repeated himself. "They knew the risks."

Jenkins shook his head. "I don't think so, Capt'n."

McDonnell frowned. "You can't take them back. Would you rather have us caught in a snowstorm and freeze to death or not reach Oregon till next year?"

"Never said I'd take 'em back. I said they ride along till Laramie. Maybe they can find another family in the next train through. Maybe that train will have enough food to spare."

"Or," Mr. Colter put in, "have a captain with Christian charity."

McDonnell apologized, and the Fullers rode with a family from Lancaster.

Just Jenkins figured out the new channels made by the ever-changing monster of a river and the rest of the train crossed the South Platte without incident, though it took an eternity. The wagon train moved on west.

Two days later, they buried little Amanda Collins, who had been bitten by a rattlesnake.

A week later, Mrs. Green just dropped dead, and they buried her, too.

As he walked, Tim considered all that had happened. Sometimes, he wished they had never left Danville.

CHAPTER 19

Kneeling, Tim studied the trail the bandits had left. He brushed the sand coating his lips, and thought about sipping water, but decided that he was not thirsty. He had taken three swallows only two hours ago.

He looked off to the north toward the mountains where he thought the trail was leading. *What was it Just Jenkins had called that range? The Winds? No. Wind River. He remembered.*

The mountain man used to camp in the Popo Agie up at Sinks Canyon. "Mighty pretty country," he bragged. "Beyond that, I can show you the grave of Sacajawea, who had been so good for Lewis and Clark and the boys."

"I'd like to see that," Tim told him.

"Well, when you gets tired of Oregon, you come back. Look me up. Ask Jim Bridger where to find me."

Tim grinned. "I just might do that," though he knew he

wouldn't. He'd be farming in Oregon. But Patricia would be there to make him forget all about being a wild man like Just Jenkins.

He shook off the thought of Patricia and looked at the tracks. The raiders had turned south and west, heading away from the Wind River Range and off toward the nothingness of what appeared to become nothing but desert.

Figuring they must have known where they could find water, Tim gathered up his packs and trudged on ahead.

He was used to walking.

Since leaving Independence, that was practically all he had done. As he walked, he thought.

When all the remaining wagons had forded the South Platte, Just Jenkins pointed at California Hill.

"We have to climb that?" Pa asked.

"It ain't nothin' compared to what you'll be facin' down this pike," Jenkins said. "Ain't big, but it is a grade. 'Bout two hundred fifty feet or so in a mile and a half. It'll take a spell. Once we reach the plateau, it's an easy jog to Ash Hollow."

Tim walked up that hill. He walked to Ash Hollow, where they found shade trees and plenty of wood, so the beans did not taste like dried buffalo dung. It was pretty, that part of the country, and he saw more sights that amazed him as they traveled along the south bank of the North Platte.

Courthouse and Jail Rock. Ma said she could see it. Pa said he couldn't. Mr. Scott said it was just a name.

Captain McConnell said, "If I had my druthers, I'd make it a jail, and leave Just Jenkins chained to it."

Jenkins smirked. "I'd like to see you try."

Tempers were short by then, and they had a long way to go.

Chimney Rock, everyone agreed, indeed resembled a chimney. When they camped underneath Scotts Bluff, they had traveled a third of the way to Oregon.

Jenkins told them, "You have a hard road ahead."

Through Robidoux Pass, they went, and across rolling prairie, where the wind blew even harder and longer, and the sky got bigger.

Finally, they came to Fort Laramie.

It was a sprawling compound and a beehive of activity, but to Tim's disappointment, he saw no soldiers.

"They'll be here, I suspect," Jenkins told him. "Army comes everywhere eventually. When there's white folks to save or land to steal."

Tim didn't know what to make of that.

"William Sublette founded the trading post along the Laramie River back in 1834 and named it after himself, Fort William, Jenkins told Tim. "Then the American Fur Company bought it from Sublette and renamed it Fort John but nobody calls it that anymore. Name changed a lot. Fort John at the Laramie River, then Fort John-Laramie, and finally they just started calling it Fort Laramie."

You could buy everything at the post, including a Conestoga wagon that some unfortunate emigrants had abandoned. The Fullers bought one and grub, but not enough to get them to Oregon.

"I wonder if we'll get to see our piano," Mrs. Fuller said.

Mr. Fuller put his hand on his wife's shoulder.

"Next year, Mother. Just you wait. Next year."

Those poor folks. They had paid a fortune to freight their grand piano around the Horn by clipper ship. The piano would have been too big, too heavy to haul by Conestoga.

Sadly, Mr. and Mrs. Fuller rode out the next morning . . . east, back to Independence, hiring a half-breed Pawnee to lead them down the trail and into civilization.

Tim wondered if they had made it back. Maybe the Pawnee half-breed had killed them. Maybe when they recrossed the North Platte, the quicksand had taken them and their new wagon. He wanted to think they were in Independence, where Mr. Fuller would work and Mrs. Fuller would have her baby. Tim grimaced. He did not even know she was in the family way until Patricia told him. The Fullers planned to join the Scotts and the Colters in the Willamette Valley the next year. Tim kept walking, re-membering, and wondering if he would ever see them again.

Just Jenkins bought a jug of what someone called Taos Lightning and got rip-roaring drunk.

That angered Captain McConnell, who chastised the red-eyed, pale guide the next morning. "From now on, I'll be giving the orders. You will say nothing more than yes, sir . . . if you want to receive payment." Mr. McConnell abstained from alcohol and did not associate with men who imbibed far too frequently.

Jenkins agreed. That's how hungover he was.

* * *

Tim stopped walking. *Fort Laramie,* he decided. That was where it happened. At least, that's how the riff between McConnell and Jenkins had started to happen. Tim wondered how maybe the Fullers had been fortunate. He wished vainly that the Scotts or his own family's wagon had broken down, or gotten lost in quicksand in the South Platte River, and that they had returned home.

They would be together.

They would be alive.

Instead, they left Fort Laramie and began a steady climb. He started walking again.

Tim carved his and Patricia's names in the soft sandstone at Register Cliff, and they walked around, reading names and dates, and wondering what had become of the people who had left their names there.

They moved onto Warm Springs and a natural bridge, and crossed the North Platte with the Laramie Mountains looming off to the southeast.

Just Jenkins took them through a gap, saying it would keep them away from the Red Buttes, and they forded the North Platte, stopping to camp and rest as he warned that the travel would be hard and dry until they reached the Sweetwater River.

John Ferguson, just a year older than Tim, would never see the Sweetwater. He slipped while hitching the team of oxen to his father's prairie schooner, and his neck landed on the wagon tongue. He did not die right away, but was gone in a week.

Two days later, Mr. Ferguson was dead. No one said how,

though, but Tim knew. He could see the grownups whispering and had heard the lone pistol shot and Mrs. Ferguson's screams in the middle of the night.

Yet all those tragedies, all those hardships, all the aches and pains, scratches and scars, all the buffalo dung and the insect bites, and the fear whenever anyone heard the whirl and clicking of a rattlesnake's warning . . . it was all forgotten when they came to Independence Rock.

They sang songs. They danced. Many climbed up the rock to carve their names alongside others. Tim took Patricia there, and they read names and dates—the earliest they found was 1829—but Tim said he did not want to carve his name. He had found some paint, and for some silly reason, he thought painting Tim Colter-Patricia Scott, 1845, would be more fitting, that it would last longer.

Just Jenkins laughed and told him, "Your names will be gone come the next thunderstorm."

After resting an extra day at Independence Rock, the train moved west, through Devil's Gate, a mesmerizing place that looked brutal yet beautiful. The Sweetwater River—which they would cross six times—had carved a gap in the high rocks. At the base, where the wagons rolled through, it stretched maybe thirty feet across, but up above, at the summit of the rocks some three or four hundred feet over them, the gap must have been ten times wider.

The fifteen hundred feet they traveled through the Gate felt like fifteen hundred miles. Tim felt chilled as he walked, and he wasn't sure if he could attribute that to the fact that the sun's rays no longer burned his hands and neck.

When they camped that night on the other side of the Gate, Mr. Longmont said, "Man back at Fort Laramie said this place was haunted. Says the Shoshones and some other injun tribe said a big giant beast with tusks—like an ele-

*phant, I guess—carved the path with its tusks after some in-
juns had cornered it and was trying to kill it. That's how
the big animal escaped. He says Indians don't like this
place."*

*Captain McDonnell said, "That is a silly superstition by
a bunch of heathens."*

*"Maybe so," Mr. Longmont said, "but I don't like this
place, either."*

*"It's behind us now, Chester," Mr. Scott said. "Don't look
back."*

Don't look back, Tim thought as he walked. He tried
to take it to heart. *Don't look back. Look ahead. Think of
what you have to do. Just keep walking. One foot. One step.
One foot. One step.*

He stopped to drink water and eat the last bit of
dried beef. And while he ate, he remembered.

*They had gone on, stopping only at Three Crossings to
bury Mrs. Ballard, whose heart had given out, a day or so
after they had passed Split Rock.*

*The Granite Mountains were to the north, hills to the
south, and beyond that, nothing but savage land.*

*They walked. The oxen snorted. Even the Percheron grew
tired and dropped his head.*

*Mountains loomed ahead. Women prayed. A few cried.
Tim wondered what folks were doing back in Danville.*

*They slipped and stubbed toes, fell and tore gashes in
hands and legs as they climbed seven hundred feet up a
place Just Jenkins called Rocky Ridge where boulders lined
the path.*

The oxen labored to pull the Conestogas up the trail. To lighten the load, Mr. Ballard tossed out his late wife's trunk and even their bed. By the time they reached the crest of the ridge, Tim could see other emigrants had followed suit. The place was littered with items that once had seemed so precious, but had become nothing but trash.

They passed another wagon, dried and burned by the sun, a reminder that not everyone who set out on the journey reached their destination.

Their lips chapped. Dust and grime almost blinded them. They made four miles that day. It felt as if it had taken them four months.

And they had not even crossed the ridge.

It would take them another day to complete the twelve-mile stretch, the wheels of their Conestogas deepening the cuts across the hard rock floor that other wagons had created. Two high shelves they crossed, then forded a dry bed called Strawberry Creek—another place named by someone with a demented sense of humor—and camped again, worn out. Too tired to eat. Too exhausted to sleep.

Tim did not think it could ever get any worse.

Until they reached South Pass. Actually, compared to Devil's Gate or Rocky Ridge or the crossing of the South Platte, it had been an easy trek.

But the Scotts' left wheel busted.

Captain McConnell told them they would have to stay behind to repair it. "You can catch up with the train at Bridger's Trading Post. Or wait to join another train."

Jenkins did not like that idea, but he was taking orders from Captain McConnell.

*   *   *

Tim had to stop to catch his breath. The wind was picking up, and he saw the clouds darkening in the west. Something caused him to blink, and he realized it had been a flash of lightning. A few seconds later, he heard the thunder.

Fear seized him. Rain would bring him much-needed water, but it could also wipe out the tracks he had been following. He took a quick step, then stopped suddenly and stared. One of the sacks slipped from his fingers and dropped in the sand.

Standing just off to the trail stood a man in buckskins. One hand held the hackamore to his horse. The other held a hatchet.

The man laughed, but Tim Colter found nothing funny.

CHAPTER 20

He was a swarthy man, with eyes as dark as his beard. Slim, though, and not that much taller and heavier than Tim. He did not move, not even blink. The only movement came from the horse, a small, black mustang, which lowered its head to graze on a batch of grass sticking out of the sand and rocks.

"Hello," Tim said.

The man did not answer.

"Do you speak English?" Tim tried again. He thought back to Danville, and that tall man with the curly mustache who had stopped at the subscription school for a week and tried to teach them French.

"Anglais?" It was the only word he remembered except for *oui*, which had made all of his classmates laugh whenever the Frenchman or anyone else said it.

The man dropped the hackamore and started walking toward Tim, who instinctively took a step back and tumbled onto his buttocks. The man did not stop, but he did grin at Tim's accident. He also shifted the hatchet.

The hat topping the man's long black hair came from a skunk. Tim knew that. The head was still on the animal, its mouth baring its teeth in a snarl that matched the look on the man with the hatchet. His buckskins were well-worn, the pants fringed from waist to feet, the shirt—of a darker color—fringed only along the sleeves. A weathered scarf of faded blue silk hung loosely around his neck, and a strange bronze ornament dangled below the bandanna, secured with a leather thong around the man's neck. The bronze piece was maybe three inches in size, sort of like a cross made of four commas, or two *S*'s with the ends much wider than the middle.

The man brought the hatchet up and rubbed a thumb over the blade.

He whispered something in a language that Tim did not understand. It wasn't French. It certainly was not English.

Wetting his lips with his tongue, Tim reached behind his back and brought the big horse pistol forward. He thumbed back the hammer.

That stopped the man.

"Leave me alone," Tim said.

The man studied the big pistol. Tim tried not to look at the gun, which shook in his hand so much that he had to use both hands to steady it. He brought the gun up higher, aiming in the general direction of the man's chest.

Tim knew he had not primed the pan with powder. If he pulled the trigger, nothing would happen. The gun could not fire. Yet he hoped that the mountain man with the hatchet could not tell that the weapon was useless, hoped the man would back away, mount his horse, and ride off . . . leave Tim . . . alive.

His mother would have paddled his fanny for gambling, but he did not see that he had much of a choice. He could not whip the man in a fight, certainly not when the wiry, dark-skinned, black-eyed man held a hatchet. Tim had also seen a long rifle in a fringed sheath leaning against a rock beside the grazing horse.

"You . . ."

Tim blinked, amazed. The man with the hatchet could speak English, though it certainly was not a language he used often. "You . . . shoot . . . *pistola* . . . kaboom! . . . in . . . *esku*." He shook his free hand to let Tim know what he meant.

Shoot the pistol, and it would blow up in Tim's hand.

"Maybe," Tim said. *If I had primed the pan, anyway.*

"Maybe not."

He wasn't sure if the man understood, but he did get the general idea. With a sigh, the man lowered the hatchet to his side. He, too, wet his lips.

They seemed to be at a stalemate. Tim wondered how long he could hold the pistol, which seemed to add pounds every few seconds, but he knew better than to lower it. Maybe the man was waiting for help. Tim couldn't tell, and he dared not take his eyes off the swarthy fellow in front of him.

Thunder boomed. The dark clouds began getting closer. Tim saw a flash of lightning, and, after several seconds, heard another distant rumble of thunder.

The dark man spoke again. "Baillarger?"

Tim squinted, not understanding.

"Baillarger?" the man repeated. He pointed at himself, and using his free hand, lifted it above his head a good foot or two.

"You?" Tim asked. "Your name is Baillarger?"

"No." The man shook his head emphatically. "Baillarger. He . . . no . . . *asasinatu.*" His head shook, trying to find a way to break the barrier caused by their different languages. "Keeel." His head nodded. "Baillarger no keeeel . . . *zu.* You. No keeeeel you." Again, he raised his free hand over his head, moved it around, indicating, maybe, a larger man.

Baillarger. Tim thought he understood. *Kill.*

"No, Baillarger did not kill me." He sucked in a deep breath, and let it out. "I killed him." He tried to repeat one of the words the man had said. *Asasinatu.* "I a-sasi-natu-ed Baillarger." He even made himself smile when he said those words, even as he swallowed down the bile rising in his throat and felt his stomach turning over and over and over.

The man laughed and pointed at Tim. "You?"

"Me," Tim said.

The skin of the skunk atop the man's head shook. The man laughed again and sighed, relaxing his shoulders. "Jackatars, no . . . *sinetsi.*" Another laugh. "Baillarger . . . *mozolo.*"

"You better go now," Tim told him, waving the heavy pistol slightly.

The hatchet fell to the ground. The man studied Tim.

"You don't go now," Tim said, trying to deepen his voice and narrow his eyes, "I'll kill you." He wet his lips again. "Sure as hell." He could almost see his parents frowning on him for using such a nasty word, but he figured he was in nasty company and wanted the man to mount his horse and ride off. Leave him alone.

The wind blew hard and Tim could smell rain off in the distance. "Go on!" he shouted. "Get out of here."

The dark man surprised him. He nodded. Even turned away and started for his horse, but he stopped after a few paces and looked back at Tim. He pointed to the hatchet he had dropped on the ground, tapped his forehead as if he were an imbecile, and stepped toward the weapon, kneeling to the ground, and reaching for the hatchet.

Tim tried to swallow, but his throat had no moisture in it.

The man's dark hands went down. One hand brought up the hatchet. The other sent a fistful of sand into Tim's eyes.

Turning, Tim heard the hammer click on the pistol, although he didn't remember pulling the trigger. He didn't remember much after that, either, because something slammed across his forehead. Orange and red flashes exploded across his eyes, and he groaned. He fell back hard, his head striking the rocky path and sending more orange and red blossoming.

Breath left his lungs. Something crushed his face. Something else smashed his nose, and he tasted blood as it poured from his nose and over his lips. The back of his head was bleeding, too. At least he didn't taste that.

Opening his eyes proved a struggle. He saw the

dark man's face, and vaguely understood that the man straddled his chest. He kept shouting something, but Tim's ears rang, and his mind seemed all befuddled. Besides, the man spoke a language Tim had never heard, and little English.

Slowly, the man came into a hazy focus and Tim seemed to understand that the dark man waved a pistol over his head. Tim's pistol. Or, rather, the pistol he had taken but failed to prime from the man he had left dead by the river. *Ballenger. No, Baillarger.* Whatever the dark man had called him.

The man seemed upset that Tim had fooled him with the pistol. He slapped Tim's cheeks—hard blows that caused tears to well in his eyes. He saw the waving pistol, which the dark man tossed aside. He wrapped his left hand around Tim's throat tight like a vise, and Tim struggled to breathe. The man leaned over, and through the tears and pain in his eyes, Tim saw the man lift the hatchet with his right hand.

He spit in Tim's face, but Tim didn't care. He tried to fight, to shake the man off him, to free the grip that crushed his throat and blocked any air. Suddenly, he understood what was happening. He was about to die. He wouldn't save Patricia or her mother or his sisters from the bandits. He had failed.

He was a stupid kid. About to be a dead kid.

The dark man grinned. He seemed to understand that Tim knew what would happen. The hatchet came up.

Tim closed his eyes.

He heard a deep voice, and the grip released his larynx. He could breathe, and did deeply, quickly.

His eyes opened again. The dark man was staring to his right, over Tim's head.

The man wet his lips, said something. There was no reply. He was looking at someone Tim couldn't see, still holding the hatchet.

Slowly, the man stood up, still straddling Tim, but only for a second or two. He moved his left leg over Tim's stomach and did a few side steps, still holding the hatchet, which he lowered, and backed away toward his horse.

"No, Abaroa," said the deep voice out of Tim's eyesight.

The dark man grinned. He had raised his hands, said something, and brought his hands forward, moving them every which way as he spoke. Tim craned his neck, but could not see who the dark man spoke to with words, fingers, and hands.

"That be your play, Abaroa," the voice behind Tim said. "*Mano-a-mano.* Me and you. No guns."

"*Bai.*"

"I drop my rifle. You drop the hatchet. We fight like that. Just like that time at Horse Creek in '37."

Tim felt certain that the dark man did not understand all the words, but he grinned. The man Tim could not see must have also been speaking with his hand. No? Not if he held a gun.

But the dark man again grinned, his head nodding, and he repeated the word *bai.* The hatchet slipped from his right hand and fell at his feet. He held his hands at his side.

Something clunked on the ground, and the dark man started to reach behind his back, still grinning.

Thunder sounded.

Tim blinked, seeing the dark man drop to his knees and then fall to his hands that kept him from crashing to the ground. Blood poured from his mouth as his head lifted weakly, and he stared in the direction of the thunder and the man Tim did not see.

Tim realized it had not been thunder, but a gun-shot.

The dark man dropped to the ground, heaved once, and then became still.

Still.

And dead.

CHAPTER 21

Tim rolled to push himself to his feet, but the world started spinning, and he fell back to the ground, squeezing his eyelids shut. He did, however, manage to wipe the blood off his face. When his eyes opened again, he saw the hideous monster leaning over him.

He was a white man . . . or once had been. He had a beard and long hair flecked with silver, and a face covered with scars . . . and was missing an eye. A patch covered that, and he, too, wore a fur hat over his head. His massive left hand held a smoking horse pistol, which he laid on the ground beside Tim. The big hands unloosened a silk scarf fastened around his neck, fisted it into a ball, and pressed it against Tim's nose. The other hand lifted Tim's left arm and positioned his hand over the piece of filthy silk. "Hold it here till the bleeding's done. Lie easy for a spell. Be back in a minute or two. Need to fetch the horses and mule."

For a big man, he moved gracefully and practically silently.

Tim wanted to say something, but his brain still felt foggy, and he wasn't altogether certain what had just happened. He managed to wet his lips, which still tasted of salty blood, and eventually rolled over, but he could not see the man anymore. Maybe it was an apparition. A ghost. Tim's guardian angel.

He would have laughed at that thought, if it would not have hurt so badly. That man was definitely no angel.

He blacked out or fell asleep, for when his eyes opened again, the clouds were black. *Night? No.* He could smell the rain in the air, and the wind was blowing harder. The storm was fast approaching.

"Here."

It was the one-eyed giant, once again hovering over him. He dropped an animal on Tim's legs.

"Skin out of them duds. Put these on."

The angel . . . or demon from Hades . . . helped Tim sit up. His head spun around a few circuits, but stopped, and slowly he seemed to feel better. He touched the back of his head, and found a piece of cloth had been wrapped around it. His nose had stopped bleeding.

Turning slightly, Tim looked at the animal. *No. Skins. Buckskins.* He sucked in a deep breath, which caused him to gasp in pain. These were the clothes the dark-skinned man had been wearing. Tim looked over, and saw the naked, bloodied corpse of the man.

"I . . . I . . . won't . . ."

"You will," the demon said. "Them duds you got on won't last a day. Storm's blowing in. Get up. Get dressed. We need to get moving."

"I . . . can't . . ."

"You will. Or I leave you here."

The monster walked away, back to the dark, naked man lying on his back on blood-drenched rocks. Tim fingered the greasy buckskins and touched something that caused his fingers to jerk back. Blood stained the tips of two fingers. Blood from the shirt of the dead, dark man. Blood from the bullet the demon had fired into the man's stomach.

Tim looked at the monster and sucked in a deep breath. He almost threw up as the demon put a knee in the small of the dark man's back. The knife worked around the dark hair. The Cyclops jerked. A pop sounded like a gunshot. After wiping blood from the knife's blade onto his buckskin leggings, the monster walked back, holding a bloody scalp in his right hand.

"Get dressed. If you want to find your sisters."

Rain fell in icy torrents, the wind howled like demons, and the sun had long ago vanished. With their backs to the wind, the three horses and a mule stood miserably in the rain, soaking wet.

At least Tim Colter was dry.

He sat underneath a shallow outcropping of rock, the fur of an animal over his shoulders to keep him warm, and worked with his fingers on the buckskin shirt, trying to scrub away the dark, dried blood over the hole that had killed the man earlier that day.

The one-eyed monster sat with his back against the stone wall, a long rifle cradled over his thighs, gnawing on a piece of dried elk. Or so he had told Tim. The weapons had been stacked in a pile far from the rain, as had a few other pouches and sacks. Most remained on the ground, covered with hide, but that was the only protection.

"I can patch that hole if that's what's troubling you."

Tim stopped with his fingers and looked over at the man. "The shirt's too big," he managed to say. "So are the pants."

"You might grow into them." The man considered that for a second. "Might not, too." He stuck the last bit of jerky into his mouth. "Warm enough?"

Tim shivered but made himself nod his head.

"Want me to patch the shirt?"

"The hole doesn't bother me," Tim said, summoning up courage.

The man waited.

"It's how it got there." Tim stiffened, figuring the monster would kick him into the rain, let him freeze or drown out there.

"Maybe you'd rather be dead back yonder," the man pointed out.

"You shot him down in cold blood. He dropped his hatchet."

The monster laughed and pointed a long, bent finger at the pile of weapons.

"See that screw-barrel .45 by you?"

Sure, enough, Tim spied a pistol he had never seen. It was close enough, so he reached and picked it up. It was small, the barrel just over two inches long. He read the engraving on the side plate above the trigger and below the hammer. *London*.

"It was behind Abaroa's back," the monster said. "He figured when I put my Hawken down, he could kill me quick enough. He just didn't think I had a pistol behind my back, too. Never been much for pistols. Bridger let me borrow it while he was fixing mine."

Tim swallowed.

"If you carry a pistol, kid, remember to prime it."

"Oh." It was all Tim could say.

The man chuckled. "Reckon that's an apology."

Thunder rumbled.

"Name's Jed Reno," the one-eyed beast said.

"Tim." He did not recognize his own voice. With a busted nose, he sounded something like a frog or a cricket. Or a girl. "Tim Colter."

The man nodded. "Your sisters got took."

"And Patricia." Tim looked at the hole in the buckskin shirt that reached to his crotch. He swallowed. "Patricia Scott. She's . . ." He couldn't finish.

"They took your ma, too?"

He had to brush away a tear, and his voice cracked as he shook his head. "No . . . Ma's . . . they . . . they took . . . Patricia's ma . . . Mine's . . ."

Lightning flashed, followed instantly by a crash of thunder.

Reno was looking at the horses and mule, but after a moment, he seemed to relax and faced Tim again. His one blue eye seemed to soften. "I'm sorry, boy. You buried them. Good graves. But how did you get past Baillarger?"

Tim felt uncomfortable suddenly, but not because

of the memories the man kept bringing back. Or Patricia. Or the attack. Or his parents, Mr. Scott, and the graves. "You knew them," he said, a challenge in his voice. "The man they left to kill me at the camp. The . . ." He looked at the hole in his shirt.

"There ain't a whole lot of folks who live in these mountains. White folks, I mean. Baillarger? Yeah, he showed up at Horse Creek near the Green in '36. The Basque? He come the next year. Neither of them was worth spit. Don't surprise me none that they joined up with the Métis breed."

Tim tried to take it all in, but his brain couldn't comprehend much of anything. "Basque?"

Reno nodded. "Abaroa."

"I don't—" Tim tried to shake the fog away from his brain. "Abaroa? Basque?"

"Name was Abaroa. He was a Basque. You recollect that funny cross he was wearin'?"

Picturing the odd bronze ornament, Tim nodded slightly.

"It's a *lauburu*. Basque version of a cross." Reno's one eye winked. "Now, you're thinking that I am a professor from some university, but I only know that because I saw Abaroa win it from another Basque by betting on a horse at the Rendezvous in '37. Don't ask me what a Basque is, though. Foreigners. That's all I can tell you. But that's what all of us is. Foreigners."

"Rendezvous?" Tim asked.

The man laughed. "Don't pepper me with too many questions. I ain't one for gab, and I ain't talked so much in a spell. Besides, you need some sleep."

Tim, however, did not feel sleepy. Questions began

to flood his brain, too many to ask, or sort out. He found one.

"How did you know?" And another. "How did you find me?"

Reno laughed. "Finding you was easy. What made you set out after Jackatars?"

"Jackatars?"

"The hombre who led that butchery."

"Jackatars," Tim repeated. Now he knew the name. He repeated it twice more so he would never forget it.

"Half-breed Métis. Dangerous and meaner than a gut-shot silvertip griz."

Lightning flashed again, but not so close. The rain seemed to be lessening, and Tim figured the animals out there would feel a little bit better.

He remembered the one-eyed man's question.

"I needed to find Patricia. And my sisters."

"You're sweet on her?"

Tim shrugged. "Well, they are my sisters, too."

"How old?"

He thought to remember. "Margaret. She's my younger sister. She's . . . twelve . . . no . . . thirteen. We had—" He stopped speaking as he remembered.

His ma made what passed for a cake at Scotts Bluff. Everyone from the train, even Just Jenkins, gathered around to sing a sweet English ballad to Margaret and wish her a long life. Someone had said that before they knew it, Margaret would be married and giving her ma and pa plenty of grandbabies. She blushed. So did Ma. Tim thought it sounded disgusting.

* * *

He needed to block out that memory. "Nancy's seventeen."

That seemed to make the mountain man's one eye darken.

"Patricia's my age. Fifteen." He straightened. "I'm sixteen. Almost."

The one-eyed man nodded.

Tim thought, shook his head. "I don't know how old Mrs. Scott is."

The man laughed. "Well, I should hope not. Women don't give them facts away so freely."

Almost as quickly as the rain had started, the storm stopped. It was as if someone had quit working the pump's handle. Tim looked out at the darkness. It had turned into night. Although the rain had stopped, the world out there got darker and darker.

"Time for sleep, boy. Close your eyes. I'll wake you up now and then, just to make sure your head ain't broke too badly."

Tim stared.

"It's just something I learned. You took a couple nasty blows. Folks been known to fall to sleep and never wake up."

Tim felt a sudden wave of fear.

"I don't think you're going to die, boy. You showed me enough grit. You killed Baillarger, which ain't no easy task. Jim Bridger been trying to put him under for four years. You survived Jackatars's raid. You buried your folks and that other gent. And instead of following the ruts and saving your own hide, you had the gumption to go off—afoot, in this country, mind you—against them god-awful vermin who took the womenfolk. I'll wake you up just to make sure."

Tim nodded. His eyes closed, but opened immediately. "I forgot your name, sir."

The one-eyed monster laughed. "It ain't *Sir*, boy. Get that through that addled mind of yours right quick."

Tim tried to smile, but just couldn't manage one.

"Reno. Jed Reno."

Tim nodded and closed his eyes. He wondered if he would ever wake up once he fell asleep. Or if he would just wake up dead. With his eyes closed, he heard himself say, "Mr. Reno . . . I'm sorry."

Silence. Then a fart.

And then, "Apology accepted, boy. But it there ain't no *Mister* to it. Call me Reno. Or Jed. Or Plenty Medicine."

BOOK TWO
GREEN RIVER

CHAPTER 22

Tim could have sworn he heard birds singing and chirping when he woke early the next morning. The air smelled sweet and fresh, though the buckskins he wore reeked. Another aroma aroused his stomach, and he threw off the big robe that had kept him warm, and sat up. Stretching, he realized his body didn't ache so much.

At the corner of the little shelter—too small to be called a cave—the Cyclops in buckskins named Reno sat against the wall pulling what looked like thick thread through a long piece of leather. On a rock near the fire, were two steaming tin cups, smelling just like coffee. Tim saw no pot, just the cups.

"Morning," Jed Reno said without looking up from his work.

Tim had to clear his throat. "Morning," he repeated, climbed over the robe, holding up his pants as he hunched over to keep from hitting the roof of their shelter, and sat across the fire.

Still focusing on his stitching, Reno tilted his head toward the cups.

"Help yourself."

Tim had to let go of the pants, but he was sitting, so there was no problem. When he unloosened the neckerchief around his neck and used it to pick up a tin cup without burning his fingers, Reno smiled.

The coffee warmed him. Strong. Thick as tar. He looked around, but still saw no pot. Nor did he find any sign of breakfast.

"How'd you make it?"

"In the cups. Pour water over some beans and let them soak. No room for a pot." Reno looked up, thinking. "I don't reckon I've seen an actual coffee-pot since eighteen forty. Last Rendezvous." He lowered the big needle and drew a knife, snipping the thick thread.

"I've never seen thread like that," Tim said.

"Sinew."

"Sinew?"

"Deer tendon, in this case. Tough. Shrinks when it dries." Reno held up the piece of leather, which Tim realized had been fashioned into a belt—five inches wide, dark brown, and complete with a cast-iron buckle. He almost spilled his coffee when Reno tossed it to him.

"That'll keep them britches on." Reno reached for his own cup of coffee, only he did not need a bandanna to keep his fingers from blistering. "Drink up. Daylight's a precious commodity out here."

After another sip, Tim looked around. He wondered if he should ask, decided against it, and then his stomach growled. After wetting his lips and fortified by another sip of the bitter, black tar, he asked, his voice meek, "What about breakfast?"

Reno finished his coffee, emptying the dregs and beans on the fire, which sizzled. "You're drinking it." He came to his knees and began scooping wet sand over the fire.

Quickly, Tim finished his coffee and tried to help Reno break down the camp, though he grew to realize he was probably more in the way than anything else. Giving up, he let Reno work while he answered nature's call and then buckled the belt over his waist. He still didn't like wearing the dead man's clothes—even the Basque's moccasins—but he knew better than to complain to that monster who had rescued him.

Reno stuck the two cups into the robe, which he rolled up and secured with rawhide. After he had cleared the overhand, he heaved it over his shoulders and walked to the mule. He secured it onto a pack-saddle, then came back to the shelter and picked up two rifles. "Come on," he ordered.

Tim Colter obeyed.

They walked a good fifty yards before stopping. The morning amazed Tim, how clear the sky had become, how fresh the land smelled. Reno spit, and, without a word, handed one of the big rifles to Tim. He almost dropped it, for it weighed at least ten pounds, maybe more, and stretched more than four feet from butt to barrel's end.

"Careful," Reno grunted. "That's a Hawken." He hefted the other rifle he held. "Same as mine. Sam Hawken made mine. Cost me twenty-five dollars, and I've been offered better than one-fifty for it since.

Mine's a fifty-four caliber. One you hold is a fifty. Look at it. Study it."

The rifle felt uncomfortable, but Tim obeyed. It was, he knew, a thing of beauty. The stock was dark maple, the butt plate was iron, as were the trigger guard, forestock cap, and patch box. Oddly, he saw two triggers, but only one barrel. He did not ask Reno about this, though, because the man already thought him to be a fool, and he did not wish to give the mountain man more evidence of that fact.

"Ever shoot a rifle before, boy?"

"Uh . . . I saw Pa . . . my father . . . shoot one." Tim swallowed. "It was at a turkey shoot."

"Whereabouts?"

"Danville."

Reno stared blankly and wordlessly.

"Pennsylvania."

He spat. "Gun like this?"

Tim looked at the heavy Hawken. "No, sir. Pa said it . . . was . . . um . . . per- . . . percussion?"

Reno spat again and snorted. "Figures. Don't favor percussion rifles much. Flintlock's easier to fire, more reliable than copper caps. Quicker to reload, too, no matter what some hardware clerk'll tell you." He butted his rifle on the wet earth, and nodded at Tim. "Let's see how you shoot."

The Hawken rifle could easily have been the wheel of a steamboat. Tim had no idea how to use it.

"It's loaded," Reno said. "All you have to do is prime it. You're lucky, too. No wind today. Come a gale, it can blow the powder out of your pan, and repriming it wouldn't be no easy chore."

Tim lowered the gun, butting it the way Reno had, and leaned over.

Reno barked something and pushed Tim back with his free hand. "Boy, don't lean over a rifle's bore like that."

"But . . . you said it wasn't primed."

"Don't lean over a gun barrel, boy. All guns are loaded. Don't look down the barrel." He gestured. "Pick it up, prime her."

Tim got the hammer to half cock, shook out powder into the pan—Reno's nod told him he had enough—and closed the frizzen. He looked around.

"Rock over yonder." Reno gestured lazily and stepped away.

Tim remembered what his father had done at the turkey shoot. The rifle came up, he braced the butt against his shoulder, and brought the hammer to full cock. Trying to steady the long gun proved awkward. Trying to look down the sights troubled him even more. The barrel moved in clockwise circles, and he could not steady it. He quickly decided that he should just pull the trigger as soon as the barrel hit the bottom part of his target. Or whenever he thought it was there.

He pulled the trigger, saw the smoke in the pan, then heard and felt the cannon blast.

Jed Reno picked up the Hawken first, examined it, laid it gently on the ground, and extended a hand toward Tim.

Tim's ears rang. His right shoulder felt as if an elephant had kicked it, maybe cleaved it all the way in two. He looked quickly at his shoulder, relieved to find it still attached to the rest of his body, accepted the mountain man's hand, and let him pull him to his feet. "Did I hit the rock?"

Reno stared.

Tim knew the answer and frowned. "Can I try it again?"

There seemed to be some glint in the man's lone blue eye, maybe even a bit of respect for Tim's gumption. The light, however, faded, and Reno picked up the Hawken on the ground. He did not offer it back to Tim, but walked on ahead, carrying both his rifle and the one Tim had just shot.

"Powder and lead are precious commodities out here, boy," Reno said as he moved back toward the camp. "When you fill them britches you're wearing, maybe you'll be able to handle a Rocky Mountain rifle. But we need to get moving."

Back at camp, the mountain man reloaded the rifle Tim had fired. Tim watched him intently, trying to memorize everything Reno did. Finished, he sheathed the rifle in a long buckskin pouch, which he fastened into a packsaddle. Easy to reach, Tim figured, if they came to a fight.

He also pulled out something black and white and hideous, which he tossed in front of Tim's feet. "Put that on your head, boy," he ordered.

Tim recognized it and frowned. It was the skunk cap the Basque had worn. He already wore the dead man's buckskins, even the moccasins. He wasn't about to put that ugly thing on his head. "No."

Reno's eye squinted. "Boy, it's a nice morning, but this ain't nice country. You wear a hat for protection and brag. The protection you'll need from the sun . . .

because you ride out here with no hat, the sun'll bake your brains and you'll keel over. You keel over, and I ain't stopping to pick you up. Them duds you had—like some girl's bonnet—that won't do enough. Pick up the hat."

Reluctantly, Tim obeyed.

"The brag," Reno said as he went about checking the straps on the mule. "That's important, too. Somebody might recognize that ugly thing covering your topknot as once belonging to miserable Abaroa. That'll make them respect you a tad. Make them think that you killed that slimy Basque."

"But I didn't kill him," Tim said. "You did."

"But I got my own hat, boy. And it's a damn sight better looking than what you got." Reno walked about camp, making sure nothing was left behind. He kicked more sand onto the dead fire and secured the Basque's black mustang to a lead rope that also held the mule. Tim noticed that it had no saddle. Reno must have left it behind.

The two other horses were saddled, with hackamores instead of bridles and reins. Reno gestured to the pinto, smaller than Reno's big dun. "You always have two horses?"

Reno swung onto his big horse. "That's the one you left behind. Belonged to the man you killed by the creek. Reckon he won't mind you riding it."

Tim's stomach churned. "But . . . I looked . . . I didn't see . . ."

"What did you think, boy? That the vermin Jackatars left behind to make sure you were dead was afoot?"

Tim picked up the hackamore's end. He wondered if he could reach the stirrup, but after finding a rock, he stood on it. It might be cheating, but he did manage to climb onto the horse's back.

The horse moved around a bit, but Tim pulled hard on the hackamore, and the pinto stopped moving around and started backing up.

"Let up, boy," Reno said. "You want him to stop, pull straight back. You keep pulling, he'll think you want him to back up. Tug the rope. He'll mind you. Unless he bucks you off."

Tim absorbed that. He hoped he could remember. "I looked for the horse," he said again.

"Not hard, I figure," Reno said.

"Well." Tim dropped his head. "Yeah. I thought maybe he was a runner."

"Sort of like Pheidippides?"

"Sir?"

"Don't sir me, either, boy. Pheidippides, boy. Don't you know your Greek? Don't you know about Marathon?"

"No, si—" Tim managed to choke back the *sir*.

"Figures." Reno rode ahead, pulling the lead rope and the mule and other horse behind him.

Tim realized that Reno would leave him there, so he kicked the pinto's sides, and felt the horse move along. After a while, as he grew slightly more comfortable in the saddle, he tired of looking at the black mustang's tail and rode up until he was alongside Jed Reno.

The mountain man seemed to smile.

"How long have you lived here?" Tim asked.

"I was born here, boy," the man said.

Tim thought the man had to be lying, but he wasn't

about to say anything along those lines. He wanted to ask more questions, but the man kept riding slowly, looking at the land, though Tim decided any trail left by the raiders who had taken Patricia and his sisters had to have vanished after the rain.

At last, Reno reined in. Tim stopped a good fifteen feet past him, then decided to test his horsemanship, and pulled hard on the hackamore. He kept pulling. To his amazement, the horse backed up, then stopped when he released the pressure.

Smiling in spite of himself, he turned toward Jed Reno. The look on his face made Tim lose the smile . . . and his pride.

Reno's long arm stretched southward.

"You could do me a favor, boy, by riding that way. Just keep south. Day or two, you'd be at the Bitter. Follow it to the Green, and you'll come directly to Bridger's Trading Post. Might be the train you was with is still there. Likely not. But Jim would hold you till I come back with your sisters and that girl who's sweet on you."

Tim shook his head.

"You could also tell Jim—and any emigrants who happen to be there—that Indians didn't kill your folks. You could help me stop a war."

Tim knew he would not even consider it.

"I'm going with you. I . . . have . . . to."

Reno tugged on the hackamore and kept riding west.

Tim caught up with him after a while.

"I have to," he said again.

"I heard you the first time, boy." Without looking at Tim, Reno continued. "Now you hear me. You want to ride out for revenge or to be some hero to your sweetie, make your sisters think high on you, that's your business. Not mine. Out here, we let a body make up his own mind. I won't argue with you. But know this. Slow me down, I leave you. Get hurt and can't go on, I leave you. Get killed, I leave you. Get lost, I won't come looking for you. You made your decision. I've made mine."

The Cyclops known as Jed Reno did not speak another word that day.

CHAPTER 23

Eventually, they came to a small creek. The water flowed but not as wide nor as fast as in the past. Tim felt proud of himself for coming to that conclusion based on the wide bed of the creek. He wasn't sure he was right, of course, but he wasn't about to ask the silent man who had studied the area for a good five minutes or more before dropping out of the saddle and wrapping the hackamore around a clump of sagebrush.

Once Tim had dismounted, he stood around like an oaf until Reno handed him the lead rope that secured the mustang and mule. Rope in hand, Tim just stood and watched Reno work his way around the camp, stopping here and there to poke at something on the ground. Why, he even picked up a clod of horse droppings . . . then broke it open and rubbed it around in his fingers. He merely wiped the manure off on his buckskin britches, frowned, and moved to another bit of sage.

Silently, Tim thought his ma would have had a

stroke had she seen anyone do that—and not wash his hands afterwards. He didn't mind standing around. After most of the day in the saddle, he felt relieved as he stretched the muscles in his aching legs. The insides of his thighs felt chaffed. His buttocks might never recover.

Reno picked something out of the sage. "Ute." He looked to the south, his frown hardening. "You're bringing all of them in, just like Red Prairie figured." After tucking what appeared to be a beaded headband inside his belt, Reno moved over a few more yards, stopping again, fingering something in the dirt, and heading toward a small rise north of the creek.

Behind Tim, his horse peed.

Tim scowled, and stepped a little bit ahead and away from the pinto to avoid any splatter.

After what seemed like hours, Jed Reno walked back down the rise and toward the creek, tucking the Hawken underneath his shoulder. Once he stopped, he held out a piece of brown cloth in his dirty, thick fingers.

"Ever seen this?"

Tentatively, Tim took the bit of calico and held it up, lowered it to brush off the sand and dirt, and examined it closer. It was more than just a patch of calico. His heart sank as he remembered the brown dress with the design of red floral—his ma had called it a "roller print," whatever that meant. The ripped piece had come from the bottom of the skirt.

He swallowed and tried to stop the tears from welling, but could not. His stomach heaved. He imagined the very worst. "Patricia's. Dress. My—" He stopped speaking and had to close his eyes. His mother had made it for Patricia on her fifteenth birthday. She was wearing it when . . . the . . . bandits . . . hit.

"Is she—?" He couldn't ask. Couldn't open his eyes.

"Smart?" Reno asked. "I'd say so. Leaving us a bread crumb, be my thinking."

Tim's eyes popped open. Patricia was alive. The ruffians had not hurt her.

"Trail to follow," Reno said. "Smart gal you're sweet on, boy. We might need some more crumbs to follow." He took the lead rope and led the horse and mule away. "Rain washed away most sign, but they camped here." He began removing the packs, talking to himself as he worked. "Rain might have done us a favor. Keep the emigrants from following the trail. Be my guess." He frowned. "They might follow ours, though. Well. So be it. They want to have their top-knots lifted, it ain't my worry."

Once the horse and mule had drunk their fill from the flowing creek, Reno hobbled them. After unsaddling his big dun and Tim's pinto, he led them to the river, hobbled them, then fetched a sack of grain and gave them each a handful to eat along with what grass they could scrounge up.

"We'll camp here," he said, breaking out the cups from the heavy robe.

Tim looked at the sky. The sun wasn't even sinking beyond the far mountains. He did not understand why they would not keep riding, especially since Patricia, her mother, and his sisters had been there. He did remember some of the things Just Jenkins was always talking to Captain McConnell about and ventured to say, "There's plenty of daylight." As soon as the words were out of his mouth, he sucked in a deep breath and held it, unsure of how the mountain man would respond.

Jed Reno looked up from a pack, his lone eye boring a hole through Tim's innards. "What do you see here?"

Tim looked around. Sagebrush. Ugly desert-like country to the south. The beginnings of towering mountains off to the north and west. He saw their horses, the packs, the Hawken rifle, and the patch of brown calico he still held in his fingers. He saw . . . "The creek," he said tentatively.

Reno's head bobbed.

"The Big Sandy. Water. We camp here. Get an early start tomorrow and take our time. Find their trail or maybe some more calico bread crumbs from that gal you fancy."

The two jackrabbits Reno had somehow managed to snare that afternoon after setting up camp seemed as big as pronghorns. The meat was greasy, stringy, but Tim did not think he had ever tasted anything so delicious. It was just meat, speared with a stick and roasted over an open flame that gave off little smoke. No salt. No pepper. No bread or dessert. Washed down by two cups of thick, terrible coffee.

By the time Tim was wiping his greasy fingers on the buckskins, and Jed Reno was sucking on the bones of his rabbit, the sun had begun sinking.

With a belch, Reno finished his coffee and leaned back, using his saddle as a pillow.

Tim decided to do the same as he watched the sky

fade into darkness. "You weren't really born here?" he asked cautiously. "Were you?"

"You calling me a liar, boy?"

Tim smiled. He could detect a little humor in Reno's voice. Maybe the rabbit and the coffee—if you could call it coffee—had softened the mood. Made him human. Almost.

"No." Tim almost said *sir*. "But you weren't really born here. Were you?"

A moment passed, followed by a long sigh. "In the physical sense, I'd have to say no. But you could say I was reborn here."

"Where was home?"

"Kentucky."

That interested Tim. "Did you know Daniel Boone?"

"Who?"

Tim lifted his head. Enough light remained so that he could see Reno grinning. He even heard a little chuckle. "You know who." He lowered his head on the saddle. To his surprise, it felt almost comfortable.

"Nah. Never run across Daniel Boone. He likely regrets never running across me."

"Did you know that Boone was born in Pennsylvania? Not near me. Not in Danville. Some place called Berks County. It's near Philadelphia, I think. That's far east of Danville."

"Uh-huh."

"Well, that's what Just Jenkins told me." He heard Reno sit up.

"Who?"

"Mr. Jenkins. Ummm. Just Jenkins." Tim lifted his

head off the saddle and propped himself up with his elbows.

"You knew Terrance Jenkins?" Reno asked.

"I don't know anyone named Terrance, but Just Jenkins guided our train."

The one-eyed man nodded. "Yeah. But Terrance don't talk to just anybody."

Confused, Tim asked, "Terrance?"

Reno chuckled. "Don't ever let him know I told you that."

Tim sat up completely. "You know Mr. Jenkins."

Turning his head, Reno spit across his saddle, wiped his mouth, and chuckled. "I don't know no *Mister* Jenkins, but I've trapped and hunted and had a few close calls with Just Jenkins, and I'm the only one in the Rockies who knows the true handle his mammie and pappie give him."

"That's—" Tim leaned back against the saddle, swallowing down the ugly feelings that always came back just when he thought he was free of the shame of running and the hurt of finding his ma and pa dead. Butchered. He wiped his eyes, hoping that Reno did not see him.

After a moment, Tim said, "They shouldn't have left us alone."

Reno cleared his throat. "Jenkins said it was the captain's orders."

"They voted on it," Tim remembered, "but Captain McConnell did his stumping. They shouldn't have left us alone."

"No. But they did. That was a risk your ma and pa and all those others knew they were taking, long before you left Berks County."

"Danville," Tim corrected. "I wish we'd never left. Danville was home. I was born there."

"Terrance Jenkins." Reno laughed, farted, and spit again.

Tim thought the mountain man had to be the most uncouth man he had ever known. He remembered the rogue at South Pass, the one whose horse he rode. He remembered the Basque, the one whose clothes he'd donned. *No, they were worse. Maybe.*

"We had some fine times together. On the Green. In the Wind. Down to the Wasatch and Uinta. He don't just talk to nobody, boy. If he talked to you, he must've seen something in you."

Tim knew what Reno was doing. Trying to change the subject, get Tim's thoughts away from all the horrors he had seen, all the tragedy. He could almost appreciate it.

Of course, Reno couldn't let it go just like that. He had to add, "Whatever it was, I ain't seen it yet from you, boy. Get some sleep. I'm done talking."

But he wasn't. About ten minutes later, Tim, still wide awake and not certain he could ever fall asleep no matter how beat he was or how much his bones and muscles ached, heard Reno speak in the coming darkness.

"You was born in Danville, boy, but you ain't really been born yet. That'll come later. If you live."

CHAPTER 24

"Saddle your horse, boy."

Tim Colter tried to give one-eyed Jed Reno the blank look of stupidity that would let him understand—as if he did not know already—just how incompetent he was. The problem was that Reno, as soon as he had washed out his coffee cup that morning in Big Sandy Creek, had already moved toward his horse.

Swallowing, Tim just stood beside the campfire Reno had kicked out. His mouth moved. He even tried to clear his throat, but no noise escaped him.

Reno took a brush from his pack and rubbed the sides of the big dun. He tossed a blanket on the big horse's back and over that went on the saddle. Realizing that Tim wasn't doing the same with his own horse, he turned on his moccasins and glared with that one cold eye of his.

Tim shuffled his feet, stared at the dead man's moccasins that he wore, and sighed. "I don't know how."

What followed was an explosion of blasphemy and profanity, the likes of which he had never heard. Had he spoke such language, his ma would not have made him wash out his mouth with lye soap. She would have kicked him out of the house and disowned him.

After the thunder faded, Reno let out a sigh of exasperation. "Well, boy, time you learned. Come over here."

Tim went over to Reno's side quickly, remembering that this mountain man did not wait around for fool city boys, and he did not want to be left alone in that country. Not that he was scared. He was just . . . well . . . slightly . . . petrified. But only slightly.

"I'll show you once. Learn it good." Reno flipped the stirrup over the saddle, knelt, and reached underneath the dun's belly to grab a strap, but then stopped what he was doing, and stood up.

"You saw what I done first, didn't you, boy?"

"Yes, si—" Again, he remembered in the nick of time to drop the *sir*.

"Horses be like people. Hot day like it is today, they sweat. So we brush them off before we put the blanket on. Like some folks, dirt bothers them. So does loose hair. You don't brush, it can wear on their back. Worse, they might start shaking off that dirt and loose hair. Do that, they's apt to shake you out of the saddle. You savvy that, boy?"

"Yes."

With a curt nod, Reno bent down to grab the wide strap, then brought the smaller strap from his side of the saddle and threaded it through the cast-iron ring at the end of the wide strap. Deftly, he looped the

strap through a hole in a strap and a circular ring affixed to the saddle. "Then you cinch her up tight."

Tim watched as the man's big hands worked, pulling the strap. The horse grunted.

"It don't hurt them none. Horses are tough animals. He's just holding his breath."

Reno looped the small strap through ring and hole
several times, then, after lowering the stirrup off the
saddle, he grabbed the hackamore and led the dun
away from the creek. He took time then to light his
pipe, and after only a few puffs—more than likely,
the ruffian was hoarding tobacco the way he hoarded
powder, shot, grub, and coffee—he slipped the pipe
back into the pouch that hung around his neck, and
tightened the cinch more.

"There. That's all there be to this, city boy. Now . . .
you do it. And remember what I said. Don't worry
about hurting that horse. If you don't get that cinch
on tight enough, that saddle slips, and it'll be you
who's getting hurt."

Swallowing down the fear rising from his gut
along with the coffee, Tim returned to the pinto and
began working, trying to remember everything he
had seen Reno do, and everything Reno had told
him. After a few minutes, he sucked in a deep breath,
held it for a while, and exhaled. He picked up the
hackamore and walked the horse toward Reno.

Blue eye scowling, Reno flipped up the stirrup and
ran his finger under the cinch. Then he dropped the
stirrup and tugged on the saddle's horn.

"You learn quick, boy. For a first time saddling a
horse, that ain't bad."

Tim straightened at the compliment, but his pride vanished when Reno turned.

"Now . . . best remember never forget what you just done. Ever. Because I'm done schooling city boys on how things work out in these parts." He went to get the lead rope and pulled the mule and spare horse behind. "Let's ride, boy. Daylight's a precious commodity."

They rode along the Big Sandy for a few miles, turning with the creek when it cut northwest, but when the stream changed directions again, cutting back to the east, they left the water and rode toward the high mountains, purple in the distance.

Every now and then, Reno would dismount and hand the lead rope to Tim, who took that as a compliment—that a mountain man would trust him to hold the rope that held the mule that held their supplies.

Once, Reno looked at something on the ground—though whatever it was, Tim could not tell—and then pushed up his hat and looked off into the distance, whispering just loud enough for Tim to hear. "Where is he going?"

Cursing slightly, Reno rose, remounted the dun, and held out his left hand to take the rope.

They rode silently as the day turned hot. Reno did not speak again until they made camp that night, and even then, he barked only orders, which Tim knew to obey.

* * *

The next morning, after a breakfast of coffee, Reno brought out a pistol and held it out, butt forward, to Tim. "You ain't filled those britches yet, so I don't think you'll be much of a hand with a Hawken. Let's see what you can do with one of these."

Tim looked at the pistol. It was the small one the Basque had tried to hide from Reno before the mountain man had shot him down. Something was different. Reluctantly, Tim took the .45 and studied it.

"The barrel," he said at last. "It's longer."

It had been maybe two inches long when he'd first seen it. Barrels did not grow, but this one had. It was six inches long.

"Remember what I called it?" Reno asked.

Tim thought back. His lips moved, but he did not speak at first. Not until he could recall and was certain he was right. Well, maybe he wasn't all that sure of his memory, but he said questioningly, "A . . . screw . . . barrel?"

Reno grinned. "That's right. You screw in the barrels. Abaroa had an extra. One thing about pistols, boy. Longer the barrel is, typically, the better the accuracy. Especially for range. Try her."

Tim looked at the pistol, which suddenly seemed heavy in his hand. His face came back up toward the mountain man's. "It isn't primed."

Reno's one eye gleamed. "That's right. Maybe you recollect what I told you earlier. About powder and shot being hard to come by."

Tim's head nodded, though he did not understand how shooting an unloaded weapon could teach him anything.

"Shooting a pistol is different from shooting a

long gun, boy," Reno said. "More instinct, I figure.
Less skill, though. I don't have much use for short
guns. Come to a fight that close, I figure I'd rather
use knife or hatchet. But they can be handy. Like
when I killed that ignorant Basque. You know how to
point a finger?"

Tim laughed. He thought Reno had to be joking,
but he quickly stopped his giggle and let his head
nod again.

"Then point at that rock yonder, only use that"—
he gestured at the .45 in Tim's right hand—"instead
of your finger."

Tim did as he was told. He thumbed back the
hammer, found his target, pretending that he was
pointing his finger instead of the small heavy pistol.
The trigger pulled. The hammer clicked.

"Squeeze," Reno said patiently. "Don't jerk. Squeeze.
And don't breathe when you're shooting. If you have
to, let out your breath, then squeeze the trigger. Just
remember, boy, when you got to use one of those pistols, you might not ever draw another breath. Keep
that in mind. You got one shot. Best make her count."

Again.

Again.

Again.

Ten more times, he dry-fired the pistol. After that,
Reno took the pistol, stuck it in the packs, and they
rode on north.

The next day, Reno made Tim dry-fire another pistol, a larger one, more of the kind that Tim had seen
around Danville. Reno said it came from Harper's

Ferry, was .54 caliber, and that he had taken it off a dead Dragoon. Tim knew better than to ask how the Dragoon became dead. He hoped and prayed that the soldier had been killed by Indians, or maybe from an accident, and not by Jed Reno. Although he would not put such an action past the one-eyed devil.

"Only reason I kept it is on account that my Hawken's a .54-caliber. You don't want different size balls for your firearms. Keeps things practical if they're the same caliber. Shoot it."

It wasn't loaded. Tim dry-fired again.

On the next morning, Reno primed the pan and handed Tim the screw-barrel .45, which felt heavier in his hand.

"All right, boy, point and shoot. Just remember she's loaded and primed. Hold her steady. Squeeze, don't jerk. Let's she how you shoot for real."

The morning's coffee splashed around in his belly, but Tim managed to stop his hand from shaking.

They had reached timber country, so he aimed at a pinecone at the side of a tall tree. He wet his lips, inhaled, let it out gently, and squeezed the trigger. The pan flashed. The pistol roared. He felt as if his arm had been torn off, but when his eyes opened, and the wind carried the white smoke away, he realized that he still held the screw-barrel. The pinecone looked undisturbed, but a ditch had been dug along to its left.

"That ain't bad, boy." Reno took the smoking pistol from Tim's aching hand. "Not bad, at all." He slipped the pistol inside his belt, then pulled the other—the big Harper's Ferry—and gave it to Tim. "She's loaded, too, and she'll kick an apt harder. You might do well to hold her with both hands."

Tim obeyed. He spread his legs out and found that using both hands helped him steady the barrel. Remembering everything Reno had told him, he squeezed the trigger.

To his amazement, he found himself still standing, and not lying on his buttocks a few yards to the east. He also had a pretty good view of the pinecone, or would have, had he been able to find the pinecone. It had vanished. Above the ringing in his ears, he heard a sharp whistle before feeling an anvil crush his shoulder.

"By Jupiter, boy!" Reno's face flamed. Tim feared that he had done something wrong, but the mountain man clasped his shoulder hard again. "That's some shooting, boy. Some shooting indeed!"

Tim grinned. He stood a little taller. Then Reno jerked the screw-barrel .45 from his waist and handed it to Tim. He held both guns.

"Reload them, boy," Reno said. "They be yours now. Keep them clean. Shoot to kill."

CHAPTER 25

On a few rare occasions, Tim Colter almost believed that the one-eyed mountain man might have been at least partly human. Like that morning. He reined in his horse and beckoned Tim to ride alongside him.

Tim had to urge his mount with several kicks before it obeyed, but the teenage boy thought he was getting the hang of things. Maybe. Pulling on the reins, then letting go, he breathed a sigh of relief when his mount stopped.

Jed Reno tilted his head and pointed the barrel of his Hawken off toward the distance. "You see them, boy?"

Standing in his stirrups, Tim stared ahead. Yes, yes, he did see something. Moving off in the distance. First he spotted the dust, and a few moments later, his eyes focused better. It was a herd of animals.

He lowered himself into the saddle.

Reno's one good eye stayed trained on the scene

off to the north and west, and, if Tim's eyes weren't
playing some kind of cruel joke, the old trapper appeared to be smiling. Shaking his head in wonderment, Reno looked at Tim. "Pretty sight, ain't it, boy?"

Tim's head bobbed slightly. He swallowed. But he
had to ask. "Are they elk?"

The smile vanished. The mountain man spit,
grunted, farted, and cursed. "Elk!" He shook his head
and muttered a few pages of profanity. "Is you that
dense, boy? Or blind? Elk? Elk! No, they sure ain't
elk. If they was elk, I'd be leaving you here with these
animals, making my way downwind of them, coming
in close, and real quiet-like, and then shooting one
of them for supper. Elk. By Jupiter! I knowed I
should have left you back down the trail when I first
come across you. Elk." He shook his head and spit.
"And they ain't antelope, deer, rabbits, coyotes. Ain't
hawks, eagles, or even sage grouse, neither. Them's
wild mustangs, kid."

Tim looked again.

"Mustangs," he whispered.

"That's wild horses, boy," Reno said.

"I know that!" Tim swallowed. He had not meant
to snap at the Cyclops.

The trapper just chuckled.

"Well, that's a good thing to learn about you, boy.
You take a little pushing, but not too much. Good."
His head nodded again at the herd. "See a lot of
them down in the Red Desert. Beautiful animals,
ain't they?"

Tim could see better. If he counted right, there
must have been at least forty, in a wild array of colors.

They were too far away to see any details, but even at that distance, he had to agree that Jed Reno was absolutely right. It was a beautiful sight.

"Got introduced by Spanish explorers, way back in the 1500s," Reno said. "You might not believe this, but before that time, there wasn't no horses in this country. The Cheyennes, the Shoshone, the Sioux, well, they didn't even have horses, hadn't even ever seen one of them. I guess a few got away from those Spanish boys. Must've bred like rabbits. Well, a mustang, he ain't got no natural enemy, excepting a catamount. You know, a mountain lion. Cougar. Panther. Whatever you want to call one of them mean cat beasts. So Indians learned how to handle those Spanish ponies . . . better than most white folks. Pretty to see."

Again, he shook his head. "When I see something like that, boy, it makes me think that maybe the olden days ain't a thing of the past. That maybe this land here will always be like this. That there will be a place in the country for wild mustangs and wilder men like me. Yeah, I know it's just a dream, a silly notion, but, well, it sure makes me feel good about the way things are, the way things used to be, the way things—and this land here—should always be. Yep."

He kicked his horse into a trot, and Tim followed, watching the mustangs ride off, thundering away. Reno galloped with them, too, and Tim struggled to keep up, noticing how small, but tough, those mustangs were. Pintos and sorrels. Roans and bays. Browns, blacks, and duns led by a proud, spirited, high-stepping stallion the color of midnight. Running like that, those wiry little animals did look free,

and Tim thought he could even hear Jed Reno
laughing as he galloped with the herd.

That night, faces of the dead haunted him, tor-
mented him, terrified him.

First appeared his mother. "Run!" she shouted. "Ru—!"

*Tim stood frozen, watching, hearing the sickening sound
as the tomahawk split her head open. It happened again and
again. He watched the man who had killed her. A big man,
almost a giant, in buckskins and a fur hat, full beard, forehead and nose painted green and gold, earrings hanging
from his ears.*

*The man left his mother dead and walked toward Tim
while other attackers killed Mr. Scott, the old dog, and Tim's
father. He saw his sisters running, pursued by the Indians
and renegade white men.*

He saw the big man well.

*The hat—which looked like a coyote—came off the man's
head as he walked toward Tim, hatchet in his right hand,
dripping with his mother's blood, her brains, and bits of her
hair.*

*His hair was long, frizzy, black, with small braids hang-
ing in front, buzzard feathers attached to the braids with
rawhide. The only gray appeared in small streaks on the
beard that fell to his heart. The forehead seemed crevassed
with ditches and scars—wrinkles deep and dirty—and the
nose appeared crooked and bent, and, likewise, heavily
wrinkled.*

Never had Tim seen a man so ugly.

The clothes, however, were beautifully stitched and beaded, the leather lighter than the buckskins worn by the other raiders, and sporting little fringe. The cream-colored shirt was untucked, falling over the rust-colored britches that became plaid wool just past the knees. Moccasins came up to the man's calf, and these were not beaded, just plain, dirty, and serviceable.

Tim could make out a bear-claw necklace behind the full beard.

As the man walked toward the paralyzed Tim, a name came to him. It wasn't spoken, unless by God. Dog . . . Ear . . . The rest of the name, he could not understand. Rose. Something foreign. French.

Tim's mouth fell open. He tried to scream, but no words, no sounds, could come out. He watched the man named Dog Ear Something-or-other raise the tomahawk, but before the hatchet split Tim's head, the man changed.

Tim saw him staring at the raider by the creek . . . the man who had basically died by an accident, falling on his knife and killing himself. Tim saw him clearly. Suddenly, the man's features changed. His face melted. Blood ran in rivulets until there was nothing left but a skeleton, then dust.

Tim awoke screaming, scared out of his senses.

He sat straight up, then felt a crushing hand knock him to the ground.

"Hush up, boy!" Jed Reno yelled.

Tim screamed again.

The blow came harder, and Tim groaned.

"Quiet. Quiet, I say."

Tim sniffed. He realized he had been having a nightmare. Suddenly, he started sobbing.

"By Jupiter, boy, don't you start bawling on me. Quiet. Buck up."

He saw the one-eyed trapper's features more than anything else, because clouds enveloped most of the stars.

Reno knelt and his big hand grabbed Tim's shoulders. "You all right now, boy?"

Tim sniffed, but he did manage to nod.

"Some h'aint come after you in your sleep?"

"Huh?"

"Nightmare."

Again, Tim's head nodded.

"Well, next time you have a scare like that in your sleep, don't wake up crying out like some banshee, boy. Let every dad-blasted injun in the Rockies know where we are. Or Louis Jackatars himself. You understand?"

"Yes . . . sir."

"Get back to sleep."

When Reno turned, Tim called out, not loud, though. He knew better than to shout in the dead of the night. "I saw my mother." His head still hurt where the one-eyed monster of a mountain man had knocked him practically senseless . . . twice.

Reno grunted, but stopped, turned, and looked at the boy.

"Saw the man who killed her."

The mountain man's knees popped as he knelt, but Tim could tell that Reno would rather be sleeping.

"Just a dream, boy. Get back to sleep. We got lots of riding to do."

"His name was Dog Ear."

"Dog Ear?" Suddenly, Jed Reno sounded interested.

"Well, in my bad dream. I don't know . . . I don't know his name. It's—"

"Dog Ear Rounsavall," Jed Reno said.

Tim blinked. He tested the name, but butchered it.

"Dog Ear Rounsavall," Reno said again.

"Yeah, Rounsavall. That's it. In the nightmare, anyway." Tim tilted his head, thinking. "But how could you know?"

"Dog Ear Rounsavall is a French cur. Big man. Part griz, part painther, not a drop of human blood runs through his veins. He's an animal. A butcher. And he rides with Louis Jackatars. He killed your ma?"

Tim nodded. "I guess. I mean . . . it was . . . just a . . . dream." Somehow, he had managed to finish that sentence without crying. "A bad dream."

"More than a dream, boy. Sounds that way to me. Big cuss. Black beard. Some braids. Ugliest fiend you'll ever see."

Tim swallowed. "In the dream, he became someone else."

"Devil most likely."

"No." Tim shuddered. "He became the man I killed . . . well, I didn't kill him. I mean, he fell . . . he killed—"

"You killed him, boy. Don't you ever forget that."

"He turned into a skeleton. Into dust. His face just—"

"Boy, you regret killing that man?"

"I didn't kill—"

"Yes, you did. Listen to me, boy. You killed a man. A man that was responsible for the deaths of your ma and pa. You remember this, too. That man—if you could call him a man—would have killed you. Wouldn't have thought more of it than had he swatted a horsefly. You killed him. That was your first killing. That's why you're having those nightmares and such, but you stop having those bad dreams. Right now. You stop feeling sorry for putting under some scum. Trust me, boy, that might be the first man you killed, but it surely won't be the last."

"I don't want to kill anyone ever again," Tim said.

"You damn well better, boy. This is wild country. Out here, you kill to survive, be it for meat to live on or to plant some scalawag who wants you for your horse, your possibles, your scalp, or the gold fillings in your teeth. If you don't kill someone trying to put you under, it'll be you who gets butchered. And if Dog Ear Rounsavall comes after you, don't give him no chance. No chance at all."

CHAPTER 26

Louis Jackatars did not like it at all. First Baillarger. Then the Basque. Both missing. And Red Coat, that wild Blackfeet Indian, had sent three braves to meet him. At least Red Coat had not come himself. On top of all that, it was snowing.

Rare for that time of year, but certainly not unheard of, not up in the Rocky Mountains. He and the braves had reached the high country and were climbing. He smelled pine and the aroma of the bighorn sheep a Frenchman had killed and quartered the day before. Jackatars wanted coffee and sheep meat, but first he had to figure out a way to get rid of the Indians. He had never cared for those red-skinned devils, not even his own mother's people. Then again, he had never cared much for anybody, except himself.

The Indians gathered around him. They were the Southern Piegans, brothers to the Siksika, Kainai, and Northern Piegans who lived in Canada, but all claimed membership in the Blackfoot Confederacy of "original people."

They did not speak English, nor Métis, so Jackatars used sign language to talk to them. The leader called himself Pinto Killer, which Jackatars understood did not mean he went about killing the pinto horses favored by many tribes. He killed Cheyenne Indians, enemies of the Blackfeet, and known to them as *kiihtsipimiitapi*, or "Pinto People."

He was a brave warrior, for his tanned deerskin shirt was decorated with porcupine quills, scalp-hair fringes, and beaded symbols of the sun, weasel, and bear. His long leggings were also heavily beaded and adorned with scalps. A Blackfoot, Jackatars knew, would not wear that outfit into battle. He probably had his war clothes on his horse. Pinto Killer wore that outfit to let Jackatars and the white men know he was a man of power.

All three braves wore their hair in the traditional fashion of Blackfeet men—three braids with high pompadours, two of which were decorated with a lone eagle feather.

The oldest brave, bundled in a heavy robe, had a face ravaged by smallpox, a blind right eye, and was missing the pinky and ring finger of his left hand. He carried only a hatchet, and from the look on his hard face, Jackatars figured that was the only weapon he needed. Pinto Killer had an old Lancaster rifle, a knife, and a lance. The youngest of the three carried only knife, bow, and arrow.

The one-eyed Blackfoot called himself Ugly Face, and he certainly was that. The younger one was called

Stupid Boy, but Jackatars figured it was the kid's first venture out of his village on a hunting or war party. The Blackfeet would give those first-timers an insulting name. If he performed bravely, counted coup or showed courage, he would earn a better name.

Jackatars signed, "Why did Red Coat send you?"

Pinto Killer answered, "To guide you to the place where we are to meet."

"I know this place already," Jackatars signed.

Pinto Killer grinned. "Red Coat knows that, too."

"You do not trust me?" Jackatars signed.

Pinto Killer shrugged. "I do not know you," his hands signed. "Red Coat does."

Ugly Face grunted. He pointed over the fire and spoke in the Piegan tongue.

Pinto Killer signed for his companion. "Ugly Face asks if those are the women."

Without looking away from the three guests, Jackatars merely nodded.

Ugly Face spoke again.

Pinto Killer grinned. "He would like one."

"When I have the gold," Jackatars signed. And added, "From Red Coat."

Pinto Killer told Ugly Face what Jackatars had said.

Ugly Face's expression told Jackatars that the Blackfoot did not care for that answer, but Jackatars did not care what a Piegan thought.

They had never been especially friendly to whites, and perhaps Red Coat tolerated Jackatars only because of his Métis blood. Or more likely, because Jackatars wasn't well-liked by the whites, either.

Things had been testy ever since.

The Hudson's Bay Company eased some Blackfeet hostility, mostly up in Canada, by trading for beaver skins, pemmican, and buffalo robes for goods—beads and blankets, coffee and sugar, and later muskets and powder and shot.

When Ashley's One Hundred came into the Upper Missouri and started trapping—without permission from the Blackfeet—war started again. Peace had come around 1830, and afterwards, the Indians let the trappers set up trading posts at Fort Piegan and Fort MacKenzie. The white men also gave the Blackfeet other gifts, ones the Indians did not want or appreciate—notably smallpox and cholera. Less than ten years ago, the Blackfeet had lost an estimated six thousand when a steamboat bound for Fort Union brought in smallpox and practically wiped out the Blackfeet. Once they had been a force to be reckoned with in this country. Now it was the Sioux and Cheyenne who ruled.

Red Coat, however, had been one Blackfoot Indian who'd refused to cotton to the whites. He hated all whites for what they did to his people, so he had agreed with Jackatars.

"If you want to hurt the white men and destroy them," Jackatars had told him, "take their women."

Red Coat had frowned. "I share my robes with only Blackfeet women."

"You do not have to like them," Jackatars had said. "I bring them. You give me gold. You do with them what you want."

Reluctantly, the old warrior, who still donned the faded red coat from an English captain that his father had killed, had agreed.

Of course, four women proved far less than what Jackatars had planned. He had hoped to capture at least a dozen, which he could divide up, so to speak. It had always been his idea to deliver at least four to Red Coat, and let the Blackfeet do as Red Coat wanted with them. Probably hand them to his young bucks, and when they were through, kill them.

The other tribes might not be so cooperative, so Jackatars had planned on pumping a few of the women full of Cheyenne arrows—after his men had had their fun. Two more would receive similar treatment, but with Sioux arrows. Others with arrows of Utes, Paiutes, and Arapaho. That should do the job, start the war.

It hadn't worked out that way, but Jackatars figured he had some extra time. Red Coat was first. He would be easily provoked to start a war. Maybe it would be enough. Maybe once the ragtag element of Blackfeet went to fight, other tribes would join in, and the country would become a bloodbath.

Yet Jackatars figured he needed at least two Indian tribes in it to turn the entire region into a battlefield, so he had also made a deal with a Sioux brave named Medicine Owl.

The Sioux had been friendly with the whites, so far, but that could easily change. He was to meet Medicine Owl along the Yellowstone after his dealings with the Blackfeet. He would give Medicine Owl one girl and a few clothes he kept well-wrapped in a buffalo robe on a pack mule. The clothes were infected with smallpox and cholera, which he figured would make the Indians blame the girl. They would kill her long before she could tell who had actually kidnapped her, and if any of the Sioux remained alive, they would be ready to fight all whites.

By then, Jackatars would be bound for Mexico, safe from the carnage.

What would he have gained from starting a war that would be long, furious, and bloody? No riches, for certain, just a little gold . . . maybe.

But he would have satisfaction. He could play God. And maybe wipe out those races he most despised. Indians. And whites. If he had his way, he would wipe out everyone on the face of the earth, leaving him alone with deer and buffalo.

The three Blackfeet Indians, however, might spoil his plan. Red Coat would want all the women, and if Medicine Owl did not get his, the Sioux would be after the scalp of Louis Jackatars. He had to get rid of these.

He signed to Pinto Killer, "If Red Coat wants these women, I need help."

Pinto Killer nodded, his face showing concern.

Jackatars continued. "White men follow us. They want the women. They come to take them from me."

The Indian looked around the camp.

"You have men," he signed. "You have many weapons. You should fight them."

"Where," Jackatars signed, "do you see men?"

Pinto Killer smiled and nodded.

"We get a woman each," he signed. "For doing your fighting."

"I have only these four," Jackatars signed. "Red Coat would not be pleased."

"You promised more women. We are not to blame."

Jackatars nodded. "You will go?"

Pinto Killer surprised him by shaking his head. "Not all of us. We leave one behind."

"You do not trust me?"

"No."

It was Jackatars's turn to grin. "I do not trust you."

"We understand one another."

Jackatars nodded. "I will send one man with you. You will leave one man behind. Which one?"

He hoped it would be the boy. He would be easy to kill. But Ugly Face spoke and stood.

Jackatars had no choice but to agree. He motioned Malachi Murchison to join them.

The fool went over, squatting by Jackatars's side, and listened, his face paling, as Jackatars told him what had been agreed upon. "Abaroa and Baillarger should have been back by now. That means someone's trailing us. These two Piegans are going with you. That one's called Pinto Killer. The kid is Stupid Boy. Find Reno. And this time, kill him."

"What"—Murchison swallowed hard—"what makes you think it's Reno? I told you that I—"

"Who else would it be? Easterners bound for Oregon? They'd have quit long ago. It's Reno. Don't play me for a fool. I want him dead. Bring me his head and not some damn lie."

Murchison actually shivered, and not because of the cold. "Where do we meet you when it's done?"

"You know where I'm going."

Murchison gave a feeble nod, and somehow managed to stand. "You keep sendin' me to cover your back trail, Louis, and you might not have no men left to fight for you when the time comes."

Jackatars smiled evilly as he looked up.
"Why do you think I'm sending you?"

When the two Piegans and Murchison had ridden
out, Jackatars filled two cups with tea and left Ugly
Face by the fire with a plate of sheep meat, which the
dirty Indian ate with his fingers, wiping the grease off
on his leggings.

Jackatars walked to the snow-covered trees where
the four white captives sat shaking from the cold and
damp. He had not given them blankets, but he did
hand one tin cup to the prettiest of the younger girls.

She took it, but instead of drinking, passed it to
the smallest. "Drink it, Margaret."

Jackatars grinned.

The girl—Jackatars remembered her name as Patricia—stared.

The mother, sitting to the half-breed's left, spoke.
"Who are those Indians?"

"Piegans," Jackatars answered, but kept his eyes on
the teen, looking her over from her shoes to her tangled hair.

"Where did they go?"

"Away." He kept staring at the girl.

"What—"

"Shut up," he snapped. "I ask questions. When I
don't, you stay silent. Or I give you to the buck the
Piegans left behind. And when he's through with
you, you won't look better than he does now." He
rose. "Drink your tea. We ride in an hour."

Jackatars walked away, sipping his own cup, and thinking that maybe, just maybe, he would not want to live on this earth all by himself with only animals. The girl, this Patricia Scott, once he had taught her how to act and how to do certain things, she might be a good Eve to his Adam.

Chapter 27

"Long about now," Jed Reno said, "I bet you're glad you got that skunk on your head, boy."

Tim Colter refused to answer. Nodding or shaking his head—even if he grudgingly had to admit that the mountain man was right—took too much effort. The skunk skin did keep his head warm. So did the other wolf skins that the one-eyed trapper had given him.

He did manage to grumble, even though moving his frozen lips hurt. "I-It's Au-Au-Au-gust." At least, he thought it was August. After everything that had happened, and all he had been through, he couldn't be certain.

"It's also nigh eight thousand feet," Reno said.

After another few hundred yards, Reno spoke again. "Don't fret, boy. This ain't blizzard season. Lucky we ain't run into hail. Storm'll pass. The moisture's good for the land."

Reno, as normal, proved correct. The snow stopped before noon, the sun reappeared, and for the rest of their ride through thick evergreen forests, Tim Colter felt himself splattered as snow fell from the limbs of the trees overhead. By afternoon, however, he was relatively dry, and had tied the wolf skins on behind the saddle. He had done that task—to his amazement—while riding behind Reno, the spare horse, and the pack mule. Done it himself, twisting in the saddle, and not getting bucked off or knocked off by a low limb.

They rode down where it was warmer, and where no snow was left. The country remained rugged, yet amazing. Tim held his breath as a herd of antelope—there must have been upwards of one hundred—bounded through the hills. They moved on, and began climbing again. Hills and forests and off to the north, what had to be the highest mountains Tim had ever seen. Danville had not been located in a desert, yet he had never seen country so green. Just a few days back, Tim remembered he had been traveling through rough, ugly, raw desert. Now he was in a paradise, albeit a paradise filled with danger. The snow had been an example of that.

Toward sundown, Reno stopped at a relatively flat place that looked as if it had been an Indian encampment many years ago. Teepee poles still rose in a few places—though the hides used to cover them were long gone—and there were fire rings, not used in ages, and remnants of whiskey kegs.

He pointed at a river. "That's the Siskeedee-Agie. The Green. Over yonder's where the padre, DeSmet, held mass. That was in 1840. Lifetime ago. Lot of water's flowed through here since then."

"That was only five years ago," Tim said.

Reno's head shook. "Feels like fifty. Lot can pass in five years, boy. By Jupiter, in five years, you might even fill them britches you're wearing. Ain't likely, though." He swung from the saddle and picked up a piece from a busted rotted keg.

"What did that padre think of that?" Tim smiled.

So did Reno. "The padre didn't come here to save our souls. He was out to convert the Indians. A good man, wise, but I swear, boy, DeSmet loved this land like I do. Held mass here, then let some Indians lead him way up there. See them rugged peaks yonder way. That's the Gros Ventre Range. Preached to more than a thousand Flatheads, Nez Perce, and Pend Oreilles. Then went back East. Tell you what, boy, I saw a lot of me in that padre, and I reckon he saw a lot of him in me."

"But he went back. You never did."

"Never had much call to see cities again. But DeSmet come back. Very next year, he come back. Only 1840 was our last Rendezvous, so he couldn't come with Bridger and the boys who guided him first time. Showed up here again, met another Flathead, and went up to preach and see the land. That time he went all the way into the Bitterroot Valley, and he built a mission—first one for the Jesuits in this country." Reno's head shook. "I was never partial to his black robes, but you got to marvel at a man like that."

He moved about then, setting up camp. Tim knew to help and before long, he knelt, holding a piece of steel between his thumb and index finger, and flint in his other hand. Quickly, he struck the steel against the rip and watched the sparks fly into the tinder he had set in the depression in the ground. He puffed when the sparks settled in the tinder, until he saw the orange glow. Cupping his hands, he blew again, but the tinder did not catch. It did less than a minute later, and when the smoke turned into fire, he fed a few twigs atop it.

When the coffeepot was on the fire, Reno squatted across from Tim and pulled off the sack that hung around his neck, from which he withdrew the pipe and what he called tobacco.

"Why do you carry your pipe and tobacco there?" Tim asked.

Reno took a burning twig from the fire and held it to his pipe. He did not answer until the tobacco was burning and he had pulled in a deep draw, holding the smoke, before exhaling through his mouth. "This?" He picked up the pouch. "This is my *gage d'amour*. That's what it's for. Other foofaraw I keep in my possible sack."

That meant absolutely nothing to Tim. He pointed at the packs that had been removed from the mule grazing with the picketed horses. "And what are those?"

Reno turned to look. "You mean my traps?"

Tim nodded.

"Six of them." Reno let out a mirthless chuckle. "Don't even know why I still carry them, beaver being practically all gone and not much of a market for them. Good money in the day, though, up to five dollars a pound. That would buy a man a smart of whiskey at the Rendezvous."

"How much was the whiskey?"

Reno laughed. "Three dollars a pint. I bet you

don't know how much whiskey'd cost back in Danburg."

"Danville," Tim corrected, surprising the trapper, who seemed to be in a halfway human mood. Maybe it had something to do with the jug he had been sipping on since the snow first started to fall and the jug that still sat by his side at the campfire. "Thirty cents a gallon."

He was a teenager after all, and boys knew about such things from listening to their fathers or the rabble that gathered about the grog shops that Tim's mother, and Tim's friends' mothers did not know they were passing—very slowly and very curiously—each day after school.

"Boy, you can be a wonder." Reno's head shook.

What seemed a wonder to Tim, though, was how a man like Reno could get robbed blind by the whiskey peddlers at the Rendezvous. Thirty-cents-a-gallon to three-dollars-a-pint was one hefty markup.

"How did it work?" Tim asked. "Trapping beaver?"

Reno puffed again, leaned forward to spit in the fire, and answered, "Well, it was *work*." He rose, weaving instead of walking straight, and made it to the packsaddle, where he reached into—*maybe his possibles sack,* Tim thought—and returned with a piece of wood, hollowed out with a stopper plugged in a hole, secured with a leather thong. Dropping beside Tim, Reno pulled out the stopper and held the wood container in Tim's face. "Get a whiff of that, boy." He seemed to be slurring his words.

Tim almost vomited.

Reno returned the stopper, tossed the container

into the grass, and dropped back onto his buttocks, slapping his thighs with both hands. "That's the bait, boy. Beavers loved it. Beaver castor. It'd draw them critters to the traps. You catch yourself a fat beaver, full grown, and take the castor out and that's your base. I doctor mine up with mustard and some secrets I ain't sharing. Put a few drops in your box with your trap. Beaver can smell a good ways, three hundred yards, maybe even farther than that. They smell that, and they're on their way to becoming a skin."

"Anything could smell that," Tim said, wiping his watering eyes.

Reno remained talkative. "So I go and fetch me one of them steel traps. They weigh about five pounds, and each one has a chain on it, five feet long or thereabouts, with a swivel and ring at the end. I fix that to my float, wade into a stream or pond or some such, put the trap in water, five-six inches deep, drive the float deep into the mud, and tie the other end to the bank. Then I set the trap, dip a small stick in that there bait, put it right above the trip. Before long, here comes Mr. Beaver. He gets caught, drowned, and when I come back the next morning, I fetch him back to camp, skin him, cure the skin. Make my pile."

He sighed, picked up the jug, shook it around while listening closely, and then stoppered the jug and put it away. He decided to smoke his pipe some more. "Ought to sell those traps to some fool who thinks the beaver's still prime."

"You ought to sell the bait." Tim did not think he would ever get over the stink.

"No, boy. Bait ain't just for beaver. It's a cure-all.

Saved many a fool from a bullet or arrow wound. That's no lie, boy. Pure gospel."

Tim wasn't sure if Jed Reno could tell anything altogether true, but he did not argue. "You did that all year?"

"Noooo." Reno puffed again on the pipe. "Indians have a way with the circle. Teepee. It's a circle. Camps. They're a circle. The earth is a circle. All things be a circle, boy. Same with trapping." Left hand holding the pipe, he raised his right hand over his head. "Winter, ponds and some rivers is all frozen over, buffalo are down in the valleys, beavers ain't around. We'd build us a cabin, or we'd find some squaw at some Indian camp. Fix traps, and do our clothes mending. Rest up for spring."

His arm rotated down to his side. "Come spring, that's when the beavers are prime. That's when we'd do our first go at trapping." The arm came down to his belly. "Then come summer, beavers are moving around, pelts not so prime, and they're looking for food for the winter. That's when we'd get ready and go to the Rendezvous, and we'd be drunker than you thought humanly possible. Fights and frolics and fun, boy. Rendezvous. Nothing like it in the world."

The arm came to his other side. "Then come fall, the beavers would find their home ponds, and we'd trap some more." The arm returned to over his head. "Then it be winter. Another year come and gone. Circle. Always a circle, boy. Life be a circle."

The coffee was ready. Tim Colter figured that Jed Reno sure could use some.

CHAPTER 28

The next morning, Jed Reno woke up, as Tim's Ma used to say, "on the wrong side of the bed." He cursed the mule, the horses, the country, Father DeSmet, the wind, the mountains, himself, and, when Tim did not react to an order fast enough, Tim.

The coffee they drank for breakfast did seem to settle him down a bit, and after he washed his face in the Green River, the mountain man seemed to be in better spirits. His eyes, however, remained bloodred, and his face still didn't have its natural color.

Once the mule's packs were loaded and secured, and all three horses hobbled, Reno motioned at the pistols Tim had become accustomed to carrying in his belt and beckoned Tim to follow him.

They stopped a good fifty yards from the animals, and Reno pointed at the remnants of what appeared to be a table. Fallen on its side, the middle plank of wood was missing. It was about fifteen yards ahead, half-swallowed by the high grass. "Screw-barrel first. Top plank."

Yesterday, the one-eyed trapper had talked like a schoolgirl. Today, he acted as if just lifting his tongue hurt like the devil. He leaned against his Hawken rifle, the stock butted on the damp ground, and groaned.

Tim drew the pistol, made sure the priming powder wasn't wet or fouled—or had blown out of the pan—and aimed one-handed at the target Reno had specified.

They had been doing that pretty much every morning. One shot. Usually with one pistol, rotating the .45 with the massive Harper's Ferry. That morning, it was the screw-barrel's turn.

The powder flashed in the pan, ignited the powder in the barrel, and the pistol roared. Tim had learned to step out of the smoke to see if his target was hit, although he heard the thud of lead against wood first and knew before his eyes confirmed the fact that his aim had proved true. The top corner of the table had been splintered by the .45-caliber ball.

Immediately, he fetched a ball from his bag and began reloading the pistol.

That was something else Jed Reno had taught him. An unloaded gun was worthless.

As Tim plunged the bullet atop the fresh powder in the barrel, he sought out Reno, expecting to hear some praise from the crusty old man.

What he heard, however, was, "Jupiter, that's loud." Reno rubbed his temple with his free hand.

After returning the pistol to his belt, Tim looked at the trapper, expecting him to walk back toward the horses.

Instead, Reno pointed at him. "Now the .54."

Tim knew better than to question anything Jed

Reno told him. The man had to have some reason for testing both pistols, so Tim drew the heavy Harper's Ferry cannon.

"Other side," Reno said. "Bottom corner."

Tim aimed, holding the weapon with both hands. The barrel steadied, he drew in an easy breath, held it for a moment, then exhaled, making sure of his target. He squeezed the trigger and felt his two hands buck from the .54's recoil.

He did not hear the thud of lead and ball, but through the white smoke, saw that the rotting edge of the table had disintegrated.

What Tim wanted to do was leap for joy. He had hit both targets, clean shots, and no matter what Jed Reno might say, neither had been luck. He was getting better. He stood there, though, reloading the big horse pistol, not even looking at the mountain man.

"All right," Reno said. "Let's ride."

As soon as they mounted the horses and rode toward the river, Reno pulled his big dun to a stop. Three men on horseback had stopped their horses at the edge of what once had been a rendezvous site. Two were Indians. The third was a white man, dressed in the same fashion as Reno.

Softly, Reno swore and handed the lead rope to Colter. "Knew we shouldn't be practicing shooting like that. Reckon they heard our racket. But one good thing about it. We're on the right trail."

He rode alongside the mule and pulled the second rifle from the packs, then rode a few yards ahead of Tim, calling back, "Stay here, boy, but keep your pistols handy."

* * *

Tim's hands turned clammy, and a chill ran up his backbone. The coffee bounced around in his gut, and most of his body turned numb.

Reno halted his horse. He guided the animal with his knees, for the hackamore had been dropped over the dun's neck, and one hand held each rifle butted against both thighs.

At the edge of the camp, one of the Indians, resplendent in his colorful buckskins, rode a few yards ahead before stopping his black horse. To the Indian's right came the second Indian, younger, thin, and stripped down to nothing but breechcloth, the hackamore in his teeth, his hands supporting a long bow already nocked with an arrow. The third man, small, thin, with a face painted black as if he were an Indian marked for war, came along the other side of the Indians to Jed Reno's right.

Even over the distance, Tim heard the big gun's hammer as it was pulled to full cock.

"Reno!" the white man called out, the word echoing in the morning air. "Who's the runt with you?"

Jed Reno did not answer.

Maybe he was too hungover from the damage he had done to the jug of whiskey yesterday, but Tim figured it had to do with something Reno had told him a few days back on the trail. "Don't waste words when it comes to a fight. Just get her done."

The next word the white man spoke sounded like a profanity. Then, the two Indians kicked their horses into gallops. The white man waited a few moments, then his horse powered forward, circling wider than the two Indians who came straight ahead.

Reno barked something and rode out to meet the charging racers.

Tim could not take his eyes off what was happening. It seemed like something out of a storybook, like one of those tales he had heard and read about knights back in England dueling each other with lances. Except Jed Reno carried no lance, just two flintlocks, and was outnumbered. He had only two shots in those rifles, and he faced three men. Tim glanced at one of the pistols in his belt. He wanted to kick the pinto into a gallop, but could not make himself do it.

Was he a coward? Was that why he had run when his ma told him to . . . when the bandits attacked their camp? Could that be why he had lived and his parents had died? Had that been the reason he had hidden out all night in that smelly beaver dam? He tried to tell himself that he was just doing what Reno had told him to do. Stay there.

The horse wanted to run. Tim had to pull back on the hackamore to keep him from joining the chase.

He heard the report of the first shot.

A moment later, he felt an arrow whiz past his head—a wild shot from the young Indian. Blinking, Tim tried to come to terms with what seemed to be happening. *Who fired the first shot?*

He saw the white smoke, though it was far beyond horse and rider, and realized it had been the Indian riding in the center. The Indian pitched a long rifle, and as if he were a magician, a long spear appeared in his free hand. Near him rode the younger Indian, who sent an arrow flying almost as soon as he had fired one. Tim wanted to see where the white man was, but he could not take his eyes off the charging

Indians and Jed Reno, who was galloping right into their midst.

If he lived to be older than Methuselah, Tim Colter would never believe what he saw nor understand how it could have happened.

Riding his dun, Reno rode right between the two Indians, ducking as the one in the center sent his lance sailing. Aiming both rifles, he braced the stocks on his hips and squeezed both triggers as he rode at a hard gallop. The guns boomed as one.

On Reno's left, the younger Indian flew off his horse's back. The horse kept galloping. He landed, bouncing several times through the grass, and then lay still.

To Reno's right, the big horse carrying the Indian in the beautiful buckskins tumbled, sending the brave flying over the horse's neck as the horse rolled head over tail, several times, before it stopped, never to rise again.

Another shot came, and Reno's horse toppled, but the mountain man leaped off before the great dun collapsed. He no longer held his rifles, having tossed them aside as soon as he fired both shots. He came up limping, whipping a knife as he ran awkwardly.

Tim couldn't see clearly as everything happened so fast.

The Indian in the fine buckskins strode toward Reno, a knife in his hand. They slashed as they ran past one another, both men leaping at the last second to avoid his opponent's blade.

Quickly, Tim looked away from the fight. He had to find the man, the white man. Sure enough, he saw him . . . galloping away, tossing his smoking musket into the grass. He had fired the shot that had killed Reno's great horse. Fired from a distance, the coward. He rode away, drawing a pistol from his belt.

Reno and the Indian locked arms. They pulled each other close. The Indian's head came forward, trying to smash Reno's nose, but the trapper jerked back, falling backwards, only to bring his knees up and catapult the Indian head over heels. Down went the Indian. Quickly, both men sprang up, Reno to his knees, the Indian all the way to his feet.

The Indian shifted the knife, brought it back, prepared to throw it from a distance of ten yards, but Reno threw his first. Over the fading echoes of the gunshots, Tim heard a piercing scream.

Down the Indian went, holding his stomach and raising his head to the sky, singing a strange song.

He had a knife in his gut, buried to the hilt, and he was singing? Tim couldn't believe it.

But he had no time to think, for that yellow-livered white man with the black face came charging with a pistol in his hand, the arm holding the short gun fully extended as the horse galloped closer and closer to Jed Reno.

Reno tried to stand, but fell. He pushed himself to his knees and moved back, away from the charging horseman. Tim tried to pull a pistol, though he knew that the horse and rider were far out of range, and that no matter how many rotting tables he had shot, hitting a moving target was far beyond his skills.

The rider yelled but did not fire the pistol, waiting to close the distance. Still moving on his knees, Reno suddenly lunged for the ground. The horse and white man were practically on top of him. The black-faced man reined hard to pull his horse to a stop then something shot out of the ground and the man was screaming, falling off the side of the horse. Several sidesteps later, it raced after the Indian horse long out of view.

Tim had to move. He slipped from the saddle, pulled the screw-barrel .45 from his belt, and left his horse, the spare, and the pack mule. Heart racing, he ran across the campground, sweating, fear rising in his stomach.

Reno stepped toward him, fell to a knee, then stood up.

The white man with the blackened face lay on his back with a post sticking up from him.

Suddenly, Tim stopped . . . and almost threw up. It wasn't a post. It was a spear. The lance the well-dressed Indian had wielded.

Jed Reno took another step, but had to stop to grip his right thigh where an arrow stuck out of his leg.

CHAPTER 29

Not one arrow, but two. Tim had seen the one sticking out from the side, but about halfway up to Reno's hip, he saw another. Blood oozed from the buckskin britches. Reno's face had turned ashen, but he kept moving. At least, he tried to. Grunting in pain, he fell to his knees and toppled forward, but managed to keep himself up with his arms.

Tim ran to his side.

The Indian kept singing that guttural chant.

Putting both hands on the mountain man's shoulder, Tim helped him back to his knees.

"Where?" Reno's muscles tightened in pain. He gasped, "Where . . . is . . . he?"

The Indian still sang.

"Mur—" The one-eyed man grunted. "Murchison. Gotta . . . talk . . ."

Tim could not believe Reno's strength and determination. The man came to his feet with only slight assistance from Tim, who had been trying to unloosen his bandanna to wrap around the man's bleed-

ing legs. Blood soaked the pant legs of Reno's buckskin britches, but he moved, leaning on Tim for sup-
port.

The white man lay in the grass, both hands gripping the shaft of the lance that had pinned him to
the ground. Blood gurgled from this mouth, his face
whiter than even Reno's—except for the black markings.

It took every ounce of strength Tim had to keep
from throwing up at the sight of the dying trapper.

His face had not been painted for war, but blackened by dirt . . . or gunpowder, perhaps. Tim had
heard of that happening, the black grains becoming
embedded beneath the skin, scarring a man for life.

"Murchison." Reno pulled away and fell to his
knees beside the little man who had tried to kill him,
and who had killed the fine dun horse.

Tim could not feel pity for the dying man. He felt
nothing.

He turned around, taking in everything. The
dead Indian—a boy not much older, perhaps not
even as old as Tim himself. The dead horses. The
smell of blood and gunsmoke and death rising in the
air. The other Indian, still clutching his belly, but on
his knees, looking at the sky, singing whatever song it
was. Maybe it was some kind of prayer. Blood also
spilled from the Indian's lips. Coughs interrupted
his song.

"Reno . . . you . . . kilt . . . me."

The words, sounding more like a boy crying than
a man, returned Tim's attention to Reno and the
man with the spear sticking out of his gut.

"Someone . . . was . . . bound to," Reno told him.

"I . . . know." The dying man shut his eyes tight.

"Where is he?" Reno asked. "Where is he going?"

The man's eyes opened, and his head turned, sending a mouthful of blood onto the already red-stained carpet of grass. As the light faded from his eyes, the little trapper with the face marked black, whispered, "Hell."

Tim waited. So did Reno. But the little man spoke no more, although his eyes kept staring at Jed Reno. It took a while before Tim realized that the man was dead, and that he saw nothing—at least, nothing near the Green River.

Still, the Indian sang, and coughed, and sang.

Reno dropped to his buttocks, breathing heavily.

Tim remembered the bandanna and handed it to him.

"Boy, get that jug. Off the mule. Need it."

Tim's legs carried him fast as he could to the horses and mule he had left to graze, unhobbled, not picketed. The pinto lifted its head, but did not run, just went back to eating the tall, lush grass. Tim went to the mule, remembering what Reno had told him. *Never come up directly behind any horse or mule. Make sure they can see you. Or feel you. If you walk around a horse or mule, keep one hand on his body. You don't do that. You're apt to wake up with a mighty bad headache or never wake up at all.*

"Easy, boy." Tim put his left hand on the mule's neck, rubbing it in a counterclockwise direction, while his right hand reached for the jug Reno had tied for easy access. He saw another sack, and remembering what was in it, he let go of the jug, which fell harmlessly to the grass, and pulled out a wooden container from the leather sack. Finally, gathering the jug and the stoppered piece of hollowed-out wood, he raced back to the one-eyed trapper, praying that he would still be alive.

Reno lay beside the dead man, eyes closed, his chest rising and falling rapidly.

Tim slid to a stop on his knees, and as Reno's eyes fluttered, he pulled out the cork from the jug and splashed the contents on the two arrow wounds.

The language exploding from Jed Reno's mouth and the fire in his eyes caused Tim to fall back, spilling more of the Taos Lightning onto the ground.

Reno had pushed the upper part of his body halfway up with his arms. He cursed more, fell back, came up wailing. Tim swallowed back fear.

"Boy!" Reno managed. "What—" More profanity. "Whiskey!"

Tim found the jug.

"I thought you wanted me to cleanse the wounds."

"I wanted . . . to . . . drink it." Reno fell back down.

Tim handed him the jug, but the mountain man lacked the strength to lift the container.

"Cut off . . . my britches." Reno shook his head, trying to keep his mind free.

Tim reached for Reno's sheath and realized that it was empty. He swallowed, knowing where he would find the mountain man's knife.

Suddenly, he understood just how quiet it was. The Indian no longer sang or coughed. Looking up, Tim saw the Indian in the beautiful buckskins lying on his side, eyes closed. Tim made himself stand and cross the few yards till he came to the dead Indian. Dropping to his knees, he reached forward, and grasped the big handle to the knife, half-expecting the Indian's eyes to open and his hands to grasp Tim's wrists. But the Indian did not move. Tim pulled the knife free, choked down more bile, and wiped the blood off on the dead man's beautiful leggings. He drew in a deep breath, let it go, and ran back to Reno.

Once he had cut away the buckskins, freeing them from the two arrows and pulling them down, he stared at Reno, who had managed to find the jug and take the last two swallows of whiskey. In stark contrast to his sun-browned face and hands, his legs were white as snow except for the dark bloodstains.

Tim wiped his mouth. "Do I . . . pull them . . . out?"

Reno's head shook. "Might leave the arrowhead in that way. No telling what the Piegans dipped them in. You gotta push."

Tim found the lower arrow first, the one sticking out from Reno's side. It seemed to be deeper, and less likely to hit any bone. He gripped it with both hands and pushed. His hands were so sweaty, they slipped off the shaft and landed on Reno's white leg.

He cried out in pain.

"Sorry." Tears welled in Tim's eyes, and, try as he might, he could not stop them from rolling down his sunburned cheeks.

"Get her done, boy," Reno said, and gritted his teeth.

Tim found the arrow again and shoved. The arrow moved. He pushed it again, and Reno cried out as the obsidian point broke free just above the back of Reno's knee.

Tim paused, wondering what to do next. He

couldn't push the arrow all the way through the man's leg.

"Cut off the head," Reno said. "Then pull the shaft out."

Again, Tim found the big knife and cut free the dark arrowhead, which he tossed aside. After wiping his eyes, and not caring about the bloody stains he had made on his tear-stained face, he grabbed the shaft higher, just below the beautiful feathers, and pulled. The arrow came free, and Reno only grunted—did not cry out—and Tim fell onto the grass. He held up the arrow then, sickened by its sight, quickly tossed it away.

"Other one . . . boy."

Tim found it, but feared it might prove more of a challenge.

"Just don't ram it into my manhood, boy." Reno even managed to smile.

Not much chance of that, Tim thought.

The arrow was higher on Reno's thigh, a few inches below the hip, but on the other side of his crotch. Tim gripped the shaft and shoved. Reno grunted again. Tim shoved again. And again. He had to push with all his might before the skin on the back of the one-eyed man's leg gave way with a sickening sound, and the arrowhead was out.

Without waiting for Reno's instructions, Tim found the knife again and cut the arrowhead free. He gathered enough strength to grab the shaft, and pull, and pull, and pull until the rest of the missile came free, and he tossed it aside.

Reno lay down, breathing rapidly as Tim stared at the ugly wounds. Mixing a few curses with prayers, he grabbed the wooden container, removed the stopper, and dumped some liquid into the holes where the arrows had first entered Reno's leg.

More profanity. More shouts. Tim had to dodge the weak attempt of a punch Reno pulled.

"What the—? What did—?" Reno could not finish.

"Beaver bait," Tim told him.

"Why . . . in—? By Jupiter, why would you—?"

"You said it was a cure-all. Fixes gunshots . . ." Tim wiped away tears.

Somehow, Reno managed to laugh as he lay on the ground. His head shook and he said in a hoarse voice, "Help me up, boy."

Tim started to, but stopped.

"Don't worry. I won't . . . hit you."

When the mountain man was sitting up, reaching down and grabbing his thigh, he stared at the wounds.

"They're still . . . bleeding," Tim said.

Reno could only manage a quick nod. After another curse, he straightened, and grabbed another thong hanging around his neck. Tim helped him remove the powder horn, which Reno handed to him.

"Pack the front holes first, boy."

"With gunpowder?"

Reno nodded, already pulling the pipe and tobacco pouch out of his gage d'amour. While Tim packed the two bloody holes with gunpowder, Reno leaned on his side and began using flint, steel, and tinder to get a small fire going.

Tim wasn't sure what Reno meant to do. Maybe gunpowder would stop the bleeding.

Once his wounds were packed, Reno discovered that the bandanna had come off when his britches pant leg had been cut off. He rewrapped it above the highest wound, tying the knot as tight as he could. "All right."

Tim looked up. Reno had sat up again, puffing on his pipe.

"Best pack the exit wounds, too, boy."

Tim nodded, and did as he had been ordered.

Reno looked at Tim and understood. "If you're going to throw up, now's a good time to do it. Over yonder. Don't want you to blow up with me."

"Mister . . ."

"Go on, boy."

Tim came to his knees, then feet, and slowly wobbled over toward the youngest dead Indian. He glanced back as Jed Reno pulled hard on the pipe, and then lowered it to the highest wound, turned the pipe over, and touched off the black powder.

Chapter 30

Tim raced to Reno, who lay on his side, alive but unconscious. He saw the ugly wound, the stench of burned flesh turning his stomach. The bleeding had stopped, but only for that wound. The three other holes poured blood, and most of the gunpowder he had packed in the wounds had been washed free by the blood.

Tim looked at the flint and steel the trapper had dropped. He had not gotten much of a fire going, just enough to light his pipe. Tim ran around, gathering what twigs and dried droppings he could carry and rushing back to Reno's side. He put just a little handful of dry grass and twigs in a depression in the grass, lay the tinder atop it, and began working flint and steel.

The weather cooperated. The fire started, and Tim added a few sticks. Next, he went back to Reno, still unconscious, perhaps dying, and grabbed the powder horn. He poured enough in the second entrance wound, the one closer to the side of the knee, reached over and grabbed a small burning stick, and without thinking or considering what he was doing, touched it to the powder.

He vomited at the stink and realization of what he had done, but kept working, wiping his mouth and rolling Reno over just enough so that he could work on the exit wounds made by the two arrows.

Twice more, he touched off the gunpowder. He wondered if Reno's legs would look like the dead trapper's face. The wounds looked ugly, and Tim remembered seeing a few old soldiers who had fought in the War of 1812. The ones with wooden legs. He wondered if a doctor would have to amputate Reno's leg.

That caused him to laugh. *Where would anyone find a doctor here?*

Looking up, he saw the mountains, the trees, the river. All loomed around him, foreboding, massive, deadly. He was all alone, except for one mountain man who lay unconscious with burned legs and sweat coating his forehead, two dead Indians, and one dead white man. He looked over at the white man. *What was his name? Murchison?*

The small fire crackled, and Tim decided he might have need of it. To heat water. To cook. Maybe to seal those ugly wounds if they reopened. He found stones to make a fire ring and added a few larger sticks and limbs until it blazed well enough that it would not die down anytime soon. He kept finding fuel and depositing it in a pile near the fire.

He looked at the fire and frowned. The smoke was rising skyward. Reno had always said to keep the smoke to a minimum. No need in letting other men see you, warn them of your presence. Well, he could do nothing about the smoke, unless he put out the fire, and that, he would not do.

Again, he checked on Reno, who mumbled in some delirium about doctors and Kentucky and why his pa had never cared a whit about him.

Tim remembered the beaver scent and picked up the container. *No,* he told himself, *use the whiskey first.* There wasn't much left, but he found a canteen and poured a splash or two inside the jug, which he swished around and slowly poured over the wounds in Reno's leg. He added the last of the beaver scent and found the bandanna Reno had used.

That was filthy, blackened some by the gunpowder. Tim raced again to the pack mule and went through the packs until he discovered Reno's possibles sack, where he uncovered a dingy pair of underdrawers. Not certain as to their cleanliness, he hurried across the grass until he reached the river. He soaked the garment, rubbed it against a rock, soaked it some more, his hands chilled by the surprisingly freezing water in the river.

A few minutes later, he had wrapped the undergarment around Reno's leg wounds. The bandanna he picked up, washed it off with the remnants of what remained in the jug, and began dabbing at the sweat on Reno's brow.

This he kept up, until at last, Reno seemed to be in a deep sleep, no longer fidgeting.

Tim made himself work. He didn't want to move Jed Reno. He seemed huge, and Tim wasn't sure if he could even drag him to some sort of shelter. Instead, he covered him with a robe, propped his head up by using the wolf skins as a pillow, and set about cleaning up the campground.

Moving the dead younger Indian was easy enough, as long as he did not look at the boy too much. He dragged him to the edge of the timbers and thought that maybe he should bury him. Yet he seemed to recall hearing that Indians buried their dead on platforms above the ground. That did not seem appropriate, but he would not disrespect the boy or the older Indian so he left him there, although he did fold the kid's hands over his chest. He remembered seeing dead men and women in their caskets at wakes, and that seemed how it was done.

The other Indian was harder to move, but he managed it, laying him beside his companion.

Finally, Tim went to the dead white man, Murchison. Bracing one foot against the man's rib cage and squeezing his eyes shut, Tim gripped the lance just beneath some feathers secured with sinew and jerked. The lance made a hideous noise as it pulled free of the ground and the dead man, and Tim flung it away as far as he could before he dared open his eyes.

Trying to keep his eyes off the dead man, Tim dragged him away, too. He started for the two Indians then stopped and looked at the dead braves. "No." His voice surprised him. It did not sound like him at all. It seemed an older man's voice, similar to how his pa had spoken.

Tim wiped his eyes and wet his lips. "No. Those Indians were brave." Deciding that he did not like how he sounded, he fell quiet again and dragged the dead trapper with the blackened face and the ghastly hole between his ribcage and navel to the opposite end of the camp.

He was sweating by then, so he stopped and slaked his thirst from a canteen, although he didn't know if his stomach, feeble as it felt, could even keep water down.

The dead horses he knew he could not move. That reminded him of his own stock. After a quick glance at Reno revealed the man still breathed, Tim went back to picket and hobble the horses and mules. The last thing he needed was to have those animals wander off and leave Jed Reno and him afoot.

That done, Tim returned to Reno's noble, dead dun horse. His fingers and hands were raw by the time he had unfastened the hackamore and saddle. He returned to Reno and laid them in the sun, the blanket atop the saddle to dry, although they had not ridden far enough for the dun to work up much of a sweat.

He looked around. *What next?*

He shook his head at his stupidity. He should unsaddle his own horse. He started for the pinto but quickly stopped. "Idiot. The guns."

He gathered all the weapons, but especially Reno's rifles, which he loaded and leaned against the saddle for easy access. Keeping his two pistols in his belt, he returned to his horse and removed its saddle.

When he finally realized that he had done all he could around camp, he returned to Reno. The man seemed hotter, so he pulled back the robe and again bathed the mountain man's forehead.

Around noon, he reached into the greasy sack he had taken from the dead raider back at South Pass, fingered out a handful of the goop Reno had called pemmican, and made himself eat it. It tasted faintly of berries, but mostly of grease, and maybe some kind of meat he could not identify and probably did not want to. He drank water, checked on the trapper, and picked up the rifle the Indian had carried. It was a Lancaster. That much he knew, for he had seen more than his share of those long rifles back in Danville.

Tim found a tree and used it for a backrest. For a few hours, he just sat, watching to the north and west, as that was the direction the two Piegan Indians and the little man with the blackened face had come from.

The birds chirped, and he even saw several elk grazing at the edge of the woods. He thought about chancing a shot, remembering just how good fresh meat tasted, but he also recalled Reno's warnings about shooting off weapons. After all, that's how the three now-dead men happened upon him and Reno. He had already eaten, the pemmican filling his stomach and not, to his surprise, upsetting it.

Satisfied that the three dead men had been traveling alone, he returned to Reno, who still slept, but no longer appeared to be sweating. As soon as he set the Lancaster on the saddle, Reno's eyes fluttered.

Tim dropped next to him.

Reno mumbled something and looked up at Tim. At first, he did not seem to recognize him, but after several seconds, he ran his tongue along his lips and somehow croaked out, "Water."

Lifting the trapper's big head in his arms, Tim held a gourd to Reno's lips. He drank till he coughed, and Tim strained to lift him up a little more, wondering if he should pat the mountain man's back the way a mother did a baby. He did not have to.

Reno stopped coughing and muttered a raspy, "Thanks, boy."

By the time Tim laid the man's head back atop the makeshift pillow of wolf pelts, Reno was asleep again.

Tim put the back of his hand on Reno's forehead. Earlier, he had found the man burning up with fever. It was not what his mother used to call "cool to the touch," but it did not feel like the fire.

That reminded him of the fire, which he stoked and added a few small limbs.

He did not remember falling asleep or even closing his eyes, but he woke with a start. The day had cooled, and the sun was sinking behind the mountains off to the west. They had wasted an entire day, but Tim knew there was nothing he could do about that. He thought about the dream he had been having, but the memory had been shattered when he awoke. He again felt Reno's head—still cool—and looked at the wounds in his leg.

A lifetime ago—when the wagon train had been crawling past the Blue River and Mr. Dawson had accidentally buried an ax blade into his thigh—someone had mentioned gangrene, how it had killed many a man, and might kill Mr. Dawson. It stank. It probably had some color to it, too, but Tim did not recall that. He did remember that Mr. Dawson had survived, though he was still limping when the wagon train had left Tim's family and the Scotts at South Pass.

He smelled the wounds, which stank of burned flesh and gunpowder and beaver glands. "I bet I looked like a fool," he said, again surprised by the sound of his—or any—voice. Shaking his head, laughing at the scene he imagined of him smelling a man's thigh, he stepped over Reno's leg, picked up the Lancaster rifle, and walked back to the livestock. He led them to water one at a time, giving each a handful of grain, before double-checking tethers and hobbles.

When he returned to Reno, he ate and drank again, leaned back on the grass, and slept like a dead man for the rest of the night.

CHAPTER 31

Patricia Scott woke up and sat up quickly, bringing her hands to her chest to tighten her chemise. She felt the rancid breath of the man staring at her, hovering over her. Yet, still not wide awake, still halfway in the pleasant dream she had been having, she whispered, "Tim . . . ?"

The animal before her chuckled. "Tim?" The breath stank. The voice mocked her.

Patricia stiffened. She knew who it was. She hated him.

Dog Ear Rounsavall came closer until she could see him so clearly in the light of the fires.

Quickly, she shot a glance at Margaret and Nancy Colter, both asleep a few yards away underneath a tree, and her mother, snoring slightly by one of the many small fires across the camp.

"They cannot help you, wench." The hideous mountain man laughed. "Nor can"—Dog Ear Rounsavall sniggered—"Tim." He spoke the name in a high-pitched voice, but quiet enough not to wake anyone nearby.

"But Jackatars can," Patricia said.

Dog Ear Rounsavall's smile vanished.

Patricia remembered the French renegade during the attack that seemed like a lifetime ago.

Hearing shots, whoops, horses, and screams, she leaped out of the back of the wagon. Tim's mom was shouting at him. Then a big bear of a hideous man had slammed a tomahawk into poor Mrs. Colter's head.

Tim's sisters screamed. Patricia heard another shot. Arrows whistled overhead. Her father's dog, Wilbur, whined, yelped, and fell silent. Several Indians—no, white men dressed like Indians—were throwing her mother back and forth, laughing as if it were some child's game.

The hideous man sprinted toward her, letting out a yell that curdled her blood. She looked for Tim, but could not see him, and then ran. She ran as hard and as fast as she could. Through the woods, feeling limbs swat at her, brambles rip her chemise. It had been so hot that day, and she had wanted to put on something new, a clean dress—or relatively clean—so she might look halfway decent for Tim.

She ran from the laughing brute, a giant, a monster. The tomahawk flew over her head, slammed into a tree, burying the blade deep in the bark.

She screamed louder and tried to run faster, only she tripped over a root, went sprawling, and tumbled down a slight incline until a tree stopped her. It felt like she had

*busted a few ribs, but when she rolled onto her back, she un-
derstood that she had only had the wind knocked out of her.
No ribs had been cracked. She was all right. But soon, she
thought, she would be dead.*

Or, she feared, worse.

*Dog Ear Rounsavall dropped beside her. He licked his
lips and tugged on the braids that hung to his ears, feathers
dangling from the dark, coarse, ugly hair.*

*He laughed and quickly snatched a knife from a sheath on
his left hip. He straightened slightly, running the blade along
his thumb, then showing her the blood, which he licked.*

Patricia felt she might vomit.

Suddenly, the man shifted the knife and brought it down.

*She screamed and saw the knife tear between her legs, cut-
ting the undergarment, pinning it to the earth. Patricia almost wet herself. Tears flowed down her cheeks. "Please," she
begged, hating herself for being so weak.*

*The bearded man with the painted face just laughed
again to mock her. Grinning, he pulled the knife up, but not
completely free of the fabric. Slowly, in a move to torture her,
the blackheart began pulling the knife back toward her, the
blade ripping the homespun muslin all the way to the hem.*

*After he sheathed the knife, he wiped his bloody thumb on
the fabric. "Now, you can ride a horse."*

*The accent was French, a language Patricia had always
found romantic, pleasant . . . until that moment. Nothing
about the man was romantic or pleasant. He was horrible,
terrifying.*

*Suddenly, he leaned forward, grabbed her right wrist,
and yanked her against him and his bear-claw necklace.
She slammed so hard against him, she came away stunned.*

*He cursed her in French, stood, still holding her wrist in
his massive hand, and then he began squeezing so hard, she*

feared that the brute would crush her wrist, break every bone in her body, or maybe just rip the hand off her arm.

He jerked her to her feet, whirled, and strode through the woods, pulling her behind him. When she fell, he did not stop, just dragged her. The flesh on her legs was torn by rocks and pine cones and briars. She thought her arm would be pulled out of its shoulder socket. She felt she would die.

A thought chilled her. She wished she would die. Now. Quickly. The way Mrs. Colter had died.

Patricia heard no more gunshots or arrows whistling by, but laughter and the unholy sounds of wild men plundering through the chests, the sacks, and the grips the Colters and Scotts had packed. The ravagers littered the campsite with items they did not want. They smashed her mother's fine China. They shattered the dreams of the Colters and Patricia's own family.

A breath escaped her, for she saw several men in buckskins surrounding Margaret and Nancy Colter. She looked for Tim, but did not see him, and cried. Her mother stepped from behind a thin man with a small mustache who pushed her back, slapped her, and turned, smiling as Rounsavall dragged Patricia forward and slung her to the ground. She landed and rolled toward the circle of men surrounding her mother and her boyfriend's two sisters.

Slowly, gasping for breath, praying for death, Patricia pushed herself up on her hands and knees.

The man with the small mustache spoke in a language Patricia had never heard. Dog Ear Rounsavall answered Louis Jackatars with a grunt.

Jackatars said something else, laughed, and took two steps toward Patricia. He grabbed her by her hair and pulled. She screamed. More tears flowed. Her mother shouted, cursed, and was slapped to her knees.

Patricia felt herself turned around. The man who held her was not as big as the brute who had dragged her back to the camp, but he was just as tough. Maybe tougher. "We ride." He, too, spoke in a strange accent.

He let go of Patricia, and she fell to her knees. They would not kill them. At least, not yet.

She started to pray, and then she saw her father. He was dead. And he had been scalped.

Over the days of captivity, Patricia Scott had hardened. She had steeled herself. No longer did she pray for death. She prayed for God to smote the fiends who called themselves men . . . or for the Lord to give her the strength to kill them—every miserable one of them—herself.

Shaking off her memories, she told Dog Ear Rounsavall, "You won't touch me."

He laughed again. "Why not?" he asked, and added some mocking French phrase she did not care to hear.

"Because I've seen what Jackatars, that pig, has done to those who disobeyed him. And so did you."

How many lifetimes in Hell had that been, when Jackatars had killed the two vermin who had attacked Patricia's mother? She couldn't remember. She couldn't remember the post at Fort Laramie. She couldn't picture Independence. She had no idea what life had been like back in Danville, Pennsylvania. Sometimes, she could not even picture Tim Colter anymore.

Was he dead? Like her father. Like Tim's parents.

Like poor Wilbur, that sorry old dog who had loved her dad with all his heart.

It felt as if her life had begun when Jackatars's fiends attacked the camp. When Dog Ear Rounsavall had caught up with her and ripped her undergarments with his razor-sharp knife.

There had been no life before that moment. And there was no future to look forward to.

Maybe she was in Hell.

She sat up, keeping the rock she had slept with hidden in her hand. David, she remembered vaguely, had killed a giant with a slingshot. Dog Ear Rounsavall was a giant. Tim Colter had once had a slingshot. She had watched one of the brutes find it, and smash it to bits back at the camp. She figured she did not need one. She would just stove in Goliath's head with the sharp stone she held.

She looked the cur in the eyes.

Dog Ear Rounsavall grinned. "Jackatars can wait. He won't live forever. Neither will you."

Of course, Patricia Scott knew she would not live forever. She might not live another week . . . or even through the night.

Traveling across some of the roughest, wildest country she had ever seen had played hell on every muscle in her body. Her backside was raw, and the inside of her thighs chaffed.

Louis Jackatars and Dog Ear Rounsavall treated their captives cruelly, brutally. Oh, those evil men had not forced themselves, or tried to, on the prisoners—at least not since Jackatars had killed the two men who had disobeyed his orders back in the flat country near the Red Desert . . . a lifetime ago.

Rarely had the rogues beaten them with sticks or cuffed them with their rock-hard hands. Some of the men even kept a respectful distance from the prisoners.

Yet they had been given practically nothing to eat, scraps fit for dogs, just enough to keep the women alive. When it had rained, they had been denied shelter. When it had snowed, they had not been given blankets or coats. They were graced with a cup of hot tea occasionally, maybe every third morning, but usually it was just tepid or brackish water, and no more than a few swallows each morning, around noon, and in the evening.

Their clothes hung in rags, and vermin lived in their hair. Patricia's forearms were covered with bug bites, and most of her skin, exposed to the harsh sun, had turned into leather, burned, peeled, hardened, bronzed, toughened.

Her mother had whispered, "God's will. They test our spirit. They break us. We will show them."

And they had. Patricia remembered hearing one of the men say that Tim's younger sister would not live more than two days on the trail. But they all still lived. They all would live. For a while, anyway.

She stared at Dog Ear Rounsavall, hating him. She wondered if she had enough strength to crush his skull with the rock she held.

"Patricia?" a voice called out from the fire.

"I'm all right, Mother." Patricia did not let go of the rock.

Men began to stir, and Dog Ear Rounsavall slowly stopped smiling. He began backing away from her, into the shadows and the dark, although she felt as though his rancid breath, his stink, and his hideousness remained right before her.

"You won't live forever, girlie," he called out, mockingly blowing her a kiss.

"But I will outlive you," she told him.

CHAPTER 32

Tim had seen how Jed Reno brewed his coffee, which was nothing like the way his ma used to make it. Following Reno's lead, he dumped some beans into the two cups, filled them with water, and set both on a rock in the middle of the coals he had raked over to one side of the pit. Another idea nestled in his head. He considered it and decided it was worth a try.

He felt certain that for a day or two, Reno would not be able to hold much solid food down. When Tim and his sisters were sick, his ma usually fed them chicken broth. He had not seen a chicken since Missouri, but he did have some jerked beef. He stuffed a few strips into another cup he found on the campground—one in surprisingly good shape, not even rusty—topped it with water and placed it on the stone with the coffee cups.

For his own breakfast, he managed to swallow a few bites of pemmican. After checking and cleaning the wounds in Reno's thigh, he added wood to the

fire, kept the Lancaster rifle handy, and waited for
the one-eyed mountain man to wake up . . . if he did.

"Boy."

Tim's eyes shot open, and he started to cock the
Lancaster rifle before realizing that Reno had come
to. Leaning the rifle against the saddle, he hurried
over to the old trapper.

Reno kept breathing rapidly.

Is that a good sign or a bad one? Tim had no earthly
idea.

The mountain man wet his lips with his tongue.

"How long have I been out, boy?"

"Just since yesterday. You want something to eat?"

Instead of answering, Reno said, "Help me up,
boy."

Tim pulled him to a seated position, which almost
wore both of them out. After a short hesitation to
catch his breath, Tim carried the coffee and the
broth to him.

Reno's head shook.

"You have to eat," Tim said, surprised to find himself arguing with a man old enough to be his father.
"Get your strength back."

Reno cursed, then laughed, and shook his head.

"All right, Mommie." He held out his hand.

Tim gave him the broth first.

The big man sipped, scowled, look at the contents, sloshed them around in the cup, and then
stared hard at Tim with that one blazing blue eye. "I
don't reckon, we got no whiskey left."

"You drunk it all."

Reno shook his head again. "No. You wasted it on
this." He pointed at his bandaged leg, but finished

the broth, and even drank the coffee without further complaint.

Pointing to the pile of wood Tim had gathered for the fire, Reno said, "Hand me that big stick." He shook his head at the stick Tim picked up. "No. The other one. Straight one. That's it."

Tim handed it to him.

Reno tested it, and it snapped, prompting a curse from the trapper, who tossed it back toward the pile. "Get me my Hawken, boy."

Using the .54-caliber rifle as a crutch, he stood up, staring straight ahead before hobbling off. He stopped a few yards away to unbutton his britches and urinate, hobbled on, then stopped again when he saw his dead horse.

A silence, dark and foreboding, hovered over the campground. Tim could have sworn he saw the man bring a hand up to his face to wipe away a tear or two. Reno, however, said nothing. He looked at the other dead horse and then noticed the living ones tethered and hobbled fifty yards away.

He looked back at Tim.

"You bury them I killed?"

"No." Tim pointed to the woods. "The Indians are over there." And nodded in the opposite direction. "The other man's yonder."

With a nod, Reno started off toward the woods where Tim had dragged the dead white man. Slowly, Tim followed him, stopping a few yards away and watching as Reno dropped the Hawken, knelt, and drew the dead man's knife from the sheath on his side.

In horror, Tim saw Reno scalp the black-marked

man, force the corpse's mouth open, and stick the scalp lock inside.

"That's for my horse, Malachi. Rot in hell." The mountain man examined the knife before tossing it away. Clumsily, he looked around for the Hawken.

"Boy," he called. "Give me a hand."

Tim obeyed, although he tried not to look at the man Reno had just scalped.

When he stood, leaning against the rifle, he nodded. "Help me back."

"To the Indians?" Tim asked, horrified.

"No. Indians was brave. Good men. Hated to have to kill them. They won't go to the Happy Hunting Ground without their topknots. But him?" Reno turned, spit on Murchison, and looked back toward the campfire. "Back there. I'm tuckered out."

He was sweating by the time Tim helped him lay back on the robe and blankets, and Tim quickly handed him a canteen.

Reno practically emptied the canteen then pulled back the bandage and examined the wounds, which he studied for several moments before facing Tim again.

"I don't remember—"

"You did one," Tim told him, knowing Reno needed the water. Besides, with water so handy, drinking so much wasn't a problem. "I did the others."

Reno pulled the bandage back up, saw the rifles, the traps, and again looked at the horses and mule. "The other mounts?"

Tim shook his head. "They ran off." He pointed south. "That way."

Reno found his pipe, blackened from touching off

the powder, and began filling the bowl with his blend of makeshift tobacco.

That has to be a good sign, Tim thought, and he grabbed a branch from the fire so Reno could light his morning smoke.

After a couple pulls, Reno removed the pipe, pointing the stem at the horses. "I won't be much good for a couple days. That's my guess. Could be a while longer. I just don't know. Can't sit a saddle, especially where we need to be going. And we can't wait around here, not if we want to stop Jackatars and get your sweetheart and sisters back. Boy, you know how to make a travois?"

Tim swallowed and shook his head.

"Well, time you learned."

Tim Colter rode ahead, the Lancaster in his arms, the two pistols in his belt, pulling the lead rope. Behind him trailed the black horse, saddled with Reno's saddle, and the mule, loaded with packs and extra weapons. Behind the mule came Jed Reno on the travois.

Tim had found straight limbs, roughly eight feet long, and secured cross sticks with rawhide and sinew to connect the two poles. After laying a robe over the travois, he secured the two poles to each side of the pack mule. As lousy as he felt in the saddle, he knew the mountain man had to be uncomfortable lying in that thing. More likely, he was in tremendous agony.

Tim's instructions were to follow the Green River till it turned east and into the Wind River Mountains.

Don't follow it, but head north, keeping Whiskey Mountain at his back.

It had taken him and Reno two days just to reach where the river turned, and still the trapper could barely sit up. Riding horseback was definitely out of the question. For now.

Tim shot an elk, and Reno told him to offer a prayer to the sky to thank the elk for his life and for helping Reno and Tim keep theirs. After butchering the elk under Reno's directions, Tim cut out the liver—at Reno's insistence—and they both ate it raw, although only the mountain man seemed to enjoy that meal. They ate some of the meat for supper, wrapped more in skins for later, but left the bulk of the magnificent animal for some grizzly, wolf, or buzzard.

Tim had seen country before, but nothing like what he was seeing. Granite mountains rose to the heavens. So did the trees, some lodgepole pines but mostly Douglas firs and spruce. He saw more bighorn sheep than he ever thought existed in the entire world, moose—he had never seen one before—and even a grizzly that, thankfully, ignored the horsemen as they rode up along a ridge.

The streams were clear, flowing rapidly, and full of trout. So they ate trout for supper and breakfast.

Or course, he would never have found his way out of the forest and mountains if not for Jed Reno.

Every now and then, Reno would get off the travois and hobble on ahead. He had managed to fashion a suitable crutch out of limbs he found in the thick forests. "That way," he would say, and limp back to the travois.

After following animal trails in the dense woods, along creek beds through rugged canyons, or climbing over rocks and fallen brush, every night Tim fell asleep sore and exhausted. Every morning he had to wake up, cook something for breakfast, and break camp.

Sometimes, he could scarcely breathe, the air felt so thin. Twice, he woke up in the morning and had to shake snow and ice off his robe. He had to lead the horses up steep ridges one at a time, and often came away with hackamore-burned hands, skinned knees, and a bleeding forehead. After that, he had to haul Jed Reno up those ridges using a rope.

Once, as he dragged Reno behind him in the travois, the mountain man called out, "Boy, we got a bit of company."

Tim stopped, turned in the saddle, and watched a bear cub following the travois. He laughed. The cub seemed curious, acted more like a puppy dog. His good humor did not last long. The bear cub reminded him of Wilbur, Mr. Scott's dog, and suddenly he remembered its lifeless body filled with so many arrows. He recalled how heavy the dog was when he had laid it in the shallow grave alongside Mr. Scott.

"Boy."

Tim stared down at Jed Reno and made himself smile. The cub had stopped, keeping a respectful distance, and started making strange grunts, then started furiously scratching near his ear.

"Sure is a cute thing."

Reno cursed. "Boy, it won't be cute and it sure won't be funny when that cub's mama comes hunting for him. That's a silvertip griz, boy, and its mama will have us for supper."

Tim frowned. "You want me to shoot it?"

"Shoot it?" Reno laid back and groaned and cussed. "That'd just bring its mama coming in madder than I'm about to get at you. And if you then shot its mama, she'd be even madder. No, boy, I don't want you to shoot it. I just want you to get us the hell away from here before we all wind up in a grizzly she-bear's stomach."

When he went to sleep thinking no day could be any worse than that one, he knew similar thoughts would be entering his mind the next night . . . if he lived through the next day.

At night, Reno would patch his pants. The sun had burned his white leg, except for where the bandage protected the arrow wounds. He stitched various skins until he had some sort of mountain man's patchwork quilt that covered his leg to his moccasin. Elk skin. Wool. Wolf pelt. Buckskin. "It ain't pretty, but it'll do."

On they went.

Through snowbanks. Through the ghost of forests in a land blackened by fire years back. Across rivers, over mountains, and into verdant valleys filled with majestic lakes, only to have to deal with another mountain, another forest, even a thunderstorm now and then in the late afternoon.

They came to a pass, and Reno pointed off to the west. "Yonder lie the Tetons."

Tim gave the wonderful mountains barely a glance. "I suppose we'll be climbing them next," he said, not trying to hide his bitterness.

"No, boy." Reno pointed. "That way."

That way looked no better than the Tetons. "Where are we going?" Tim finally asked.

Reno answered with one word. "Hell."

When they reached the South Fork of the Shoshone River, Reno decided he could ride. Tim didn't believe him, but the trapper insisted. "We've wasted enough time. I'll ride. Or die."

The first day, Tim thought Reno would die, but he woke the next morning to find the one-eyed mountain man cooking trout for breakfast.

The second day, Tim thought he would die.

The third day, Reno did not need Tim to help him into the saddle, although he grunted and swore and struggled to make it to the stirrup on his own.

Meat roasted on a spit that night, for Reno had gone hunting that evening. Tim leaned over and cut off a chunk with his knife. He felt satisfied, full. Leaning back, he stared at the stars, so bright, so inspiring. A million of them stretched across the sky. He could see the Milky Way. He felt as if he could almost touch it.

"Jed?" Tim called out.

"Yeah, boy."

"What did you feel the first time you were out here?"

"Huh?"

"How did it feel, I mean? Being here. Seeing all this. For the first time."

"Boy, that was more than a few years ago. Lot of whiskey drunk since that time. Lot of getting my head knocked around, my arse halfway froze off, and two eyes I had."

"You know, some things you never forget." Tim frowned, remembering the dream, that nightmare, and the face of that brute of a man, Dog Ear Rounsavall. He would never forget that. He made himself focus on the stars, the night, the warmth of the fire, and the fullness of his stomach.

"You're talking nonsense, boy," Reno said.

"No, I'm not. You know. How did it feel?"

The one-eyed Cyclops spit into the fire, grunted, farted, and sighed. "Felt like I was blessed, boy. That's right. Blessed. That I was put there, at that very moment, to see it. With both of my eyes. 'Cause I had two back in them olden times. Felt like I was the luckiest person on the face of God's green earth. That answer your question, boy?"

Tim laughed. "I guess so."

Reno sat up, tore off a hunk of meat, and shoved it into his face.

"But like I said, boy, that was some time ago. Back in 1822 or thereabouts. Now, I know better. I know that this country will kill you if you ain't careful, and even if you are careful, you can wind up just as dead as some green fool kid who ain't got the sense to follow the ruts left by a passel of immigrants and walk his way to safety at Jim Bridger's place."

Tim laughed again. "I'm still alive, Jed."

"For the time being. Maybe not tomorrow. Get some sleep."

Tim leaned back, chewed the meat. It tasted sort of funny. "Jed?"

"What now, boy?"

"What is this we're eating?"

"Marmot," Reno said.

"What?"

"Marmot."

"What's that?"

"Well, it ain't no bug and it ain't no painther or elk, boy. It's a damned marmot."

Tim sat up. He spit into his hand what he hadn't swallowed and stared at it.

"It tastes like—"

"Lichen and moss, I figure. It's a marmot. Kind of like a otter, and kind of like a groundhog. A big, swimming type of prairie dog, I guess. A marmot, boy."

Tim tossed the remnants into the fire and heard the meat sizzle on the coals.

"Boy," Reno said, "I ain't exactly partial to the taste myself. But it was handy, and after I killed it, I thanked its spirit for letting me take its life so we could live. I'd rather have elk, boy, but the marmot was handy. I'd rather have some Taos Lightning, but I couldn't find that, neither. Marmot. Just tell yourself it's roast beef and stewed tomatoes."

The fourth day, Reno sharpened his knives and hatchet. He looked up, his cold eye burning through Tim. "Trail's about over, boy. Tomorrow . . . maybe the next day, we'll be there. Let's hope Murchison wasn't lying when he told me where to find Jack-atars."

Tim's head shook. "He said 'Hell.'"

Reno grinned without humor. "That's right. I've thought about that. Wonder if your being here is something the Almighty planned or if maybe you're kin to him. You've sure proved your salt, kid. I ain't saying you've grown into them britches, but you got us this far. I sure wasn't no help."

"What are you talking about?"

"I'm talking about Hell, boy. That's where Jack-atars plans to trade them women to the Blackfeet. *Hell. Colter's Hell.*"

BOOK THREE
COLTER'S HELL

CHAPTER 33

The way the story went, or at least the way Jed Reno had heard it most often and told it to Tim was something like this. "John Colter came to this country with Lewis and Clark. He hailed from Virginia, or maybe Kentucky, or possibly Kentucky via Virginia. In any event, he joined the Lewis and Clark expedition in Pittsburgh, and when they set out, Colter quickly proved himself as the best marksman and best hunter in the group.

"Around 1806, when the company was returning from the Pacific and had reached the Mandan villages, Colter asked to be discharged from Lewis and Clark's Corps of Discovery so he could stay in the wilderness and trap for furs. He was doing that along about 1809 when he and a trapper named John Potts met up with hostile Blackfeet Indians along the Jefferson River . . . this was long before the pox and other diseases almost wiped out the entire Indian nation. It was no small hunting party. Five- or six- hundred Blackfeet were not happy about white men hunting in their hunting grounds.

"Blackfeet being Blackfeet, they captured Colter and shot Potts to pieces, hacking up what was left of the dead trapper. After that, Blackfeet being Blackfeet, they stripped Colter of all his clothes, pointed, and signed at him to run.

"John Colter did.

"It was a game to the Blackfeet. They were sporting about such things, giving him a head start of three hundred yards.

"What the Blackfeet did not know was how fast Colter could run. The Indians sent their fastest warriors after him, thinking they would overtake him quickly and kill him the way they had killed John Potts. But Colter ran. And ran. And ran. He seemed tireless and rarely slowed down.

"He left most of the Blackfeet far behind him, but one Indian seemed only slightly slower afoot than Colter. They ran through forests, and branches and brambles tore much of Colter's flesh. His nose was bloody. His feet were raw.

"With only one Indian nearby—maybe twenty yards behind—Colter turned to face the closest Blackfoot and held out his arms as though awaiting death. Maybe he was. Maybe that's what he wanted. The sudden move caught the Indian by surprise. He threw his lance, but worn out from running . . . and the shock of seeing the bloody white man . . . the spear fell short. Colter snatched it up and ran the Blackfoot through, pinning him to the earth.

"He pulled the lance free of the dead brave and grabbed the blanket the Indian had. Armed, Colter continued to run. Five miles later, he ran to the banks of the Madison River, and there he saw the beaver dam. Wading into the water, with only a spear and blanket, he swam to the animals' lodge and hid inside."

Just like I did, Tim thought, *when Jackatars's men attacked us. Only I had no spear. No blanket.*

Reno continued the story. "That night, Colter came out from the dam. He had a spear. A blanket. And many years of experience living and surviving in this country. He walked, hiding his tracks, surviving on berries, bark, grass, whatever he could find to eat.

"Eleven days later, John Colter, browned by the sun, still naked except for a blanket that stank and was filled with holes—he had lost the spear shortly after leaving the beaver dam—stood outside the gate to Fort Raymond near the Big Horn and Yellowstone rivers. Fort Raymond was a trading post. The men up in the watchtower stared down, wondering what kind of creature he was.

"Colter told him his name.

"At first, no body believed him.

"Cactus spines were embedded in both feet. He was more skeleton than man, but that skeleton recovered. John Colter had walked two hundred miles to survival.

"He lived only three more years, marrying a girl called Sally, who bore him a son. He died of jaundice. He died a legend.

"That's John Colter," Reno said.

Tim marveled at the story, although he did not know how much he could believe. "Did you know him?"

Reno cursed. "Boy, how old do you think I am? He was dead before I ever heard of the Rocky Mountains."

Sipping his coffee, Tim thought more about Reno's tale. "But what's Colter's Hell?"

"That run from the Blackfeet might be why folks back East talk about John Colter, but he done his share of exploring, too. Probably was the first white man ever to see a lot of this country. Including Colter's Hell.

"Shortly after leaving the Corps of Discovery, he joined a party of fur trappers heading up the Platte River under command of Manuel Lisa. Colter had been paddling a canoe, heading back to civilization in St. Louis, but he already missed the mountains. So he joined the keelboat and returned to the Yellowstone and built Fort Raymond.

"In the winter of 1807-08, Lisa sent men off on explorations in different directions. Colter went up the Big Horn, and in the dead of winter, found Hell.

"In those days, they called the Shoshone the Stinkingwater River—it give off a foul odor, like rotting eggs and sulfur. At the mouth of the canyon cut by the wild river, Colter wandered into a place that smelled even worse than the river. He saw bubbling earthen cauldrons of foul-smelling hot springs. Geysers that sent steam shooting hundreds of yards into the air. And ground that pulled a struggling buffalo into the depths of Hades like quicksand. Vents in the earth shot out gasses. Boiling water carved ditches that carried the evil water to the stinking river.

"It was Hell, but it was Hell in the middle of a Garden of Eden. Maybe that's the way it was supposed to be." Reno saw the disbelief on Tim's face. "After all,

Heaven can't be far from Hell, can it? Where else could it have been?

"Colter returned to the trading post and told of his discovery. Most of the men laughed at him. They said he could sure tell a whopper. Some called him a liar, regretting it after getting a taste of the mountain man's knuckles. No one believed him . . . at first.

"Others soon confirmed Colter's Hell. A few years back a Crow Indian chief named Plenty Coups told me about camping there. I heard descriptions of Colter's Hell from Joseph Lafayette "Joe" Meek when we shared a few jugs at the Rendezvous way down south in the Willow Valley.

"'Ye ne'er seed the likes, Jed,' Meek told me. "'Everywheres ye turnt, ye found the whole land just a-smokin' from the mists of 'em boilin' springs, an' the springs was a-burnin' with gasses. Stank, I means to tell ye, but it wasn't just the stink or the gas or the hot water. It was the noise. 'Em craters jes kept a-whistlin', an' a-whistlin' sharp. It was Lucifer his-self, I reckon, a-whistlin' for us sinners to come join him. But as frightenin' as it was, as horrible as it seemed and sure, by thunder, smelt, it was a beautiful place, Jed,' he told me. 'Inspirin', I reckon be the word. God put his hand on that land, son. Maybe the Devil wants his share of her, and that's why 'em pits and that smell be thar.' "

Stiff as Reno's leg was, the trapper still managed to climb into the saddle on the black. He seemed glad to be rid of the travois, but Tim wondered if maybe they should keep it—just in case.

"No," Reno said. "It'll just slow us down, and we've wasted enough time."

They were out of the mountains, although the land remained rugged. The sun turned hotter. They crested a hill and rode down the eastern side where the evergreens had been carved away by long-melted glaciers or mudslides from years past. Antelope grazed below, but both men knew better than to fire a rifle. Sound carried a long way, and Jackatars and his raiders would be alert. To the west rose more mountains, maybe not as inspiring as the Tetons that Reno had pointed out some days back, but brutal and dark and menacing. He led his horse away from those tree-lined peaks.

It was morning, though hot. Wisps of white clouds seemed to reach only halfway up the mountains to the east. Even though they remained snowcapped but tree-lined, it was as if they rose out of the sky itself. Closer to the valley and grass, the gray and brown rocks turned red. In the low country, where Reno and Tim rode, antelope loped away from the horses and mule.

The creeks they crossed were shallow, rocky, and cold. The animals splashed across. Reno did not give them time to drink. He did not drink himself.

Tim followed him.

That night, they camped beside a hot spring along a river that Reno did not name. When Tim started to unsaddle the black, Reno stopped him, and Tim did not ask why. Maybe the trapper wanted his horse ready in case they had to leave in a hurry. Besides, Tim was so stiff and sore, if he didn't have to unsaddle a horse, that seemed fine and dandy to him.

They built no fire and finished the pemmican Tim had been carrying for longer than he could remember. He brought a scarred hand to his face and brushed away the dirt and grime and . . . what was it? He rubbed harder, feeling bristles like peach fuzz.

A few yards away, Reno sat massaging his bad leg, though he kept looking at the teenager with his one good eye.

Finally, the mountain man grinned. "That don't come off, boy."

Lowering his hand, Tim asked, "What?"

"You'd call it a beard, I guess. Though I don't."

Amazed, Tim brought his hand up again, brushing the fuzz on his face gently, careful not to knock any of that hair off.

The hot spring gurgled. A nighthawk screeched. Clumsily, painfully, Reno began removing his moccasins. That he could do by himself, but he needed Tim's assistance to pull off his patched buckskin britches.

When he removed the bandage, Tim frowned.

"It doesn't look good." His voice sounded hollow.

"Hurts worse than it looks," Reno said, and jutted his jaw toward the steaming spring. "Help me over there."

Tim sucked in his breath as Reno eased both legs into the hot spring. Well, it wasn't bubbling, so that meant the water was not boiling. Maybe it would not scald the trapper to death. Reno sank in to his armpits and gave Tim a wink and a grin.

"Want to come in?"

Tim's head shook.

"If you reach my age, you'll like it. Indians say some of these springs can cure what ails you."

"It stinks."

"Most medicine does."

While Reno soaked, Tim found a muslin sack in the packs. He emptied its contents—two twists of tobacco, a pouch of beads, and a dried human ear—and returned to the spring. He cut the sack into strips and then soaked them in the water.

"Boy, what are you doing?"

"Making you a fresh bandage for that leg."

"You're a regular surgeon, ain't you." As Tim kept working, the mountain man added, "Smart thinking, though. My leg and I appreciate it."

When it was full dark, and the moon had yet to rise, Jed Reno used his crutch to push himself to his feet. He carried the two Hawken rifles with him, first to the packs the mule had carried, then toward his horse. Tim could not understand how the man, using a makeshift crutch, could handle two rifles, but Reno did, at least until he reached the black's side.

"Come here, boy," he ordered.

Under Reno's direction, Tim took some pelts and secured them with leather cords to the black's four feet. Reno told him that the pelts would cut down on noise—the ground they'd be traveling was hard—and make it hard for anyone to follow him, should he get back.

"Where are we going?" Tim asked.

"I'm going. You're staying." Reno tossed his Hawken to Tim, who caught it as if he had expected it.

"Hold the rifles while I climb up," Reno ordered. "Don't shoot me out of the saddle."

When he was seated, keeping his wounded leg out of the stirrup, he reached for the smaller rifle, which he turned and strapped behind the cantle. His own rifle, he held in his right hand.

"Your crutch?" Tim asked.

Reno shook his head.

"Boy, I'm making a scout. You wait here. If I ain't back before sunrise, I'm dead." He frowned. "Don't look at me like that. It happens to everyone. It'll happen to you one day, but with luck, maybe by then, them britches will fit. If I ain't here, you take the mule and your pinto and ride north and west." He gestured. "Eventually, you'll come to the Yellowstone River. Follow it downstream. Follow it forever. If you're lucky, real lucky, you'll come to the Missouri. Near the confluence, there's a trading post. Called Fort Union. They'll get you back to any kin you might have left."

Tim stiffened and felt his face flushing. "I have kin near here, Reno. If you're not back by sunrise, I'll find them myself."

Reno spit. "Boy, if I ain't back, your sisters and your gal and her ma will likely be put under, too. And if they ain't, they'll all be praying to God that they were."

CHAPTER 34

Over time, the Shoshone River had carved a deep gorge through the granite and sedimentary rock of the sharp rough uplift someone had named Rattlesnake Mountain. As the moon began to rise, Reno rode easily along the bank, watching the canyon looming before him. The river roiled, but it would be worse in the steep canyon.

However, Reno knew he would not reach the canyon. He'd come to Colter's Hell first.

Twice, he stopped and looked down his back trail, thinking that he had heard horses. He didn't think the fool kid would be dumb enough to follow him, but he had not much experience dealing with teenage city boys. If someone was trailing him, they were smart. They had stopped their horses, too.

For fifteen minutes, he waited before deciding that he was just growing old and starting to hear things.

On he rode.

The hot-spring soak had relieved the ache in his leg, but he still kicked free of the stirrup and stretched it out as he rode. The hard climb from the Green River and over those vicious mountains had taken its toll, and the leg remained stiff. Despite how bad it looked before the soak and how awful it felt, he saw no signs of infection. No gangrene. He might live just long enough to be buried with all his body parts intact, unless you count the three or four teeth he had lost in drunken rows—not to mention that missing eye and earlobe.

He smelled the sulfur long before he heard the first boiling pits, and the black snorted its distaste. Vapors rose as he rode between the two cracks in the earth. Ahead of him came a faint twinkling, too low to the ground to be stars. He knew it must be fires.

The horse stopped without Reno pulling on the hackamore.

Knowing horses had an instinct, he sat still in the saddle, looked at the horse and at the dark, eerie ground before him. He climbed from the saddle, remembering the oft-told story about how John Colter had seen a buffalo bull pulled down through the soft, stinking ground. He led the black back to the Shoshone and down to the bank, looping the hackamore around a heavy stone. "Stay here." Taking the extra rifle from behind the cantle, he moved back toward the stinking place.

The vents in the earth whistled, and he moved carefully across the ground, testing often before he stepped. Once his foot started to sink, and he felt the heat burning through the soles of his moccasins, but he stopped before he died like that old buffalo, and backed away, finding another path toward the flickering campfires.

An hour later, he could hear the voices. With his dying breath, Malachi Murchison had spoken the truth. Louis Jackatars was there.

Reno checked his knife, hatchet, and the two rifles. The moon was larger than usual and brighter than it needed to be. But a man could live only so long, Reno figured, as he began crawling over the stinking ground, slowly, carefully, stopping to listen and careful not to head into a boiling pit or come across a geyser as it erupted. He went down an incline and up again, peering at the camp of the half-breed Métis and his rogues.

He frowned and mouthed—but did not speak— the curse on his lips. Jackatars was doing more than getting the Indians blamed for murdering and kidnapping white emigrants. He was fueling the war he intended to start.

Only two men in buckskins were unloading kegs from three mules. At first, Reno thought that the containers were filled with whiskey, but they were being stacked underneath a lean-to, far away from the campfires.

Powder. Gunpowder.

Louis Jackatars barked orders to the men. Reno could have killed the Métis right then, but he knew he would never make it back to Tim Colter alive if he did that. It would also get those women killed.

One of the trappers carrying a keg was clean-shaven, rare for a mountain man. On his head, he wore a red beret. Reno studied the man helping him. With his hooded coat and the way he spoke and carried himself, it had to be Donald Baker. Reno did not know the one in the beret.

So, the Hudson's Bay Company is helping Jackatars with his plan.

That figured. The British wanted the Oregon country for its empire, and Hudson's Bay wanted that trade with the Indians and the furs and whatever else Oregon had to offer.

Keeping out of sight, Reno worked his way down to the camp until he came to a ditch. Stopping, he stared. The fast-flowing water that had carved the ditch smelled as it moved toward the Shoshone River. In front of another lean-to that had been set up near the reeking spring that fed the ditch, he saw the women.

Four of them. A full-grown woman and three kids, although two of those looked like they were practically grown up. He let out a little sigh of relief. All alive. A few yards in front of the lean-to and the women, five men squatted by the fire, but only one of those looked at the women. With curiosity and concern, the rest watched the dancing going on in the center of the camp.

That's where the whiskey kegs were. And the Indians. Blackfeet, all right. Twenty of them. He cursed when Red Coat himself—though his coat had turned pink—stumbled out of the center of the circle, fell to his knees, and crawled to the nearest jug.

Red Coat . . . Donald Baker . . . Louis Jackatars. Three dangerous men.

How many more? Reno did a rough count before he spotted the horses. He looked back at the gunpowder and the ditch. *The ditch. That could be it.*

Sliding back, away from the camp and down a slope, he eventually turned and crawled alongside the ditch. Two feet deep, maybe just as far across. Too small for a man the size of Jed Reno, especially with a bum leg, but . . .

He followed the ditch all the way to the Shoshone. He tested the water that spilled into the river, smelled it, tasted it, and spit out its bitterness.

After reading the moon, he moved along the banks of the river, heading back to his horse. He ran, for the banks of the river would keep anyone in Jackatars's camp—half a mile deep into the basin of geysers and hot pits and poison water—from seeing him. He ran as best he could with the bad leg. Ran until he heard the shout and saw the Indian, silhouetted by the moon, leaping at him.

Reno got only a glimpse of the blade of the knife as it flashed underneath the white moon, but he felt it bury into his side that Malachi Murchison had ripped back at Bridger's Fort so many days before.

The rifles fell to the ground, and Reno knew better than to reach for either one of them. He needed both hands if he wanted to live.

Gritting his teeth, he felt the Siksika brave jerk the knife free. As the hand came down again, Reno reached up with both of his to stop the blade from piercing his heart. The Indian grunted, tried to pull back, and Reno let him do just that. The brave had expected resistance, but Reno went with him and then jerked to his left. Both men slammed onto the ground and rolled through more stinking water as it sped to the river.

The Indian was young, strong. He refused to release his hold on the knife, and Reno didn't have the strength to keep up. He let go. The Indian rolled over, came up, and charged.

His side bleeding, Reno grabbed a smooth stone and threw it as hard as he could.

It caught the Indian in the chest, staggered him, and sent him tumbling to the right. He dropped the knife, but came up to his knees and reached for it. Yelling out a Siksika battle cry, he held it up and then felt the hatchet that Reno threw slam into his chest. The Indian gasped, fell back, and died.

Reno grabbed a fistful of mud and slapped it on his side against the burning knife wound. He crawled to the dead Indian, ripped the medicine pouch from his neck, and slapped it against the side, too. That would have to hold him for a while. He wanted to scalp the Indian, but lacked strength and time. Back he stumbled, stopping only to pick up the two rifles, which he clumsily carried as he wove through the rocks.

He was sweating, and knew the bleeding would not stop, for the Indian had buried that blade deep. Losing his balance, he fell into the river, came up and caught his breath. He had to fish the two rifles from the cold water and drank before he washed the knife wound. It still bled, but the blood was not abnormally dark, so the blade had pierced neither liver nor kidney.

The two rifles he had to use as crutches to push himself to his feet. He felt sick, but kept moving, and when he saw the black where he had left him, he even managed to thank God.

Only then did he see that the black horse was not alone. Six pinto horses stood just to the black's side, partially hidden by the turn in the river. On each horse, sat an Indian, and each Indian held a weapon.

CHAPTER 35

"What?" Instantly, Tim Colter came awake, screaming and pushing himself up only to feel a coarse hand slam against his mouth, cutting off his cry and pushing him back against the robe. He tasted dirt and blood on his tongue. His frightened eyes sought out the man who had him pinned down. He tried to bite the hand only to realize that he couldn't even open his mouth.

His mind raced. What had he been dreaming? It didn't matter. What time was it? Still dark. Where was he? Still along the river by the hot spring. Maybe. It was too dark to tell. Where was Jed Reno?

"Boy."

That answered the latter question. Tim's eyes began to adjust to the night.

"It's me."

The hand still had not moved, at least not until Tim relaxed his muscles when his brain finally emerged from the fog and he recognized the one-eyed trapper's voice.

When the hand withdrew, Tim slowly rose off the robe into a seated position.

Reno muttered something and stood up, the joints in his knees popping. Tim wiped his mouth, spit out the bitter taste, and realized blood covered his palm and lips. He spit again. At first, he thought that Reno's hand had crushed his lips, but on further inspection, he realized he was unhurt.

"Jed?" he called out in an urgent whisper.

No answer. Tim rolled to his feet and followed the shadow that was moving about the mule and packs. He stepped past the hot spring and came to the figure that was lighted slightly by the moon. The waxing moon was not full, but bright enough. Pretty low in the horizon, there were maybe two hours before it set. Three hours, Tim guessed, till sunrise.

The fact that he knew that made him stop to think. He had come a long way from Danville, Pennsylvania. He had come even farther over the past week or two.

Grunting, Reno managed to throw something on the mule's back, but the exertion knocked him to his knees. Tim sprinted to him and refused to let go even when Reno tried to shrug him off, and say that he was fine.

"You're bleeding," Tim said.

"Quiet." Reno relaxed. He took a deep breath and let it out. "All right, boy, here's about the time you grow up. We gotta get your sisters and them gals out of camp—"

"You found it? You found *them*?"

Reno nodded. "But we need to get her done before daybreak."

"You're still bleeding," Tim told him.

"Got stabbed. That's all." Reno said it as if he had been bitten by a mosquito. He gestured toward a dark-colored horse that Tim had not noticed. "But the Indian that done it left us this present."

"But—"

"Time's wasting, boy." Reno made himself stand. "Don't fret over me none. I stitched it up a mite with a needle and some sinew."

"You're still bleeding."

"I'm also still breathing." He gathered the end of a hackamore he had fashioned to the mule and motioned for Tim to follow with the horse that had belonged to the dead Indian . . . well, at least Tim assumed the Indian was dead.

Something was different about Reno, but he could not put a finger on it. He shook off that thought, deciding that the mountain man needed some doctoring in a hurry. "Maybe you should soak in that hot spring again," Tim suggested. Even though the water stank, it did seem to ease Reno's pains earlier.

"No time. We're riding."

Taking advantage of the moon before it sank below the mountains off to the west, Reno and Tim rode hard, the trapper pulling the mule behind him, and Tim guiding the Indian horse—a nutmeg color with two white forefeet and a white star on its head— along behind him. They rode east, and for the most part, followed the river.

Tim lost track of time, but the moonlight soon faded. Reno slowed his horse to a walk, and Tim followed suit, worried sick. They rode past a dead Indian. As the horse he led grew skittish at the smell of death and blood, Tim assumed it was the Indian that Reno had killed. He wet his lips.

Some while later, the mountain man reined in and slid from his saddle. In fact, he slid all the way to his back, groaning and cursing softly. Tim leaped from his horse and raced to the wounded man.

"I'm all right, boy," Reno said as Tim helped him up.

"No—"

"Don't argue. We got to hurry."

Tim realized what was different. "Your hat's gone."

"Yeah."

He thought that Reno must have lost it in the fight when he killed the Indian, but Reno chased that notion away when he said, "And when you see it again, remember, that's a bona fides. Trust him."

"What?" Hardly anything Reno had said since coming back to the hot spring made a lick of sense to Tim.

Suddenly, the sky lighted up all around them.

"Thunderation!" Reno smiled. "Look at that, boy."

Tim turned, amazed at the sights above him. The black sky had turned bright with colors, mostly pale green but with jets of pink, violet, and yellow streaking and flashing and dancing. It was a beautiful, somewhat macabre, pirouette. The lights danced across the sky. Through them, he could see the glow of stars, especially now that the moon had disappeared. His mouth hung open.

"Good sign, I think," Reno said, pulling himself to his feet.

Tim stared. He swallowed. Eventually, he spoke, his voice unsteady. "What . . . is . . . it?"

Reno worked at the rifle behind his cantle as he explained. "An omen of war, some say. Spirits of the dead, say others. Reflections from campfires down here. The Menominee back East believe those are the spirits of great fishermen and hunters. It's actually the Aurora Borealis—the Northern Lights— named after Aurora, the Goddess of the Dawn. You're blessed, boy."

Tim made himself look away.

"We don't have much time."

"How do you know so much?" Tim asked. "Not just about surviving out here, but Greek things and about Indians and . . . ?"

Reno was pointing at another rifle that he had strapped to the mule. Tim hurried to get it.

"Aurora ain't Greek, boy, she's Roman. I disremember her Greek goddess cousin's name. And you know some about those things yourself."

"Well . . ."

Reno made a slight gesture, and Tim knew to check the powder in the rifle's pan.

"You knew about Marathon. I'd never heard of it," he pointed out.

Reno pointed at his eye patch. "You knew about Cyclops. Called me that a time or two."

"I . . . never . . ."

Reno smiled. "You talked a mite in your sleep, boy."

Tim could only give an awkward shrug.

"No more time for gab." Reno pointed at the

horses and mule. "Take the hackamores and secure those mounts to those rocks. Hurry."

"Should I hobble them?"

Reno's head shook. "No. I figure you'll have scarcely enough time to get your hands on the hackamores."

After Tim had completed the task, Reno walked away, holding a rifle in each hand, while gesturing with his head for Tim to follow.

They walked to a stinking gulley where bad water flowed and steamed its way into the river. Tim frowned at the smell, and through the still dancing colorful lights overhead, he studied the ditch.

"It's smaller here, but it'll widen and deepen when you follow it," Reno said.

The rifle Tim held began to feel heavy.

"Just follow it. Don't gag. Don't talk. Stay low. Be quiet. A few places you'll have to crawl along that ditch in that awful water. Don't let it foul your powder, because come daybreak, you'll have need of it. There's gonna come along a disturbance about then. That's when you'll have to move, and move fast."

Tim adjusted the powder horn, and checked his possibles sack to make sure he had plenty of leaden balls. Already, the colorful lights overhead had started to fade.

"Four horses," Reno said. "Well, three horses and a mule is what we got. You have yours. The other three are for that gal you're so sweet on, her ma, and your two sisters. I figure your little sister will have to ride with you. We only got four horses."

Tim's mouth turned dry. His stomach felt queasy,

and not from the stink of the ditch. "W-w-what . . . about . . . you?"

"I won't need a horse, boy. Get moving. Now."

"But—"

Reno silenced him with a wave of his bloody hand. "You remember what I told you? About Fort Union on the Missouri?"

Tim nodded, but he didn't remember doing it. Things were happening too fast. His heart raced, his fingers grew numb, and he felt fear . . . so intense, he kept hearing his mother's screams, telling him to run. He kept wondering if he had run away because his ma told him to or if he ran because he was a coward? Would he run away again? Leave Patricia and his sisters? Leave Jed Reno?

"Follow the Yellowstone . . ." a voice sounded, and Tim realized he had spoken.

Reno nodded. "Follow it forever. Till you reach the Missouri. Then look for the trading post."

"What . . . should we . . . maybe . . . Bridger's place?" Tim asked.

"You got a better chance of living if you head for Union, boy," Reno said. "Remember the hard time we had getting over them mountains."

Tim indicated that he understood. He wanted to say more, to ask Reno another question, another ten or twenty or five hundred questions.

But Jed Reno had turned and hurried off, weaving more, with one arm pressed hard against his side even while carrying a heavy rifle.

Tim blinked once but knew he had to move. He stepped into the ditch, ducked, and began to move to the south, his moccasins splashing in the foul water.

He slipped once, and the nasty water burned his knees and hands. He came up, trying to control his breathing, and wiping the muck off his palms before checking to see that the reeking mud had not ruined his weapon. Satisfied, he moved on, but no longer in such a hurry. He looked off to the east and realized he likely had some time. He also knew better than to splash about in the water.

At some places, he had to turn on his side, inching his way from the bitter water, and the closer he got to camp, the nearer he came to the stinking springs that had carved the ditch. The water grew hotter and hotter, and the odor turned even more nauseating. Grimacing, he fought back the pain, the urge to vomit, or just say that what he was doing was a crazy idea and run back to the river and cleanse off the putrid stench.

The wondrous, colorful lights overhead were gone. What had Reno called them? Northern Lights. The Aurora Borealis? A graying sky had replaced them, and the stars began fading.

Voices sounded from the ground above the ditch. He was nearing the camp. His heart raced. He was nearing Patricia. He was closer to his sisters and Mrs. Scott.

A voice barked from right over his head, and Tim froze as he heard footsteps above him. Another man, farther off, called out something. The footsteps stopped far too close, and the voice answered in French.

Tim held his breath and tried to press his entire body into the near side of the ditch.

"What are you doing?" called one of the raiders from afar.

"Purifying this water," the man above Tim called out, his accent French though the words were English. Water began spraying on the opposite side of the ditch. Yellow water, stinking. The man was relieving his bladder.

The urine splattered on Tim's skunk hat, his forehead, and his nose.

He wanted to cock the hammer on the rifle, but knew better. Any movement would give away his location. He held his breath, knowing that he could not move, blink, or even think.

"Ahhhh." The Frenchman laughed as his footsteps faded away.

Tim felt his heart begin to beat again. He pushed himself a little bit farther and turned his head to see that he had only about ten more yards to go.

He wondered, *Then what?*

Wait, he told himself.

Reno had said there would be a disturbance. What had he said exactly? Tim tried to recall.

"There's gonna come along a disturbance about then."

Tim ran that sentence through his head a couple more times.

A disturbance. Near dawn. All right. But then what was he supposed to do? Reno had not told him that.

Tim kept moving and did not stop until he reached the end of the ditch. The miserable water boiled over from the pit and into the ditch. He kept clear of the poisonous, heated water, and tried to cover his nose and mouth with his left hand.

Already, the sky was light. He could hear voices

around the campground. If anyone came near the ditch, unless he was blind, he would see Tim . . . and kill him.

Wood crackled. Horses snorted. Men laughed and belched and cursed.

Another voice, though sleepy and worn, called out, "Mother."

Tim's heart jumped. It was Patricia Scott.

The next sound he heard was a gunshot.

CHAPTER 36

Hoofs thundered, and above the sound of the galloping horses, Tim Colter heard Jed Reno shout, "Get them home, boy!"

Another shot sounded then the yipping and guttural chants of Indians.

Tim had no plan, no orders other than to get them home, but he knew everything he had to do, everything Jed Reno wanted him—trusted him—to do. The trapper and the kid from back East had not spent much time together, but in that little time, they had developed an understanding.

Tim knew.

Reno knew.

They did not need words or written plans. They acted. They reacted.

Thumbing back the hammer on the rifle, Tim sprang out of the ditch.

"Kill the women!" a man yelled.

Tim did not see the man who yelled, but he saw a

skinny trapper with a red beard and floppy hat charge toward him across the land of bubbling springs and terrible odor. Leaning forward, Tim used the ground to steady his aim The musket kicked, and he climbed out of the ditch, ramming in more powder and shot. "Patricia!" he yelled. "Nancy! Margaret! Mrs. Scott!"

He could not look back toward the lean-to where the women were being held. He stopped loading the rifle, and grabbed the barrel, lifting the weapon and swinging it like a club. It caught another man in buckskins—maybe an Indian, or a half- or quarter-breed—across the skull as he charged Tim with a hatchet. Bone crunched, and the man fell into the boiling pit that fed the ditch. If he was lucky, Tim thought, he was dead before the water scalded off his skin.

Across the camp, Tim watched Reno ride a brown and white pinto he had never seen. His mind flashed. *Where did he get that horse?* Tim watched and marveled as Reno fired a Hawken and then clubbed another man as he rode past, losing hold of the fine rifle as he loped around. Spread out behind him came four—no, five—Indians in nothing but breechcloths and feathers.

Quickly, Tim reloaded the rifle, brought it up, and took aim at one of the Indians closest to Reno.

Tim's mind worked and he held his fire. No. Those Indians were not chasing after Reno. They were riding with him.

Tim shifted his aim, found a man with a hooded coat and a red beret kneeling by a cookfire. He drew

a bead on the hood and squeezed the trigger. The
man straightened, turned, knocking off his red beret.
He had no beard, not even a mustache, and even
though he was at least fifty yards away, Tim could
read the expression of shock in the man's eyes before he fell next to the fire.

"The pony herd, Red Prairie!" That was Reno's
voice. "Run off the ponies!"

"Reno!" came another shout, a yell of pure hatred.

Tim glanced over his shoulder and wet his lips. He
ran, leaping over the boiling pit with the dead body
in it, and handed the rifle and powder horn to Mrs.
Scott.

"Timothy . . ." Her eyes seemed vacant.

"Reload it, ma'am. Quick!"

He grabbed his younger sister, who stared at him
as if he were a ghost, pulled her aside. He wanted to
kiss her, to hug her, to tell her he was sorry for every
bad thing he had ever done to his baby sister. Instead, he pointed to the ditch.

"In the ditch, Margaret. Now!"

She blinked.

Tim saw Patricia, but footsteps sounded behind
him, and he whirled. Two bearded men came at him,
one with a hatchet, the other with a pistol and a
hatchet.

Dropping to his knee, Tim drew the Harper's
Ferry pistol from his belt. The man aimed his flintlock and fired. Tim saw the flash in the pan, the
white puff of smoke from the pistol barrel, and what
seemed like a lifetime later, he felt a tug below the
left armpit of his buckskin shirt. The big pistol

bucked in his hand, and the man who had just shot at him buckled to his knees and fell onto the dirt, writhing in pain.

With the screw-barrel, he shot the man with the hatchet, too, and that one fell back, eyes open but no longer seeing, just ten yards in front of Tim, his sisters, and the Scott women. Shoving both pistols back inside the belt, he moved, picking up Margaret, and carrying her to the ditch.

He tossed her into it, hearing her scream above the din of battle. He remembered the Northern Lights. Reno had said some people considered them a sign of war. Well, the morning gave credence to that theory.

"Timothy!" Margaret called out.

"Follow the ditch!" he screamed. "Run. Run. We're right behind you."

Patricia seemed the first to come out of the trance. She grabbed Nancy's hand, and pulled her out of the lean-to. Tim pointed. He yelled. "Get in the ditch. Get in the ditch."

They came to him, and he helped his sister in first. Another bullet burned his neck, and he felt the blood seeping from the wound, but he did not turn. Did not run. He helped Patricia into the ditch, and saw Nancy already lifting Margaret, and begin carrying her down toward the river, toward the horses, toward safety.

"You son of a—"

Tim turned, just managing to avoid a hatchet blade that would have cleaved his head in two.

The Indian swinging it fell to his knees, but came back with the blade. Tim leaped over it, but lost his footing and fell, hearing the cauldron inside the hole in the earth, feeling the splash of boiling water on his face, and breathing in the wretched odor of the poison spring.

Before he could get up, the Indian was atop him. He'd lost the hatchet, but all he needed was his hands, which locked on Tim's throat. Tim tried to buck him off, but the Indian was tough, wiry, and strong. He grinned, and the fingers tightened, pressing down, about to crush Tim's windpipe.

At least Patricia and my sisters have a chance, Tim thought.

A second later, blood and brains exploded from the Indian's left eye, and the muscles in the Indian's hands relaxed. Tim pushed the arms away and watched the Indian fall to his right and lie still, the one eye still in his head staring sightlessly at the water that fed from the bubbling water into the ditch.

Tim stood up, not bothering to massage his throat. Mrs. Scott was already reloading the rifle. She had shot the Indian in the back of the head, and the ball had exited through the brave's eyeball.

"Get in the ditch, Mrs. Scott." Tim picked up the hatchet the dead Indian had dropped, and spun around at the sound of curses and a whoop from an Indian. He reminded Tim of the ones killed back along the Green River, those who had ridden with the black-faced man named Murchison. Piegans . . . with the high pompadour of black hair.

The brave swung a knife, which Tim just managed to avoid by sidestepping and sucking in his stomach.

Tim swung the hatchet, but the brave somehow managed to parry the blow with the big knife.

They whirled, struck out again, both missing.

"In the ditch, Mrs. Scott!" Tim barked again, backing away from the point of the blade as the Indian lunged. He swung. The hatchet went over the Piegan's head after the Indian ducked.

The knife slashed, and Tim sang out in pain as the blade ripped through the buckskin shirt and carved a furrow across his side. Blood oozed from the wound, but Tim thought that a good sign. It *oozed*. It did not gush.

It did, of course, hurt like hell.

He saw Mrs. Scott bring the rifle to her shoulder, saw her pull back the hammer, then suddenly swing the long gun away from the Piegan. The rifle roared. Tim did not look to see the man she had shot, figuring she had just saved his life again, but if he wanted to keep that life, he needed to kill the brave with the knife.

Hatchet met knife. Both men grunted. They came back, swung, missed, struck again, and Tim saw sparks fly from where the blades struck. Even as he fought, he hoped that Patricia and his sisters were moving as fast as they could through the stinking ditch as Mrs. Scott tried to reload the rifle.

The Indian lunged. Tim backed up, felt his moccasins rub against something—a bunch of cookware—and he stumbled through the empty plates and cups, hearing the clatter of tin above the roar of the battle around him. He cursed, lost his footing, and fell on his backside, figuring that was when his life would end.

His eyes sought out the Piegan and saw him lunging toward him, only to straighten, and stagger back. Tim saw the arrow buried almost to the feather in the Indian's sternum. As the Indian sank to his knees, Tim rolled over and came up.

He expected to see one of the Indians riding with Reno. He figured one of those braves had just saved his life, but it was one of the Blackfeet warriors. He was nocking another arrow on his bow.

The Blackfoot had shot at Tim, but when Tim had fallen over the tinware on the ground, the arrow had slammed into the Piegan Indian. Luck had saved him that time.

The hatchet saved him next time.

He brought it up over his shoulder and then threw it, shattering the warrior's breastplate and chest. The Indian fell backward, and he too, landed into the cauldron of bubbling water.

His screams, Tim thought, would remain in his mind for the rest of his life—which might not last much longer.

He hurried to Mrs. Scott, took the rifle from her hands, and practically shoved her into the ditch. "Follow the ditch!" he screamed again. "There are horses! Near the river. It's your only chance."

She finally understood, turned, and hurried, ducking below the bank and chasing after her daughter and Tim's two sisters.

He had no intention of going after them. He went for Jed Reno, but stopped when he saw him. The pinto he had been riding was on the ground. Three Indians—one in a coat that reminded him of the drawings he had seen of British soldiers from the Revolutionary War—came at Reno, who had a hatchet in one hand.

Without taking his eyes off the opponents, the mountain man sensed Tim staring at him and simply yelled.

CHAPTER 37

"**R**un!" Reno yelled. "Run, Tim! Run!" He held his hatchet in his right hand and a knife in his left as he backed away from Red Coat and two other Blackfoot Indians.

Through the steam rising from the pits, he caught brief glimpses of several things. One of Jackatars's men was screaming, sinking to his thighs in the hellish quicksand, trying to struggle out of the scalding soft dirt. The more he struggled, the deeper he sank. Soon, he would disappear.

A geyser was spraying its steam a good one hundred and fifty feet into the morning sky, spooking a horse and sending its rider flying over the roan's neck.

Several white men in buckskins were running furiously after Red Prairie and two of his fine Cheyenne braves as they ran off the horses and mules. The brigands screamed and cursed, but they kept running away from Colter's Hell, futilely chasing the Cheyenne braves.

All of the women captives had made it into the ditch, disappearing from view, although every now and then, he caught sight of a head or some hair as the girls weaved through the canal.

What pleased Reno most was that he saw Tim Colter. The boy looked at him, and Reno feared he would run into the thick of battle, away from the girls they had traveled so far to rescue.

Yet the boy stopped and listened to Reno's yell. *Run, boy,* Reno silently prayed. *Get them women folks out of here.*

Tim Colter was no coward, but he knew his duty. He jumped into the ditch and followed the girls.

Good, Reno thought. *Now back to the business at hand.* He did not see the Hudson's Bay Company man, Donald Baker, nor Louis Jackatars, and knew he could not look for them until he killed Red Coat and his men.

The old Indian's knife came at him, but Reno leaped back. The blade cut only the nasty-smelling air. A brave thrust his lance, but Reno ducked underneath it, bringing his hatchet up and knocking the brave off balance. At the same time, he swung his knife in a wide arc, watching Red Coat and the other Indian leap back.

Reno's side ached. It still bled. Yet he did not feel weak. Fact was, he figured he had never felt more alive.

Red Coat barked out a short batch of orders, and all three Indians spread out, causing Reno to grin. They knew his shortcomings. His one good eye limited his peripheral vision, but he had a plan that might circumvent Red Coat's attack. He shifted the knife in his left hand and let it fly.

Red Coat yelled something, but too late. The brave with the spear turned too late, and Reno's knife struck him in the center of his chest. He fell back, dropping the lance at his feet, bringing both knees up, and dying like that.

That started the ball, just as Reno had expected.

He swung the hatchet to parry the blows from Red Coat and the remaining Indian. Sparks flew as iron met iron, and Reno backed up. He felt a rifle ball whistle past his head. He did not know if that had been a stray shot or if someone else had joined in on the fun—but from a relatively safe distance. He knew two of the Cheyenne warriors had remained behind, covering Red Prairie as he and the others stole the livestock. They could still be around . . . if, Reno thought, they weren't killed already.

Red Coat lunged, but Reno sidestepped the point of the Indian's knife. In the corner of his one eye, he caught sight of the other Indian, who had grabbed his bow and was reaching back to find an arrow.

"Coward." Reno swung the hatchet at Red Coat's head and watched him duck and dive onto the wet earth. He threw the hatchet, and it slammed into the throat of the other Indian just as he brought the bow up.

As the blood sprayed, Reno leaped back from Red Coat's knife.

The old Blackfoot grinned as he saw Donald Baker charging across the camp, leading two of Jackatars's renegades. Knowing he had to act fast, Reno did the unthinkable.

Unarmed, he charged Red Coat.

Confused, the old chief stopped and turned back. Reno rammed his shoulder high up on the Indian's chest. The Blackfoot grunted, and Reno felt the knife cut into his shoulder and back as they fell onto the soft ground. Quickly, Reno rolled over and dived to his right.

Old as he was, Red Coat had not lost his senses, nerve, or quickness. He came up to his knees, realized Reno's intentions, and switched his grip on the knife to throw it. A split second later, Reno picked the lance up off the ground and hurled it, piercing the Indian's heart.

Red Coat died instantly, with a snarl on his lips and a knife in his hand—died in battle the way he would have wanted it.

Before the old Blackfoot fell, Reno was up and running toward the lean-to. He passed another dead Indian, and leaned over to snatch up the Blackfoot's stone-headed war ax. A bullet dug through the sand in front of him. Another grazed his thigh.

Ahead of him, a white man with a gray beard stepped out of the lean-to, raised his Hawken, and fired. The ball whistled over Reno's head, and the man stopped to reload, butting the Hawken on the ground, fetching the ramrod, and spilling powder onto the ground.

He had the rifle loaded and primed, and even managed to cock the hammer before Reno brained him with the ax. Jackatars' man fell dead, and Reno tried to grab the Hawken, but it slipped from his fingers and landed on the ground. He cringed, expecting the weapon to discharge, but it did not. Another shot slammed through his left hand, and he cried out in pain. Still holding the war club in his right, he went to the nearest keg and smashed it twice, spilling powder as the keg rolled over. He smashed another.

And knew he was out of time.

Donald Baker and two men came at him, but their weapons were empty, although one desperately tried to reload his pistol.

Reno killed the third man with the war club, smashing his skull with a sickening crunch. He ducked underneath the hatchet Baker swung, and brought his right foot up into the Hudson's Bay man's groin. Baker grunted, gasped and tried not to sink but could not stop himself. As he went to his knees, Reno smashed the man's face with his mangled left hand.

Down went Baker—only temporarily, Reno knew—and the one-eyed wonder turned toward the other man. He was bringing down a knife from well over his head in a killing thrust, but Reno reached out and grabbed the man's right hand with his two hands. Reno's left hand screamed in pain, bleeding, one or two bones broken more than likely from the ball, but he still managed to stop the blade about a foot from his face.

Purposefully, Reno fell backwards, bringing up his knees, and rolling. He shoved with hands and feet, and the man somersaulted over, screaming, landing with a splash as the boiling hot spring silenced his cries.

Reno came to his knees. Baker was trying to come to his feet. Reno looked at the ground, hoping to find a rock or some other weapon, but saw nothing so he rammed his head into the Hudson's Bay man's face. The nose gave way, as did his lips and a few teeth. Both men went down, and Reno came up.

He could not understand where the strength came from, but he was lifting Donald Baker over his head, heaved, and watched the British felon crash against the kegs of gunpowder. Rolling kegs buried the unconscious man, and Reno moved toward the loaded Hawken.

He stopped, his chest heaving, his body bleeding from a number of wounds.

"I will kill you myself," Louis Jackatars said.

Reno said nothing.

Jackatars called out in French and in the Métis tongue. He called for help, but there was no one to hear him. Most of his men were unconscious, dead, dying, or running away, trying to catch up with the horses that Red Prairie had stolen.

"I thought"—Reno had trouble catching his breath—"you wanted . . . to do me . . . yourself."

Jackatars spit.

Reno grinned. "Now you got to." He backed up, lowering his hands, and said in a dry whisper, "If you can." He leaped back from the sawed-off saber the half-breed swung.

The blade was about two feet long. It was the only weapon Jackatars had. But Jed Reno had none. Nothing . . . but his wits.

Again the blade came, but Reno dodged it. Jackatars thrust, and it would have killed the one-eyed trapper had not the Métis devil tripped over the powder horn dropped by the dead man with the Hawken. Reno looked at the Hawken, but it seemed too far away for him to reach. He kicked out at Jackatars's face, but the bad man recovered quickly and almost chopped off Reno's foot with the saber.

Reno came back as Jackatars sprang to his feet. He was a quick man. He had always been quick and deadly. He grinned and tossed the pig-sticker to his other hand. Reno belted the breed in the nose.

Down went Jackatars, screaming, but still gripping the saber in his hand. Reno lunged, stopped, and leaped back as the breed's weapon came close to gutting him.

Jackatars leaped to his feet, sliced once, twice, three times, then stopped to spit out blood and wipe his face with his free hand.

The half-breed swore . . . in English.

Reno ducked underneath the arcing saber. Both men came up to catch their breaths, and that gave Reno just enough time to work up saliva in his mouth.

He spit into the breed's bloodied face.

Enraged, Jackatars raised the saber high over his head and brought it down. Reno sidestepped it and reached out with both hands. Somehow, he managed to latch onto Louis Jackatars's other arm, and turning in a semicircle, he swung the breed around in a crazy dance. He let go and watched Jackatars fly into the lean-to just as Donald Baker was coming to and pushing a keg away.

Swinging the breed sent Reno to his hands and knees. He heard the crash of Jackatars against Baker and the kegs and came up on his knees, blinked, and saw six more of Jackatars's men running toward him. They were a mix of Blackfeet Indians and white brigands, and all were armed with rifles or muskets.

"Plenty Medicine!" Jackatars came to his feet among

the barrels of gunpowder. He heard the footfalls of the charging men, turned and saw them, and faced Reno again with an evil grin shining through the blood and dirt.

Reno dived to the Hawken. He had only one chance. No chance, really. One shot. That, with God's luck, would kill Jackatars, Baker, maybe the charging men.

And probably Reno himself.

He rolled over, gripped the Hawken, lifted it only slightly.

"No!" cried Jackatars. *"Mon Dieu!"*

Laughing, Jed Reno squeezed the trigger.

CHAPTER 38

Just as Tim Colter stepped out of the ditch and saw the flowing river, the horses and mule left there, and just when he thought that he and Patricia and the others might get out of there alive . . . the earth rumbled and shook, causing him to fall to his knees.

The explosion deafened him. He pushed himself up, turning back to look toward Colter's Hell.

Hell, indeed.

He thought the basin had erupted like a volcano, for smoke and flames rose high in the morning air. More explosions followed, echoing across the river as smoke curled into the air. He turned quickly toward the livestock and yelled, "Grab those horses!" He heard nothing, though, nothing but the rumble of the earth, yet Patricia grabbed two hackamores, Mrs. Scott another, and Nancy was sliding on her knees, waiting to release the mule's rope until it finally stopped kicking and squealing.

Tim started to help, but stopped abruptly and

brought up his rifle, even though he had not found time to reload it.

A young Indian was mounted on a fine black and white horse, his braids blowing in the wind. He, too, looked in awe and terror at the smoking and fiery land off to the north.

Margaret screamed. Patricia and Mrs. Scott stepped back, but kept their hold on the horses. Nancy scooted to the other side of the mule.

Tim lowered the rifle and reached for his knife.

The Indian turned away from the fire and smoke and held out something. Tim sucked in a deep breath. It was Jed Reno's hat.

Tim's first thought was that the Indian had killed the one-eyed trapper, but his brain still worked, and he remembered what Jed had told him earlier. That his hat was his bona fides. Whatever that had meant.

The Indian stuffed the hat under his bone breast-plate and pointed off to the north. He said words Tim could not understand, and for all Tim had learned during his time with Reno, sign language was not one of them.

But he understood. He could not hear anything anyone said, but it seemed as if Reno was speaking to him. Reno's voice came to him clear as a bell.

"Mount up. Everybody on a horse." Tim went to help his younger sister. "Margaret. You get on behind me."

The Indian swung from his horse and hurried to Mrs. Scott, who backed away from him, screaming and cursing.

"It's all right!" Tim told her. "He's a . . . friend."

Mrs. Scott's face turned white as the Indian came

to her, and helped her onto the horse's back. Tim boosted Patricia onto the dead Indian's horse. She said something, but, again, Tim could not make out her words. Nancy managed to climb onto the mule without any assistance.

The Indian barked words again as he leaped onto his pony's back.

Tim found his horse, but did not mount it until he had reloaded the rifle and his two pistols.

The Indian gestured again, and Tim nodded, pointing to the north. "You lead." He told the girls, "Follow him."

Patricia looked at him once and then pulled on the hackamore to turn the horse.

He watched them ride off as his heart sank.

Another explosion rocked the world and caused his horse to turn in a circle.

"Easy," Tim told him, and once the mount had calmed down, he looked at the ugly smoke-filled sky.

"Jed," his voice croaked. "Oh . . . Jed." He did not cry. He figured he had no tears left in him.

"Run," Jed had told him. "Run, Tim. Run." Just like his ma had told him. Save yourself, had been her thinking. Save the girls had been Jed's.

Fort Union, Tim told himself. He would not look back at the burning hell. He saw the Indian and the girls crossing the river, nudged his horse into a walk, and followed them.

Once across the river, they kicked their horses into a lope. Tim did not look back as they rode away from Colter's Hell.

*   *   *

When the moon rose, Tim tightened the cinch in his saddle. The Indian tossed him a leather pouch, which he opened, spooned out a handful of the greasy mixture, and stuffed it into his mouth. Wiping his hands on his buckskins, he walked over to his younger sister first and held the bag out toward her.

"What . . . is it?" Margaret asked.

"Pemmican. Good for you."

"It stinks."

"Eat it. We're riding."

"But—" Seeing the look in Tim's eyes, she choked back whatever excuse or argument she had been about to say and grabbed a handful of the mixture. She ate.

He let Nancy have some, too. His older sister stared at him blankly, questions forming on her lips, but she had no strength to ask—which suited him fine enough. He wasn't sure he wanted to talk.

Mrs. Scott ate the pemmican without a word. She just kept staring at the Indian as he watered the mounts.

Tim went to Patricia Scott last.

"Tim," was all she could say . . . at first.

"We'll ride out," he said.

"We've ridden all day."

He nodded. "I know. Know it's hard on you. But we have to keep moving."

She chewed the pemmican and blinked. Her lips moved, but no words came. Finally, she shook her head in disbelief. "Tim . . . is it . . . really . . . you?"

He smiled, reached out, and took her hand in his own. "Yeah, it's me."

"We thought . . . you were . . . dead."

He had an answer for that, but he knew she would not understand. He merely smiled and squeezed her hand, although what he really wanted to do was take her in his arms and kiss her. That, he knew, would be wrong.

The girls . . . women . . . had been through hardships no one should ever have to face. They were fragile. It would take them a long time to recover, and he could not imagine the hell they had been through, riding all that time with the likes of those blackguards. The farther they rode from Colter's Hell, the closer they got to Fort Union, the better off they would be.

The Indian had finished watering the horses. He swung onto his pony's back, and his head thrust off toward the east.

"Time to ride," Tim said, and heard the women moaning, but they moved. They mounted. They rode after the Indian, and Tim trailed them, every so often looking back, hoping to find Jed Reno.

He saw only the night.

What he had wanted to tell Patricia Scott was that he *had* died. He'd been lost, dead spiritually and mentally, and soon to be dead physically. Then he had met a one-eyed mountain man named Jed Reno.

He remembered talking to—Tim grinned—the Cyclops. *"How long have you lived here?"*

"I was born here, boy."

Reborn. That's what Reno had later said. At that time, Tim had not understood what the trapper was talking about, but now he did. For Tim Colter had been reborn in these mountains. He had found himself.

As he rode, Tim realized he had been wrong about something, though. Thinking of Jed Reno, he reached up and brushed away a tear. He could cry after all. The tear rolled through the fuzz that might become a beard . . . if he ever filled the dead man's britches he wore.

Tim heard the thundering of hooves and brought up the gun. *Buffalo,* he thought. He hurried with the Indian to the horses and mule. They grabbed the hackamores and watched the dust rising.

Not buffalo, Tim realized, but horses.

He thought they were running wild, for he had heard stories of wild mustangs running across this country—indeed, he had even seen a few from afar—but these, he soon realized, were being driven. By Indians.

The Indian boy grinned with excitement and said something that Tim did not understand.

He looked back at the women. "It's all right," he told them. "More friends."

I hope.

He figured it out without sign language or reading the Indians' minds.

They had been the ones riding with Jed Reno when they attacked Louis Jackatars's camp. They had stolen the horses and mules, leaving the men—if any survived the horrendous explosion—afoot. Horses, Tim had learned, meant wealth in most Indian cultures. Those Indians would return to their lodges with much, much wealth.

Maybe that's why they had ridden with Reno. Maybe he had bribed them.

Tim frowned. Even though he knew it was rude, he turned his back on the Indians as they talked their grunts. He went to the women, who still feared Indians. Feared everything. He tried to steady his breathing, tried to dam the tears that wanted to flow down his face like a waterfall.

Patricia Scott stood at his side and put a hand on his shoulder. "Tim?" she said softly. "What is it?"

He sniffed, wiped away a tear, shook his head.

"Tim."

His voice cracked. "It ain't fair. Indians get . . . rich. I get . . . you and my sisters. Jed . . . Jed . . . Jed Reno. He saved us all. And he's . . . dead."

She pulled his head onto her shoulder, and he sobbed once and then felt her hands on his dirty, long, greasy hair.

"Boy."

Tim jerked away from Patricia, startling her, and he turned to the voice he thought he had imagined.

Jed Reno staggered toward him, pulling a big horse behind him. "You look peaked, boy."

Tim blinked. Wiped his eyes. His mouth hung open.

"Is this the gal you're sweet on?" Reno asked, and Tim could not even blush. "By Jupiter, boy, I'd be sweet on her, too, even if I'm partial to Crow squaws."

Tim could not help himself. "Jed!" he screamed at the top of his lungs, and ran, leaping into the mountain man.

Reno grunted and cursed. "Don't kill me, boy. I didn't survive that scrape in Colter's Hell to get killed by my pard."

When Tim let go, Reno tugged on the hackamore to the big horse. "Recognize this elephant, boy?"

Tim blinked. It was his pa's prized Percheron stallion.

"The explosion?" Mrs. Scott asked.

Reno sipped the tea he had brewed out of something the women did not want to know.

"Touched off the gunpowder Jackatars and that Hudson's Bay rogue meant to give the Blackfeet scoundrels."

"But how"—Tim shook his head—"how did you survive?"

Reno grinned. "They don't call me Plenty Medicine for nothing, boy. That ditch. I rolled into it." He touched his buckskins, one sleeve and leggings blackened and burned by the blast. Much of his beard and hair on that side of his body, likewise, had been singed. "I figured I'd just follow your trail. Catch up to you at Fort Union."

"Afoot?" Tim asked in wonderment.

"Boy. I'm a free trapper. I don't really need no horse." Reno sipped tea and stretched his legs out before the fire. "But Red Prairie"—he gestured at one of the Indians—"he come back. Good Cheyenne, Red Prairie. They's good people. Hate to say goodbye to them."

"Good-bye?" Nancy asked.

Reno nodded. "Well, they're headed for their village. I figured we'd go our own way. Your way."

"Fort Union," Tim said.

"Fort Union?" Reno chuckled. "Why on earth would you want to go that far? Boy, I thought y'all was bound for Oregon."

CHAPTER 39

Tim laughed. He was about to step up to Jed Reno and give that great big, grizzled, one-eyed, hard-as-granite Cyclops a hug when a terrifying war cry filled the air. Tim and Reno whirled toward the sound.

Another figure rode up, reining a lathered horse to a stop at the crest of a hill just to the south. "Let us finish the fight!" the rider called out.

Tim heard Patricia's gasp.

The rider on a big black horse yelled, "Come, Reno. I shall put you under!"

Tim did not recognize the man, but he was big, with dark hair and a full beard, wearing what remained of a fur cap atop his head. He had to be one of Jackatars's men.

Tim's stomach heaved. *Just when I thought everything was over . . .*

Reno spit. "Well, I reckon this affair ain't quite done. At least, not until I kill Dog Ear Rounsavall."

The name made Tim wince. He could not make out the rider's face from that distance, but he could picture the man clearly—the face and the figure that had haunted Tim's sleep for so long, the evil Goliath in buckskins who had split his mother's head with a tomahawk. A feeling rose in Tim's chest that he had never known.

Hate.

The one-eyed trapper picked up his Hawken rifle and walked to his horse.

Tim stopped him.

"Jed, this is my fight."

Reno's eye filled with fury. "Boy!" he snapped, pointing the barrel of his rifle toward the waiting giant of a killer. "That there's Dog Ear Rounsavall. He's a holy terror, maybe even worse than that cur-dog cutthroat Louis Jackatars. Maybe he's the devil himself. It's time someone planted him, and I figure I'll be the one to do it. That scoundrel has killed—"

"My mother," Tim said.

For once, Jed Reno couldn't think of anything to say.

"Remember my nightmare?" Tim asked. "That time . . . you told me that I'd have to kill more folks, if I wanted to live. Remember?"

Reno's head moved slightly. He started to speak, stopped, looked again at the waiting Dog Ear Rounsavall, and tried again. "I reckon you done your share of killing back at Colter's Hell, Tim. This here be my fight."

Tim shook his head. "No. It's mine." Without waiting for any more argument, he tugged on the old horse pistol, checked the powder in the pan, and then did the same with the screw-barrel .45. He shoved both inside the sash and walked to his own horse.

"Tim!" Patricia Scott ran to him.

"Patricia." He dreaded this, remembering the spring in Independence when he had kissed her, practically promised to marry her . . . someday. He remembered how he had felt after the attack on their camp at South Pass, wondering if he would ever see her again. Now he feared she might cry, and that might weaken his resolve.

Still, he stopped, turned, and told her, "This is something I have to do."

"I know." She smiled and kissed him on the cheek. "Good luck. God be with you."

"By Jupiter, boy!" Jed Reno called out. "Haul off and kiss her back. For luck. Don't keep Dog Ear waiting."

Grinning, Tim kissed Patricia on the lips. It might not have been as electric as that kiss had been back in Missouri, but he felt contented. If something happened in the next few minutes, if Dog Ear Rounsavall somehow managed to kill him, well, at least he had kissed Patricia Scott one more time. At least he would die knowing he had been loved . . . by his girl . . . by his sisters . . . by his parents . . . and even by that one-eyed Cyclops who had saved his life, taught him how to survive and how to live.

By Jupiter.

As a strange silence descended on the country, Tim tightened the cinch on the saddle, checked his weapons one last time, and swung onto the horse's back. He kicked his mount into a walk and rode to meet the awaiting Dog Ear Rounsavall.

He laughed when Tim reined up. "You send a boy

to do your fighting, Reno?" Dog Ear Rounsavall called out, adding a few curses in French and English.

"Boy's man enough to kill you, Dog Ear!" Reno yelled back. "But don't wet your britches, you damned rapscallion. I won't let the boy scalp you. I'll save that pleasure for myself."

The French renegade cursed again as his horse fought the hackamore, dancing, feeling the approaching danger, the death in the air. He kicked the horse and thundered toward Tim Colter.

Tim waited, counted to five, and kicked his horse's sides hard. The mount exploded into a gallop. He could see the big man with the black beard and short braids. He could feel the wind blasting his face. Death he could taste. Yet somehow, Tim Colter felt no fear.

Letting loose of the hackamore, Tim drew both pistols.

"Tim!" cried out his sisters and Mrs. Scott. Patricia sucked in a deep breath. Jed Reno wondered if his heart would stop.

The thundering horses came closer. Dog Ear Rounsavall dropped his hackamore and brought up his Hawken to his shoulder.

"Not yet, boy," Reno said softly. By Jupiter, he realized he was sweating and he wasn't the one dueling with that sorry, low-down killer. "Wait," he whispered. "Wait till you're in range."

Reno remembered all those stories he had heard— and a few he had even read—about the Middle Ages and the knights and jousting. Mostly, though, he remembered that time on the Green, all those years ago, when a strapping young kid well on his way to becoming a man had dueled Joseph Chouinard in that Rendezvous.

"Waghhhh!" Reno shouted. He raised his Hawken over his head, cheering on the boy he had taught, the kid making him proud as a peacock.

Dog Ear's Hawken roared, answered immediately by Tim Colter's big pistol. White smoke blocked out horses and riders for a moment as Tim's sisters screamed and Mrs. Scott let out a gasp and a prayer. Patricia stood with her hands clasped, watching the smoke.

One horse galloped on, riderless. To the south, Tim Colter and his mount appeared out of the cloud of smoke. He tossed one smoking pistol away and leaned forward, grabbing the hackamore. He turned the horse—as if he had been born in the saddle—and loped back toward where the wind was carrying off the gunsmoke.

Dog Ear Rounsavall staggered, hatless and no longer holding the Hawken he had fired, yet still very much alive. He stepped back and drew his tomahawk in his right hand and that razor-sharp knife in his left. He yelled French insults at Tim, who kicked the horse hard, lowering himself as he approached the giant, the killer, at a gallop.

"Tim!" his sisters screamed.

"By Jupiter," Jed Reno called out. "That boy has growed up to be a hell of a lot like me. Only a damned sight better!"

Dog Ear Rounsavall threw the tomahawk, which sailed harmlessly over Tim's back. The screw-barrel .45 boomed—definitely not as loud as the bigger pistol—and Dog Ear Rounsavall spun around, falling to his knees as Tim rode past him.

Again, Tim pulled the horse around and rode back, slowing to a trot, then a walk before he reined up right behind Dog Ear Rounsavall.

Echoes of horses and gunshots died away. The sisters, the Scott women, and Jed Reno watched as Tim kicked a foot loose from the stirrup, planted his left foot against the back of Dog Ear Rounsavall, and shoved.

The Frenchman fell on his face and did not move again.

Slowly, Tim Colter wheeled his horse around.

"Let's see if that boy remembers everything I taught him," Reno said, speaking mostly to himself.

Sure enough, Tim rode back to pick up the first pistol he had fired and dropped. He swung from the saddle, blew off the dust, checked the action, and reloaded it. He reloaded the screw-barrel. Finally, after climbing back into the saddle, Tim loped toward his sisters, Mrs. Scott, Reno, and a beaming Patricia.

"That's my boy." Reno shook his head and laughed. "Be back directly, folks." He strode toward the corpse of Dog Ear Rounsavall.

Jed Reno was a man of his word. He would lift that dead man's scalp. Then he would come back to the camp, and tell those womenfolk all about Kit Carson and the time he had dueled Joseph Chouinard. That was one for the legends.

Reno had seen both fights and the way he figured things . . . Tim Colter had just topped it.

* * *

Reno grimaced when he saw the furrow Dog Ear's shot had carved across Tim's head. Mrs. Scott and all those women were pampering that boy too much, fretting over how the wound might get infected, how Tim had almost gotten his brains blown out, how . . . how . . . how . . .

Reno made his way to the kid, grabbed his head, turned it, and stared at the wound. "It ain't deep, ladies. Boy's cut hisself worse shaving. Or will . . . once he starts shaving." He looked at the wound closer, then let the women finish their pampering. "Might leave a scar, though."

"You think so?" Tim called out, excited.

Reno grinned. Tim Colter was all grown up in some ways, but he was still a kid.

The mountain man just shook his head. "Let's get you folks to Oregon."

CHAPTER 40

More and more emigrants kept crowding up the country, Jed Reno thought, as he watched Tim Colter help his sisters and the Scott women into the back of one of those ugly prairie schooners. Behind the Conestoga trailed the big Percheron. Tim had told Reno he could keep the stallion, but Reno said he didn't ride elephants.

Conestogas were meant to haul supplies. The emigrants walked. Usually. But after all those women had been through, another train bound for the Willamette Valley had agreed to take the Scotts and Colters along. They had chipped in to buy an abandoned wagon from Jim Bridger. Some of those wayfarers, dumb as they were as city folks, did show decency. Bridger had a sentimental side, too. He had taken a loss when he sold that prairie schooner.

Colter walked from the wagon, and Reno sucked in a breath. The kid held out his right hand. Reno stared at it.

"Reckon this is good-bye, Jed," the boy said.

"You must be joshing me, boy. Out here is where you belong. Knowed that the moment I first laid eyes on you." Reno lifted his hand and gripped the boy's firmly. Feeling a strange thing in his own eyes, he pulled the kid close and squeezed him in a bear hug. "But . . . I reckon . . . if I had a gal as pretty as that, I might take up growing apples or tilling the land or teaching school."

Tim stepped back.

"But you get bored, boy, you light out here. We'll find us beaver. Live the life. But don't do it, boy, till them duds you got fit."

"I'll remember that, Plenty Medicine."

Reno grinned. "I know you will, son."

They shook again, hugged one last time, and then Reno sat down on a barrel next to Jim Bridger. He watched the boy climb into the saddle of his pinto. The wagon master barked out his command, and the oxen began pulling the prairie schooners. Tim rode out ahead with the scout, Carroll Smith. He wasn't quite as good as Just Jenkins when it came to scouting—and had lost that stupid bet that Malachi Murchison would kill Reno in that fight all those weeks ago—but he could get the train to Oregon, even if he did not have Jenkins's experience. Or Bridger's. Or Reno's. By thunder, Smith had not come to the mountains to be born until '37. Or maybe it had been '36.

Reno grunted and fetched his pipe and tobacco. Beside him, Jim Bridger was already smoking. They watched the oxen and the prairie schooners and the emigrants walking along. And the Percheron stallion trailing the Colters' Conestoga. They watched the dust.

Bridger said, "Jug's at your feet, Jed."

Reno picked it up. "I know."

"Well, I'm thirsty if you ain't."

"I am a mite parched." Reno took a slug and handed the jug to Bridger.

Bridger drank.

They drank. They smoked. They watched.

When the last wagon on the train had been swallowed by dust, and the jug was half empty, Bridger tapped the bowl of his pipe against a wooden log of his trading post. "Jed, what makes a boy like that want to settle down and become a farmer"—he spit—"in Oregon?"

"Can't say I know for sure, Jim, but I expect it's of the female variety." Reno sloshed the contents around in the jug, took another sip, and handed it to his friend.

"That kid be a mite puny, Jed. You reckon he will ever grow into 'em duds?" Bridger passed the jug to Reno, who set his pipe down, took a healthy swallow, and placed the jug on the ground between them.

Reno found his pipe, had to relight it, and drew deep on the steam, savoring the taste of real tobacco. He couldn't see Tim Colter anymore. Couldn't even seen the train. Maybe because of the dust. But maybe the tears in his one eye had something to do with that, too.

He smiled.

"Jim, them duds fit that boy. And they have for some time."

TURN THE PAGE FOR A RIP -ROARING PREVIEW!

**JOHNSTONE COUNTRY.
WHERE BOOT HILL IS FULL OF MEN WHO
PULLED THEIR TRIGGERS WITHOUT AIMING.**

As hardworking families and ambitious dreamers set down roots across the American West, others swooped down to prey upon them. And after the smoke cleared, those who lived by the gun found themselves facing justice—and vengeance . . .

It was supposed to be a simple robbery. A fortune in gold for the taking. What Hack Long and his outlaws hadn't figured on was the Texas Rangers pouncing on them like a pack of rabid wolves. Desperate to escape, Long led his men south of the Rio Grande, where they ran afoul of Mexican Rurales and were imprisoned.

Unwilling to die behind the bars of the hellish prison where life is worth less than a peso . . . Long's band of desperadoes break out of jail and split up to escape. Now, Two-Horses, Luke Fischer, Gabriel Santana, Billy Lightning, and Long are scrabbling along a desolate landscape, heading for Texas to reclaim their ill-gotten gains, hunted by dogged lawmen, merciless Comanches, and a violent gang of bandits who also want the stolen gold.

Though they be thieves and outlaws, Long and his men aren't nearly as deadly as their pursuers. They may not deserve forgiveness for their sins, but only death passes judgment on both the good and the bad. . .

Chapter 1

The bare prison courtyard deep in Coahuila, Mexico, was hot as hell's foyer, and Hack Long would have given anything to be somewhere cooler. Dirt and rocks packed by decades of hooves and human feet reflected the desert sun's rays back against the brick, rock, and adobe buildings, making the enclosure feel like a massive oven.

He sat on the ground in a sliver of shade with his back to the rough exterior wall, chewing at a tough piece of meat that could have come from a cow, bear, horse, donkey, or wolf. Dog, for all he and the others knew. He'd eaten plenty of dog in Two-Horses' village over the past few years, when they were in the Indian Nations.

It didn't matter. The plain, familiar stew was nourishment and they all needed to keep up their strength for the next struggle to survive that was sure to come. Bland food was strange down in Mexico, because the smell of onions, peppers, and spices wafting from the *comandante*'s office and the adjoining guard's barracks made their stomachs rumble several times a day.

He and the boys figured the grub they brought to them was boiled up well before anything else was added, other than the salt needed for the prisoners to survive, providing another form of punishment for all those locked up in that hellhole. Only on Sundays were their tortillas and beans flavored with *nopales* and chilis so hot they seemed to be an added punishment instead of a treat.

Hack and the hard-eye boys with him ate every bite of whatever the Mexicans dished and were proud to get it. They had to stay strong, because only the fit could survive in a world of bandits, murderers, and thieves.

There were two kinds of men in *Purgatoria.* Predators and prey. Sometimes Hack was of the mind that only the wicked survived, while the dead were finally released from the tribulations that delivered them to dry graves outside the penitentiary with startling regularity.

The Long gang, as they were known both inside and out of the prison, long ago proved capable of protecting themselves, but it was essential they continued to project a sense of menace worse than what they'd been dragged into.

That made them harder men than when they stumbled through the gates of the Mexican prison in chains. None of them were without scars, and over half of those they shared were earned in attacks and fights that usually resulted in the deaths of the instigators.

With only fifteen minutes to eat before going back

to the copper mines, though it always seemed much shorter, Luke Fischer lowered himself to the hard ground beside the gang leader and adjusted his position to keep an eye on the other prisoners. "You feel it?"

"I do." Jaws aching, Hack shifted the tough piece of meat to the other cheek and chewed some more.

One of the newer inmates with a wispy mustache passed the American prisoners, looking with dead eyes for a safe place to eat from those wolves who stole food. Swift attacks to take the weaker men's twice-a-day allotment usually spilled more than they gained. The slender young man named Escobedo had only been there for a week, and in those few days he'd lost half of his portions, as well as his shoes.

Eyes glassy with hunger, work, and fear, he sat only a dozen feet from the *norte americanos* and wolfed down his meal. Two fresh cuts from an altercation the night before marred the smooth skin over one eyebrow and the opposite cheekbone.

Andelacio Morales rose from where he squatted with a clot of other prisoners near the long row of cells and swaggered across the bare yard. Hack couldn't *stand* that man because he stank so bad. That's part of why he and the boys steered clear of him whenever possible.

He was also the worst, most black-hearted human being Hack had ever seen. Morales's worn-out shoes crunched on the gravel and yard packed hard by decades of footsteps. Even the hot air stilled as the man towered over Escobedo, who kept his eyes lowered to the tin plate between his knees. Escobedo seemed to collapse inward as his spirit vanished. Hack sensed that he wished to sink into the ground.

Morales towered over Escobedo and spoke to him in Mexican. "Your portion."

The younger man quickly tilted the bowl and swallowed without chewing. His Adam's apple bobbed as he swallowed, and Hack wondered how he got any of that gristle down without chewing.

Morales's face twisted. "The rest of that's mine."

Like a child, Escobedo twisted sideways to protect the bowl until he could get the last mouthful.

For the past several months, the Long gang stayed out of the trouble that swirled around them like a *chiindii*, the Navajo word for dust devils. That's what those little fights in the yard reminded him of, the skinny twisters of sand that walked across the desert floor. Those kinds of fights were as common in *Purgatoria* as breathing.

Knowing what was coming next, he put down his empty bowl and rose, using only the muscles in his stout legs. The corners of his eyes tightened and Hack wondered why he was getting involved in someone else's business.

It didn't matter, that familiar tingle in his head rose with a hum. There were some things in this world the wanted outlaw wouldn't tolerate, and one of them was people who preyed on other, weaker men. The red tinge at the edges of his vision would soon narrow down to a tunnel with only Morales at the end. It had happened more times than Hack or his best friend Luke cared to admit.

He shifted over to make Morales see a fresh target, rather than his young victim. "Go away and leave him alone."

The hulk of a man didn't take his eyes off Escobedo and the tiny bit of food left in the wooden bowl. "I'm not talking to you, *gringo.*"

Across the yard, Juan Perez perked up. From the corner of his eye, Hack saw the head guard grin at the incident boiling to life in the hot sun. That evil man liked nothing better than watching a good beating, and didn't give a whit about who was on the wrong end.

When he was a young man, Hack's old daddy always said to get the first lick in on a fight, and to use anything that came to hand. The only things he had nearby were his fists, and Morales was as hard as the packed ground under their worn-out old boots.

"But I'm talking to you, *estupido.*" Hack's right fist shot out in a blur and landed squarely against Morales's jaw, spinning him to the side. A hard left landed on the point of his nose, which exploded in a gout of blood that gushed from both nostrils. The cartilage crunched under Hack's large knuckles and the man's expression went dull.

Morales staggered backward before regaining his balance. Pursuing his advantage, Hack followed up with two more swings that immediately split the skin over Morales's eyebrow and split his cheek. The stunned man blinked several times to clear his watering eyes. Half a dozen of his *compadres* gathered behind him like regimental troops, as if preparing for a charge, shouting and urging him on.

Still behind Hack, Luke Fischer barked a laugh and rose to square off with the others. Using his fingers to comb back a tuft of brown hair from his forehead, he set his feet in case somebody charged. "Damn, son. I think I just saw water shoot out of six holes in his head."

The other members of the incarcerated Long gang heard Luke chuckle. Two-Horses, Gabriel Santana, and Billy Lightning put their bowls on the ground and stood as one. The boys drifted behind Hack and scattered out. Had the members of the Long gang been armed, it would have the makings of a shootout with deadly results. They were all experienced gunmen and had done their share of killing both good and bad men.

Instead, they faced Morales's lackeys and prepared to fight.

Morales was an experienced prison brawler, and a couple of hard licks and a little blood didn't faze him all that much. A large man, he'd survived innumerable fights by using his weight and power. He shouted and rushed in to get his hands on Hack where he could use his considerable prison experience gained from years of preying on weaker men.

Hack was far from weak and had no intention of letting that happen. Planting his right boot, he cocked his arm as if ready to swing. The instant Morales ducked his head to plow a shoulder into his chest, Hack settled back to use his own motion against him.

A former town marshal, train and bank robber, and range rider who'd fought his way across most of Texas, bustin' knuckles with someone else was nothing new to the gang leader. He'd learned long ago to let a man use his own leverage against him and almost felt comfortable with what was about to happen.

When Morales charged, Hack swiveled and dodged, at the same time grabbing the inmates arm, and used the man's momentum to swing him headfirst into the prison wall. The convict's skull and shoulder hit the solid rock and brick with a crack. The impact stopped the man's charge and his knees buckled.

Morales went down for a second, but using the wall to steady himself, he regained his feet and pushed off with both hands, addled for a second time in fifteen seconds. He shook his head to clear it and blood flew. Gritting his teeth, he growled like a furious coyote and rushed at Hack.

Those friends of his were moving in, and Hack had to finish up fast. Only men who lost their tempers wanted to continue a fight, just to maim and hurt. He wanted that mad dog down for good in the eyes of those who saw him as their leader, so he wouldn't have to look over his shoulder every day for the rest of the time they were there.

Morales shook his head a second time to clear the cobwebs, and droplets of blood flew like rain once again, splashing on those nearby. His face was a mask of blood that poured from his nose and a gaping split in his forehead wide enough to look like a second mouth. The edges separated enough to show his white skull that was soon covered in red.

Hack reluctantly gave him one thing, the Mexican prisoner was tough as a horseshoe nail, and had no intention of stopping. He came in again and Hack swung a soft left that inmate easily blocked, but it left him open and an uppercut that started at Hack's rope belt and aimed at the top of Morales's head finished the fight. His teeth clacked from the impact that shattered his jaw and he dropped in his tracks like a puppet with the strings cut. He hit the ground blowing bloody bubbles mixed with broken teeth.

Breathing hard, Hack faced Morales's friends and squared off with them. "This'll be the rest of you if y'all take one more step. This is over." He pointed at Escobedo. "And you leave this man alone."

Still making eye contact to maintain their machismo facade, they drifted off like leaves in the wind, leaving Morales unconscious in the dust. Hack's boys stayed planted where they were, in case someone whirled to charge. When all the inmates were back to their places in the shade, they relaxed and went back to their own small pieces of ground.

Escobedo nodded his thanks and pushed his back closer to the rock and mortar wall, as if ensuring no one could get in behind him. He tipped the bowl into his mouth and finished the food Hack fought for.

Hack licked his thumb and rubbed at the now raw knuckles on his left hand. All the roosterin' over with for the time being between them, he picked up his own wooden bowl and returned to his previous spot in the shade to suck in another mouthful of now cold stew.

The shirt hanging on his thick shoulders wasn't much more'n a thin rag, but a new rip in the back that ran from shoulder to waist parted when he sat. "It's a good thing this storm is coming." He picked up the conversation as if they'd never been interrupted. "They won't make us work for a day or two while it passes through and Escobedo there can rest up."

Luke scratched at his brown whiskers. "I'm surprised you stood up for that feller."

Hack chewed for a moment longer and nodded at Escobedo, who watched his tormentor's lackeys haul the unconscious man off. "He'll make it now, maybe. Did you hear what happened in his cell last night?"

Luke swallowed the last of his meal. "Escobedo's tougher'n you think. He whipped Torres one on one."

Two-Horses stood in the sun, picking at a callus on his thumb. His face was wide, jaw solid, with prominent, protruding cheekbones. It was his white man's blue eyes that set him apart from his Comanche roots. Round in shape and always narrowed against the light, they spoke of mixed blood that almost no one, white or red, could abide.

He seldom spoke, but seemed surprised that Hack had waded into a fight that didn't have anything to do with any of them. "So why'd you help him?"

"Because what they did wasn't right. Torres paid one of the guards, and I figure it was Perez, to open Escobedo's cell after lockup. Torres slipped in and about five minutes later they had to carry what was left of him out. They locked the cell again and nobody said a word. That's why I think Escobedo can handle himself, but two fights so close together can drain a man down to nothing.

"The truth is, I don't like it that Perez is playing games with everyone in here. Next time it could be me, or you, or any one of us who's not up to snuff at the moment and can't defend themselves."

"Why did he let Torres into Escobedo's cell in the

first place?" Gabe Santana wanted to know. Besides Luke, Gabe had been with Hack longer than the others. A lithe, slender man with black hair, olive complexion, and somber eyes, he'd been a man to ride the river with from the first time Hack laid eyes on him up in Llano County.

"Because I heard there was a bet over who would win."

The youngest of their group, Billy Lightning scratched at a red spot on his forearm where a scorpion stung him a week earlier. Looking more like a schoolboy, Billy had only a few light whiskers along his jawline and a dusting of blond strands on his upper lip. "Torres woke up in the hotbox this morning. He's still in there as far as I know.

"I knew a guy who spent three days in the Yuma hotbox," Luke interjected. "Killed him deader'n Dick's hatband. Fell out about five minutes after they let opened the door. It was a crying shame for a tough man like that."

"I bet Torres wishes he'd never tangled with Escobedo." Santana stretched his legs into the dry sunshine, studying what was left of his worn-out boots.

Billy used his thumb to rub at the knot left by what he'd grown up calling a stinging lizard, which was a local description of scorpions. "You could have let Escobedo handle himself. Now you'll have Perez thinking about you, and what he can do to us."

"Don't matter. I dislike Morales, and now that's settled," Hack answered. "Sometimes you have to refresh folks' memories, too."

Taking advantage of the time out of their cells and the mine, Hack adjusted himself in the narrow shade thrown by the twelve-foot wall to keep the sun off his head. The guards allowed each man a cap, of sorts, but it fit so snug that the hot material against Hack's skull felt like it had been baking all day. He'd often thought he'd give anything for one of the tall sombreros worn by the locals that provided a cushion of air on top, and wide brims to shade a man's face and shoulders.

Shoot, he'd even settle for one of the military style caps with the leather bills the guards wore. They were a byproduct of the French influence there in Mexico, but Hack really wanted a good, soft felt Stetson he'd worn across the river. All Texans love their hats, horses, and depending on the man, their dogs or women.

Only one prisoner had a hat of any sort, and that was Torres, but it would go into the grave with him if the hotbox took his life. The guards took what they wanted when a man died, and the rest was either distributed to the peasants in the nearby community, or buried.

As the boys finished their thin stew, the Long Gang sat quietly for the last few minutes allotted for dinner until an old man with sunken cheeks stopped beside them and spoke in Spanish.

"Ah, *los terribles cinco*. Do you feel it, the air?"

"The five of us aren't so terrible, unless these boys get riled, but it seems a little hotter out here than usual," Hack said. "Of course, this place is only a couple of notches below the boiling point in hell anyway."

The man smiled, revealing only two bottom teeth left in his head. "The wind, it comes from the south.

There is a storm on the way. *Muy malo.* This time of the year they blow off the *baja* and bring rain and life to the desert."

The last to finish his stew was Billy Lightning. He paused with the bowl still against his mouth and swallowed. "I *thought* I felt something in my bones."

"I am an old man and have seen it once for each decade of my miserable life. If I was much younger, I would ready myself to escape from this hellhole when the storm hits."

As was his habit in the Mexican prison, Hack glanced across to the guards huddled around a water bucket in the shade of a stick and timber portico leading into the *comandante*'s office. They were laughing and paying more attention to a dice game than their prisoners, knowing the noonday heat would dampen any ideas of trouble.

"Have you ever seen it done, an escape from this place?"

"No, but I've heard about it. No one has broken out of here in nearly twenty years. The last time was the dark of the moon, but the one before my time was when fifteen men climbed the wall. Only five got away. The others were killed by the Apaches they used to track them. For every man killed, the one who did it received two pieces of gold."

"Apaches working with Mexicans?"

"Civilized Apaches who live that way, in the Chisos mountains."

A tingle ran up Hack's spine and an idea formed, making him feel more alive than he had for months. "How long does it take them to get a tracker from out there?"

"It would be at least a day, unless a couple were in the village for supplies or mescal."

"There's no way to get out of the cells, though, once it starts storming."

"You can be like Torres. Bribe Perez there to let you out for a midnight fight. If it was me, I would tell him you knew Escobedo outside and needed to settle with him. Perez loves to gamble like he's doing over there right now, shooting dice, and would welcome to see a match with you and Escobedo, and he'd bet on you to win."

"Well, I've already stood up for him."

"So you could kill him yourself."

Hack forced a grin off the corners of his mouth. He'd been there for so long his mind didn't seem to work, and that idea had never occurred to him. And here it was, an old man giving them all a way out, served on a platter. "Then I could take Perez, get his keys, and let the others out."

"That is a good plan."

"Why're you telling me this? This is your plan, not mine."

"Because I am too used up to fight and run. I will die here, but the other reason is that I don't like Perez and would like to see his dead eyes open and collecting dust."

Luke drew in the dust with a forefinger. "Mighty hard talk, just because you don't like the man."

"He cheated me in a dice game when I first came here and took my shoes." The old man looked down at the worn out *huaraches* on his feet. The pitiful sandals had been repaired so many times with strips of leather they almost looked like small mops. "My good shoes would not fit him, but he sold them in the village and used the money to entertain one of his whores."

Close enough to hear, the rest of the guys remained silent, but they were working things out in their own minds. They'd learned not long after arriving at the prison that groups involved in too much discussion brought suspicious guards. They were Hack's men, but had their own minds and did what they wanted. They came and went when the Long Gang was working north of the river, though these were his core group, there were others from time to time.

Instead of gathering to hear, Two-Horses and Gabriel Santana were stretched out along the wall, pretending to sleep. Billy Lightning sat four feet away, sanding a callus off his hand with a rock. They were all listening, and if one were close enough to feel the rising tension and elation, it was easy to tell the men who'd resigned themselves to incarceration were once again ready to ride.

CHAPTER 2

The chief guard, Juan Perez, rose from an arbor shade reserved only for he and his men, and sniffed the air like a dog, filtering much of the scorching air through a mustache that sprouted thick and heavy against his nostrils. In addition to dust and manure coming from a corral outside the walls, there was a hint of dampness.

He kicked a resting guard's foot and poked another's shoulder, prodding them from the raw wooden benches against their quarters' wall. "Get up. These men need to work and a storm is coming. The *comandante* will want one last shift back to the mine before the rain falls."

Though he and the *comandante* Raul Mendoza would have preferred for their prisoners to work from morning to night, they long ago discovered that a full day in the mine would kill them, and a dead prisoner couldn't make money for the *jefe*'s pockets. Instead, they dug for half a day, then returned to the prison as the second shift took up shovels and picks to worry copper from the mine, then they'd switch again.

Although he acted as if irritated, Perez was pleased with the changing weather. He heard the day before that his favorite cantina server was back at work. Juana'd been taken to Mexico City by a soldier loyal to Porfirio Diaz, the country's president, but for some unknown reason he'd sent her packing, and that was fortunate for Perez. A rainy day meant he could leave the prisoners in their cells and visit with her to spend his money.

It wasn't that they couldn't work in the mines while it rained, but *Comandante* Mendoza was afraid the inmates would use the weather in an attempt to escape as they were moved back and forth between them and the prison. Better to let them remain behind bars, and besides, everyone wanted some time off, and that went for him and his men.

He paused to stare in the direction of the little mining village that lay between the ancient structure that was once a mission run by friars, and the entrance into the low, barren mountain that looked like an animal's burrow.

Against a backdrop of gathering storm clouds, and lit by the sun that was not yet covered, two spirals of buzzards turned lazy circles over areas of interest. Perez studied the scavengers, wondering if they were human or animal bodies that lured them to those particular portions of the sky. He loved the scavengers, and once even had the opportunity to share a *trabajador*'s pleasures while letting her do all the work as he lay on his back and stared out of an open window to watch the carrion birds float overhead.

Maybe it would happen again sometime soon. With that pleasant thought in mind, Perez remained where he was in the shade as the guards kicked the afternoon shift upright while those who'd been in the mines that morning went to their hot cells. Spending time in those hot, airless cubicles was a different kind of punishment, and wasn't considered as a pleasant gift.

Finally bestirring himself, Perez used a fingernail to pick at the dirt crusted in the corners of his eyes and followed the men past the hot box. He paused beside the sun-baked door in the windowless structure made from hand-packed adobe. "Torres, are you still alive in there?"

The man who'd been beaten within an inch of his life by the newest inmate groaned an answer and Perez chuckled. "It seems that you are. Feel better, my friend. We need another match between you and the boy who put you in there." He gave the hot box a slight kick, doing nothing but dislodging crumbling sand and rocks. "You cost me a lot of money, amigo. That's why you're in there. You need to earn it back, and possibly your life."

It was a blistering afternoon with not a cloud in the sky. He watched the prisoners march out of the front gate and went inside the *la oficina del alcalde* to cool off a little and visit with the *comandante*. Raul Mendoza always had interesting stories to tell.

Visit our website at
KensingtonBooks.com
to sign up for our newsletters, read
more from your favorite authors, see
books by series, view reading group
guides, and more!

Become a Part of Our
Between the Chapters Book Club
Community and Join the Conversation

Betweenthechapters.net